W9-AQC-052

WITHDRAWN

Ortega

Ortega

Maureen Fergus

KCP FICTION

3 3210 1865597

*For my dad, a loving and generous giant among men,
and for Sheila, who believed in me*

KCP Fiction is an imprint of Kids Can Press

Text © 2010 Maureen Fergus

All rights reserved. No part of this publication may be reproduced, stored in a
retrieval system or transmitted, in any form or by any means, without the prior
written permission of Kids Can Press Ltd. or, in case of photocopying or other
reprographic copying, a license from The Canadian Copyright Licensing
Agency (Access Copyright). For an Access Copyright license, visit
www.accesscopyright.ca or call toll free to 1-800-893-5777.

This is a work of fiction and any resemblance of characters to persons living
or dead is purely coincidental.

Many of the designations used by manufacturers and sellers to distinguish their
products are claimed as trademarks. Where those designations appear in this
book and Kids Can Press Ltd. was aware of a trademark claim, the designations
have been printed in initial capital letters (e.g., Ping-Pong).

Kids Can Press acknowledges the financial support of the Government of
Ontario, through the Ontario Media Development Corporation's Ontario Book
Initiative; the Ontario Arts Council; the Canada Council for the Arts; and the
Government of Canada, through the BPIDP, for our publishing activity.

Published in Canada by   Published in the U.S. by
Kids Can Press Ltd.   Kids Can Press Ltd.
29 Birch Avenue   2250 Military Road
Toronto, ON M4V 1E2   Tonawanda, NY 14150

www.kidscanpress.com

Edited by Sheila Barry
Designed by Marie Bartholomew
Printed and bound in Canada
Jacket photos © Shutterstock Images

CM 10 0 9 8 7 6 5 4 3 2 1

This book is printed on acid-free paper that is 100% ancient-forest friendly
(100% post-consumer recycled).

Library and Archives Canada Cataloguing in Publication

Fergus, Maureen
    Ortega / written by Maureen Fergus.

ISBN 978-1-55453-474-6

I. Title.

PS8611.E735O78 2010   jC813'.6   C2009-906522-3

Kids Can Press is a *l***©**l***S™ Entertainment company

Prologue

Eleven years ago, an infant lowland gorilla was acquired by my privately funded laboratory. His inexperienced mother had abandoned him shortly after his premature birth, and my lab offered a humane, ethical and cutting-edge alternative to traditional zoo placement.

Within days of his arrival at my specially designed facility, an elite surgical team undertook the first in a series of radical procedures designed to make it physically possible for the infant gorilla to acquire speech. After the surgeons finished reshaping his tongue, modifying his palate and implanting an artificial voice box, speech therapists and handlers took over, working around the clock to model and teach spoken language.

So began a ground-breaking experiment that would allow me to test my belief that if they could speak, higher-order primates would push the envelope of intellectual development beyond what has previously been exhibited by apes who successfully communicate using American Sign Language.

Over the past decade, this young gorilla's progress has exceeded my wildest expectations. He has acquired a vocabulary that compares favorably to human children his age, he has learned to read and write and his IQ has tested as high as 98 on a scale where 100 is considered "normal" for humans. He consistently demonstrates reason, original thought and the ability to understand and express complex and abstract concepts.

Today, we stand on the brink of the next phase of this groundbreaking experiment: integration of the gorilla into social situations with humans of his approximate age and level of development. Ladies and gentlemen, I thank you for your continued interest in "Project Ortega," and I look forward to being able to provide you with future updates on the progress of this remarkable young ape.

> Introduction to a scientific paper presented by
> Dr. E.B. Whitmore at the Thirty-Second Annual
> Conference of Behavioral Psychologists

Chapter One

"Hurry *up*, Ortega," called Dr. Susan. "We're going to be late for school!"

"I can't find my knapsack," Ortega replied in a muffled voice. He lay on his back with his head under the bed, being as perfectly still as he could be and not looking for his knapsack at all.

"Ortega?" Dr. Susan peered under the bed.

He closed his eyes.

"We talked about this," she reminded him gently. "You said you'd try."

He began to snore.

Dr. Susan regarded him thoughtfully for a long minute before reaching down to give his big bare feet a vigorous tickle. When his snores turned into reluctant chuckles, she stood up, walked over to his desk and began making notes.

Ortega ignored the sound of her scribbling for as long as he could, which wasn't long. Scrambling out from under the bed, he loped over to where she sat. "What are you writing about me now?" he asked, poking his head under her arm.

"Who says I'm writing about you?" she replied with a smile, closing the notebook. She gave him a poke in the ribs that made him jump, and then a kiss. "Your knapsack is right there beside Mr. Doodles," she said, pointing to a ratty stuffed bear slumped forlornly at the edge of the messy bed.

"I guess Mr. Doodles wants to come with me," said Ortega, taking a flying leap onto the bed that nearly bounced Mr. Doodles onto his head.

"I don't think so," said Dr. Susan, chasing after him.

"He does, otherwise why would he be trying to steal my knapsack?" said Ortega, jumping up and down so hard that the reinforced-steel bed frame squeaked in protest.

"He doesn't, otherwise why would he be doing things to make us late?" said Dr. Susan, giving Ortega's leg a sudden tug.

With a tremendous crash, Ortega flopped into the sitting position; Dr. Susan expertly wrestled the knapsack onto his back.

"He does. He's afraid of being lonely," said Ortega, giving Mr. Doodles a ferocious squeeze.

"He'll be fine," said Dr. Susan. She pried the stuffed bear out of Ortega's arms. "Why don't you show him how to be brave?" she suggested.

"I'd rather show him how to eat ice cream," said Ortega.

"Maybe later," said Dr. Susan, taking him by the hand.

"And chocolate cake," he added.

"Don't push your luck," said Dr. Susan.

Don't push yours, said Ortega, in his mind.

———

He burst out of the clean, cool, quiet marble foyer of the lab building into a messy, misty morning drizzle. He didn't often get out at this time of day, and certainly not in this kind of weather. He grinned at the low gray sky, and at the squelching feel of the wet ground beneath his bare feet. His nostrils twitched, savoring the moist, wormy smell. He smacked an open hand against the front of his rain poncho once, softly.

"Oh, for goodness' sake," came Dr. Susan's exasperated voice behind him. "Get out of the flower garden!"

"I can't help it if I'm a nature lover," he replied, blowing her a noisy kiss.

Holding a dripping clipboard over her head to keep off the rain, Dr. Susan chased Ortega out of the garden and across the lawn to the parking lot, all the while complaining about how irritated fussy old Dr. Whitmore was going to be when he discovered that Ortega had trampled though his favorite tulip patch. Again.

"Look on the bright side," Ortega suggested as he climbed into the backseat of her rusted Chevette Scooter and buckled himself up. "At least I didn't get my ugly, uncomfortable new pants dirty."

Dr. Susan stared pointedly at the muddy stains on both cuffs.

"Well, nobody's perfect," he sniffed, closing the door.

It was a long drive to school — past the gates of the laboratory complex, past the ice-cream and pizza parlors, past the road that led to Grandma's house, deep into the noisy heart of the city and beyond. Dr. Susan tried to talk to Ortega about how he was feeling, but he pretended to be deaf.

"You're not deaf, Ortega," she said, smiling at him over her shoulder.

"WHAT?" he asked loudly, cupping a hand to his small ear.

"I SAID YOU'RE NOT DEAF."

"It comes and goes," he shrugged, tuning her out again.

They drove in silence through the pelting rain. Traffic thinned and the city fell away. Just past an isolated truck stop, Dr. Susan spun left onto a bumpy gravel road flanked by brimming drainage ditches. A soggy prairie landscape unfolded before them — plowed fields and muddy pastures, log fences and lonely farmhouses. The occasional clump of spindly poplar trees dripped and drooped.

Ortega flopped back in his seat. "This is ridiculous," he complained. "I could have flown to the moon and back in the time it's taking to get to this place! You really should have tried to find me a school in the city, Dr. Susan," he admonished.

"We did try."

"You should have tried harder. You should have made sure people understood how good-looking I was."

"I told them you were gorgeous," she smiled.

"So what was the problem?"

Dr. Susan's smile faded, and she stared straight ahead without saying anything for so long that Ortega wondered if *she'd* gone temporarily deaf. "Oh ... you know," she finally said with a lame little shrug.

Ortega sucked his lips in annoyance. "No, I *don't* know. If I knew, I wouldn't be asking."

"Well ... they were afraid."

"Afraid?" he snorted. "Why? What did they think I was going to do? Rip off the gym teacher's arms? Eat my locker partner? Master the nine-times table and take over the world?"

"No, no, nothing like that," assured Dr. Susan as she motored through a series of watery potholes that sent the small car flying. "They were afraid of getting involved in something controversial. A lot of people have strong feelings about you."

"A lot of people don't even know me!"

"I don't mean they have strong feelings about you *personally*," corrected Dr. Susan hastily. "I mean they have strong feelings about Project Ortega."

"And that makes it okay for them to be mean to me."

"No, of course not," she said, flushing slightly. "It's just that —"

"So how come the people at this school decided to accept me?" Ortega interrupted. "Did they realize how stupid it was to tell someone he couldn't go somewhere just because he happened to be the star of the world's most boring experiment?"

"Not exactly," said Dr. Susan hesitantly. "The school is located in a small town whose biggest factory shut down a while back. When that happened, a lot of people were forced to move to the city to look for work. With so many tax-payers gone, the town was slowly going broke, so when we, uh, offered to pay them to participate in the study, I guess they felt they had no choice but to accept."

"YOU OFFERED THEM MONEY TO TAKE ME?" screeched Ortega, feeling more than a little insulted by the idea. "How much did you offer?"

"It doesn't matter how much we offered," said Dr. Susan, as the car bounced off the gravel road and onto the paved street of the town. "What matters is that we found you a school, and now it's up to you to do your best — to fit in, to learn, to make friends." She reached back and squeezed his knee. "Your best is all Dr. Whitmore and I have ever asked of you, Ortega."

"What if my best is being a dummy with no friends?" he asked.

"It won't be, unless you don't try," she said.

"But what if it is?" he insisted, as they pulled up to the only stoplight in sight.

"Then we'll be proud of you."

Ortega snorted derisively at the thought of Dr. Whitmore proudly introducing him as the dummy with no friends who had ruined his life's work and made him the laughingstock of the scientific community. Then he noticed the woman in the car beside them staring, so he squashed his face up against the streaming window and mouthed swear words at her. He laughed out loud when she gave him a shocked look and abruptly turned right.

"Knock it off," said Dr. Susan.

Ortega hooted at her as loudly as he could.

"Use your words," she reminded.

"Okay," he said, and then he mouthed swear words at the back of her head until he noticed her staring at him in the rearview mirror.

"Other words," she suggested sternly.

"Fine," he snapped, as an overpowering odor filled the car. Like the eye-watering reek of a hundred unwashed armpits, it was the smell of gorilla fear. "How about these words: my stomach hurts and I want to go home."

"You're going to be okay," soothed Dr. Susan, resisting the urge to crack open the window and let in some fresh air.

"That's your opinion," he whispered.

"What was that?" she asked, giving him another look in the rearview mirror.

"NOTHING!" he hollered.

Dr. Susan was so startled that she swerved into oncoming traffic and nearly sideswiped a pickup truck carrying several bales of hay and a fat, mottled pig in a crate. Ortega saw the bushy red eyebrows of the grizzled old driver bunch up in a scowl for only an instant before flying upward in surprise at the sight of Ortega sitting in the backseat of the offending vehicle, grinning and waving merrily as the truck trundled by.

Ortega felt better. He leaned forward and tickled the back of Dr. Susan's neck. Without turning around, she reached up and patted the callused knuckles of his hand. "It's going to be all right, Ortega."

"That's your opinion," he mouthed, sitting back again.

They drove past an old-fashioned movie theater, several crumbling brick buildings and a lunch counter with faded posters of meat sandwiches in the window. On the corner, a woman in a plastic shower cap swept the sheltered cement stoop of a fussy-looking beauty parlor; across the street, a man in a soiled apron arranged open crates of fruit on a table under a red-striped awning. Dr. Susan hung a right at

Harding's Fine Leather Goods, and two blocks later, the car screeched to a halt.

They had arrived.

The school was a cement box tinged green, like the face of somebody about to throw up. Several of the windowpanes were cracked; one was boarded up completely. There were no flowers in the flower bed, no flag on the flagpole. The open field behind the school was nothing but flat, empty space. In the distance, half hidden by trees, a dilapidated factory loomed.

"It looks like a prison for the criminally insane," announced Ortega.

"It does *not*," chuckled Dr. Susan, stepping out of the car.

"It does. The only thing missing is the bars on the windows," he said.

Dr. Susan opened the backdoor of the car and tugged on his hairy bicep. "Don't be ridiculous, Ortega. We don't have you scheduled for a stint at a prison for the criminally insane until next weekend."

"I can't believe you're making jokes like that at a time like this!" he screeched as he climbed slowly out of the car, dragging his knapsack behind him. It landed in the puddle beside him with a wet plop. "Is this what Dr. Whitmore meant when he said that he hoped your nurturing presence would help ease me into my first day of school?"

With a long-suffering sigh, Dr. Susan apologized for her insensitive joke, picked up Ortega's dirty knapsack and helped him slip the straps over his long arms. "Now, don't forget — as much as possible, Dr. Whitmore wants you to walk upright when you're at school."

"It's unnatural *and* uncomfortable," he complained, pushing her hands away. "Why should I?"

"Because you've practiced it, because it'll leave your hands free to do other things and because it'll mean one less difference between you and the other children," she said, leaning into the car for her purse. "Also because I don't know if the seams of those new pants can take the strain of you bent over on all fours all day long. Dr. Whitmore had them designed for a biped — you know, for someone who walks on two legs."

"I *know* what a biped is," crabbed Ortega. He thought it was pretty typical of Dr. Smarty Pants to do something like designing biped pants without even consulting him, but before he could mention this to Dr. Susan, she'd started up the cracked cement walk to the front doors of the school. Ortega hurried after her, knuckling defiantly through the puddles she so carefully stepped over. He wondered what she'd do if he bolted. In his much younger days, he'd been a runner — darting through open doors when people's backs were turned, solemnly agreeing to walk nicely beside Dr. Susan and then galloping away the minute the leash came off. Many times he'd been apprehended wreaking havoc in his little kitchenette or inciting mayhem in the animal-testing laboratory downstairs. Once, Dr. Whitmore forgot to lock his office door, and Ortega spent an unforgettably joyful half-hour overturning filing cabinets, upending plastic potted plants and sampling the tasty pages of Dr. Whitmore's more expensive scientific texts. He'd been harshly punished for his behavior — no tapioca pudding and sliced strawberries for a whole week — but it had been well worth it.

"Don't even think about it," Dr. Susan warned, holding the door open for him.

Ortega sighed heavily. He wasn't really going to bolt. Even he knew he was getting too old for that kind of behavior. Besides, where would he bolt *to*?

Inside the empty entrance hall they paused — Dr. Susan to wipe her sneakers on the mat, Ortega to contemplate the enormous, gilt-framed picture that dominated the stark and silent space. It was a portrait of a withered old crone in a hanging black dress. She looked as though she'd been surprised in the act of sucking lemons.

"Please tell me she's not in charge of this place," said Ortega, his voice echoing pleasantly in the high-ceilinged, white-walled emptiness. "I've never felt comfortable in the care of the undead."

There was a snicker from the stairwell at the far end of the hall.

"Who's there?" boomed Ortega, enjoying the sound of the echo.

A shriek, and the sound of small feet pounding up the stairs.

"Lower your voice, Ortega," shushed Dr. Susan, heading for the stairs. "I purposely arrived late — and a day early — so we'd be able to get you settled with a minimum of fuss. If you start shouting in that big voice of yours, everyone is going to come rushing out to get a look at you. It'll turn into a complete mob scene."

"I love mob scenes," lied Ortega in a loud whisper. "They make me feel like a rock star."

With a smile that said she knew he was lying — and scared — Dr. Susan drew him close and pressed her lips against his leathery forehead for a long, quiet moment. Then she briskly turned and started up the stairs. Reluctantly, Ortega followed. The stairwell smelled like old gym clothes, fresh photocopies and forgotten lunches. He could hear the sound of murmuring voices and the distant hum of office equipment. Somewhere, someone with very long fingernails was pecking at a keyboard. He eyed the dusty photographs that lined the walls. He supposed that to each other the students in the pictures all looked pretty different, but to him they all looked pretty much the same. And in spite of his talking, walking upright — even wearing ugly, uncomfortable new pants — there was no mistaking how different he looked from them.

Halfway up the stairs, he seized a handful of Dr. Susan's sweatshirt, dragging her to such a sudden stop that she nearly lost her balance.

"They won't like me," he said.

"They will."

"They won't, they'll think I'm a freak."

"You're not a freak, Ortega."

"Gee, thanks," he said sarcastically. "I feel much better now."

"What I *mean* is that being different from others doesn't make you a freak," she soothed as she peeled his fingers off her sweatshirt. "Being unique doesn't make you a freak. In our own ways, we're all different and unique. That's what makes each of us special and interesting."

Ortega yawned loudly in order to show Dr. Susan what he thought of her little inspirational speech. Then he said, "These pants itch."

"They'll be fine," she said, resuming her climb. When she reached the second-story landing, she turned right down a corridor lined with battered blue lockers. Ortega followed.

"They itch. They're uncomfortable. I don't like them," he insisted.

"There's a dress code at this school — no sweats allowed. Everyone else will be wearing regular pants," said Dr. Susan, stopping in front of the last door on the left. "Don't you want to be like everyone else?"

"Regular pants are not going to make me like everyone else," he muttered, looking around. A door opened halfway down the hall, and a small boy with glasses popped his head out. He stared at Ortega, who stared back — ambivalently at first, but with growing defiance. Ortega didn't like being stared at — but more than that, he didn't like being stared *down*. He folded his arms across his massive chest and lowered his head, settling in. He wouldn't be the first to break eye contact. Oh, no. He'd stand there all day if he had to.

"Okay, here we go," breathed Dr. Susan, leaning over to fuss with his shirt collar one last time.

He swatted her hands aside and craned to see around her, but the boy had disappeared. Ortega hoped the boy realized that Dr. Susan's interference meant the contest had ended in a tie. He hoped the boy didn't think he'd won.

But there was no way to find out what the boy thought — at least not at that particular moment there wasn't — because with a sense of timing that made Ortega want to give her a pinch, Dr. Susan chose that particular moment to step forward and rap sharply on the classroom door.

———

Almost immediately, Ortega heard the sound of sensible shoes padding across the floor of the classroom. Then the door swung open and his new teacher stood silhouetted in the doorway. She looked like an ancient tortoise might if it had crawled off and left its shell behind somewhere — scrawny, wrinkled and slightly put off. Her mouth was tight but not unkind; she wore what hair she had in a bun fixed firmly to the top of her head.

Ortega had met Miss Rutherford before — several times, in fact. On her first visit, she'd given him three caramels. On her second visit, she'd reprimanded him for not telling her that Dr. Susan didn't allow him to eat caramels. After her last visit, Ortega had overheard her promise Dr. Whitmore that she'd treat him just like any other student. Since then, he'd often wondered whether that would be a good thing or a bad thing. He hoped it would be a good thing.

Carefully closing the door behind her, Miss Rutherford peered through her wire spectacles — first at Dr. Susan, then at Ortega.

"Good morning," she said in a faintly accented voice.

Dr. Susan said good-morning; Ortega said nothing. Up until this moment he'd been rather distracted — by the picture of the lemon-sucking witch, by his itchy pants, by the boy with the glasses. Now, the enormity of what he was about to confront struck him full force. In a minute, Dr. Susan would turn around and leave him here to face a roomful of strangers. He'd faced strangers before, of course — many times, at Dr. Whitmore's boring scientific conferences — but he'd never had to do it alone. And the strangers had never been eleven-year-olds. And he'd never had to worry about trying to befriend them, because their interest in him had never been personal. He'd never enjoyed being observed, monitored, tested and debated over, but at least he'd always known where he stood. He had no idea where he was going to stand with the strangers he was about to meet — assuming they were going to let him stand with them at all.

After a moment of silence, Dr. Susan gave him a little nudge and said, "Miss Rutherford said good-morning, Ortega."

His muscles bunched beneath him as he was gripped by an almost overwhelming urge to flee. "I don't think I can do this," he croaked.

"You most certainly can," said Miss Rutherford.

Dr. Susan — who'd seen him tense up — didn't look so sure.

"Really, I can't," he insisted, with a pleading look at Dr. Susan. Not for the first time, he wished that gorillas could cry. If there were big, salty tears coursing down his leathery face, there would be no mistaking how upset he really was. Of course, if he suddenly started charging up and down the hall, slapping at the decrepit blue lockers and pounding on his chest, there would also be no mistaking how upset he really was. However, that sort of behavior was unlikely to elicit a lot of sympathy from Dr. Susan, and her sympathy was the only thing that was going to get him out of here.

He leaned his head up against her arm and sniffled.

"You can do this, Ortega," repeated Miss Rutherford, without giving the least indication that she'd noticed his pitiful state. "I would not have accepted you as a pupil if I thought you couldn't. That you are nervous is entirely understandable, and yet where would the world be if we turned back at the first flutter in our bellies? Courage is the cornerstone of progress, Ortega, and I know you know this because I know your remarkable history — the skills you have mastered, the expectations you have defied, all that you have endured. Time and again you have made great personal strides in difficult, demanding circumstances."

"Like I had a choice," he said, sniffling more adamantly.

"Choice or not," continued Miss Rutherford, holding a quivering index finger high in the air, "we must face the challenges that life lays down before us, else we will never know how high we might have climbed." She paused, savoring her words like a choice broth. "Besides, I have found that the anticipation of a thing is often worse than the fact of it, and I believe you're going to be surprised by how smoothly your introduction to the class unfolds."

Ortega snorted. It was a rude thing to do and he knew it, but who did she think she was kidding? Those kids were going to stare and whisper; the girls were going to scream and faint. And who knew what the boys would do? Dr. Whitmore's nephew, Rupert, liked to jump out at Ortega unexpectedly and fling rubber snakes in his direction even though he knew perfectly well that Ortega had a pathological fear of snakes. And Rupert was only seven! Ortega could just imagine how much worse an eleven-year-old could be.

"No, I don't think so," he said. He shook his head regretfully. "I've changed my mind about attending school. These things happen."

Dr. Susan started to speak. Miss Rutherford cut her off.

"As I understand it, Ortega, this is one of those situations where you have no choice," she said crisply. "Arrangements have been made. Commitments have been given. And I would remind you that you felt ready two weeks ago. You told me that you were sick of being treated like a baby. That you were tired of being spied on all day long. That you wanted to get out from under Dr. Whitmore's pasty white thumb."

Dr. Susan gave him a look at this last one, but he ignored it.

"Well, I've changed my mind, and I don't feel ready now, and Dr. Susan won't make me go if I don't feel ready, will you, Dr. Susan?" he asked. Reaching for her hand, he made a noise that sounded something like a purr.

It was a nasty shock when she untangled her hand from his and gave him a gentle shove in Miss Rutherford's direction. "Miss Rutherford is right, Ortega," she said with an encouraging smile. "You *can* do this."

Ortega glared — first at Dr. Susan, then at Miss Rutherford. Dr. Susan frowned. Miss Rutherford neither frowned nor smiled. She simply looked at him as if to say that she'd stand there all day if she had to. It was too much.

"Well, maybe I can do it," he growled, dumping his knapsack and dropping to his knuckles. "But you can't make me!"

With that, he darted in the direction of the stairwell.

And very nearly barreled into the boy with the glasses.

They both screamed at the top of their lungs; the boy tripped on his own untied shoelaces and fell backward. There was a pattering of feet from the classroom, but Miss Rutherford held the door firmly shut and called to the excited students on the other side that everything was fine.

Easing his hulking body forward, Ortega glowered down at the boy who had given him such a fright. He looked no older than nine, with an awkward, skinny body and hair like a helmet. The gray eyes behind the glasses were probably overly large at the best of times; as the boy lay sprawled and quaking beneath Ortega, whose knuckles were planted firmly on either side of his head, they were positively enormous.

"Please don't eat me!" he blurted.

In his mind, Ortega barked that even if he *were* in the habit of chasing down his protein and eating it raw, making a meal out of such a pipsqueak would hardly be worth the effort.

Out loud, he said, "I can't make any promises. Do you taste like chicken?"

The boy squawked in terror.

Dr. Susan marched over and hauled Ortega up by the back of his shirt collar. "Stop it!" she ordered. "Stop it this instant! Honestly, Ortega, why go out of your way to scare the first child you meet? Are you *trying* to ruin your chances here? Do you *want* to fail? Is that it?"

He huffed and shrugged her hand off his collar. "Cut it out," he muttered out of the corner of his mouth. "You're embarrassing me."

Dr. Susan threw her hands in the air.

"I wasn't scared," panted the boy, skittering out of Ortega's reach.

"I wasn't scared, either," said Ortega, pushing himself up into a standing position.

The boy hesitated. He didn't seem to know what to say to this — evidently, it hadn't occurred to him that a two-hundred-pound talking gorilla *could* be scared. Tentatively, he ventured, "Well, if I were as big as you, I wouldn't be scared of anything."

"I'm not. I sure am big, though, aren't I?" said Ortega, throwing out his barrel chest. "And you know what? I'm going to get even bigger. I'm going to get huge!"

"Not in the next few months you aren't!" said Dr. Susan with a strained chuckle.

Both youngsters ignored her. Appearing suitably impressed by Ortega's prediction of his future hugeness, the boy adjusted his thick glasses with one hand and looked quizzically at him. "So, if you're not afraid of anything, why were you running away just now?"

"I wasn't!" said Ortega indignantly. "Why were you sneaking up on me?"

"I wasn't," said the boy. "I was coming back from the bathroom. Why did you avert your eyes when you first saw me looking at you?"

Ortega bristled. "I didn't! She stepped in front of me," he cried, poking Dr. Susan in the belly.

"Oh," said the boy in a disappointed voice. "I thought maybe you were acknowledging my dominance. My name is Peter, by the way, and you should know that when I found out you were coming, I read everything I could on the subject of gorillas."

Ortega sucked his lips in annoyance.

"Don't worry, though. I didn't mind the extra work a bit because science is my second favorite subject," continued Peter. "That's why I think it's so great that you're here. I mean, how many kids get a chance to participate in a ground-breaking scientific experiment?"

Before Ortega could stuff his fingers into his ears to spare himself the torture of having to continue to listen to this future Dr. Smarty Pants, Miss Rutherford intervened.

"All right, Peter," she said with a sharp clap of her hands. "That's enough — back to class, please."

"Yes, Miss Rutherford," nodded Peter. He stepped past her and opened the classroom door, but before he went inside, he turned back to Ortega. "By the way," he said. "I know from my studies that gorillas are mostly herbivores. I know you were never really going to eat me."

In his mind, Ortega screeched, *Don't be so sure of that!*

Out loud, he said nothing.

———

"Well, Ortega, I am pleased to learn that you are not afraid of anything and that you were not running away," said Miss Rutherford, the minute the door closed behind Peter. "I confess I had a moment of doubt there, but you have proven me wrong in the most unequivocal terms, and I shan't underestimate you again. Now, why don't you pick up your knapsack and say good-bye to your Dr. Susan? You may have a moment alone with her while I do one final check to ensure that the class is prepared for your introduction. Excuse me," she said, slipping into the classroom.

Feeling distinctly outmaneuvered — by the teacher, who was treating him just like any other student, and by the boy, who would think he'd won if Ortega ran away now — Ortega slowly picked up his knapsack.

"I like her," whispered Dr. Susan, smoothing back the hair on his brow. "She's going to take good care of you, Ortega."

Ortega didn't answer. He strained to hear what was happening on the other side of the door, but it was impossible to hear anything over the pounding of his heart.

"She is," insisted Dr. Susan in a voice that sounded almost pleading. "If I didn't think it was true — if I didn't think you'd be okay — I'd never leave you here. You believe me, don't you, Ortega?"

Before he could say anything, Miss Rutherford returned.

"Ready?" she asked.

The door behind her was wide open. Ortega could see the feet of the children sitting in the front row of desks. He swallowed hard and clutched his knapsack in his arms more tightly.

This was it. There was no turning back now.

"I'll see you after school," said Dr. Susan, who was back to speaking in her usual cheerful voice. "What about a hug before you go?"

With a small huff, Ortega leaned forward and gave her several businesslike pats on the back. Then, without a backward glance, he loped quietly after Miss Rutherford into the classroom, where the world's first talking gorilla was about to make history.

Again.

Chapter Two

Ortega entered the classroom with his eyes sharply averted from the children, steeling himself for the outburst of excitement that the sight of him was sure to bring. When it didn't come, he hesitated for a few seconds, then looked over in puzzlement.

Every child in the classroom was wearing a blindfold of black silk.

And rather than staring or whispering or screaming or fainting, every last one of them was sitting stock-still. Waiting.

The silence in the room stretched. Ortega felt almost breathless — it was like being on the right side of a two-way mirror for the first time in his life. He watched, unwatched, for as long as he dared, then reluctantly looked a question at Miss Rutherford.

"It's something I do when introducing new students to the class, Ortega," she explained. "After all, don't we all deserve the chance to be judged first and foremost for who we are rather than what we look like? Your classmates have generously agreed to afford you that opportunity —"

"Like we had a choice!" someone griped.

"— and they know that anyone attempting to sneak a peek at you before I've said that the blindfolds can come off will be *severely punished*." She emphasized these last words in the direction of a big boy in the back row who had tilted his head back in an effort to see out of the gap at the bottom of the blindfold. He righted his head, grinning at no one in particular.

"So," she concluded, "why don't you come over here, Ortega, and we can all spend a few moments getting acquainted before returning to our lesson."

"Okay," he said.

There was a *whoosh* as the students exhaled in unison. "Was that him?" breathed a boy halfway back.

Ortega nodded. Then, realizing the boy couldn't see him, he said, "Yes, it was."

The boy threw himself against his seat back, the tails of his blindfold flapping behind him. "Geez!" he exclaimed. "You sound just like a normal person!"

"So do you," said Ortega.

The class laughed. Ortega snuck the tiniest of smiles in Miss Rutherford's direction. It died on his lips the very next instant.

"Ew," gagged a girl in the front row. "What is that *smell*?"

Ortega was mortified. The smell was him, of course — a combination of wet hair, fear and possibly the garlic in last night's salad. The girl made a face and pinched her thin nose with her bony fingers. Several girls nearby followed suit, one after another, their collective insult choreographed to such perfection that it was hard not to be impressed, particularly given the fact that they were all still blindfolded. This was obviously a team that was used to working together.

"I don't know what that smell is," drawled a girl in the far corner of the room. "Did you forget to wash under your arms again, Myra?"

Everyone laughed except Peter, who cleared his throat importantly and said, "I believe that smell is the juvenile version of the silverback odor. In stressful situations, adult male gorillas — also known as 'silverbacks' — release it. Scientists believe that in the wild, it may act as a signal to the family group, warning them to flee danger."

He smiled, blissfully unaware of the manner in which Ortega was glaring at him.

"Yeah?" said Myra. "Well, it stinks."

"Well, so do you," snapped Peter.

"Enough," said Miss Rutherford.

"And you know what else?" said Myra. "I'm not sitting beside that thing. My mother says I don't have to. She says he's an abomination — you know, like a monster — and she says the fact that he's being allowed to attend school is just one more sign of how sick our world really is. That's how come she planned a protest march for tomorrow morning, which was *supposed* to be his first day of school. When she finds out he showed up a day early —"

"I said *enough*, Myra," said Miss Rutherford severely.

Myra gave her pointy shoulders an insolent shrug, but stayed quiet.

"Miss Rutherford, the gorilla can sit beside me," called the big boy at the back. "At home my mom makes me take out the garbage all the time, so I'm used to things that stink."

Several boys nearby guffawed. Ortega did, too, sort of, even though he wasn't exactly sure what was so funny.

"No!" cried Peter, jumping to his feet. "Miss Rutherford, the gorilla should sit beside *me*. I've already met him and plus I've done so much *studying* on the subject and ..."

"Take a chill pill, Peewee," said the big boy in a bored voice.

"Shut up, Duncan!" said Peter shrilly.

"Ortega will sit beside Eugene," said Miss Rutherford smoothly, pointing at the empty seat in front of Peter, and beside an enormously fat boy, who hastily shoved some sort of plastic food wrapper into his desk at the mention of his name. Peter looked triumphant. Duncan shrugged carelessly and began to twirl a pen between his long, slim fingers with such practiced ease that it made Ortega's heart ache. His own thick fingers could barely hold an oversized pencil, let alone manage something like *that*.

"Can I ask him a question before he sits down?" asked the girl who'd mentioned Myra's armpits. Her position behind Eugene shielded her from Miss Rutherford, but from where he was standing, Ortega could see her perfectly, and his heart leaped when he realized that she had pushed the black silk up over her thin, arched brows and was staring straight at him with the clearest, bluest eyes he'd ever seen in his life. With her blindfold tied kerchief-style over her long, dark hair and a pair of thick gold hoops dangling from her ears, she looked like a pirate. "After all," she continued, her gaze never leaving his face, "he's hardly said a word, and listening to other people talk about him isn't exactly the same thing as getting to know him, is it?"

"No, Janice, I don't suppose it is," admitted Miss Rutherford.

"Good," said Janice. "Then my question for him is this: are you more like a gorilla or more like a person?"

"I never really thought about it," said Ortega. He put a finger to his lower lip and frowned, thinking hard. "I guess I'd have to say I'm like both."

"That's not a good answer," declared Janice.

Ortega shrugged. "It's the only answer I have."

"Then I'll rephrase the question," she said. Dropping her voice a notch, she asked, "If you were caught doing something illegal — like, say, trespassing on private property or robbing a bank — could they put you in jail?"

"I don't know," blurted Ortega, shocked by the question. "I don't think so."

"Well," smiled Janice, her voice dropping even lower until it was hardly more than a husky whisper. "*That* is a good answer."

———⚬⚬⚬———

Other questions followed. Everyone wanted to know how come Ortega could talk, so he explained about the surgeries he'd had as a baby, and about how he'd spent practically his entire life being pestered to do speech exercises designed to bore him half to death. Eugene asked Ortega what he liked to eat. Ortega replied that he *liked* to eat brown sugar and cherry suckers, but that he was mostly fed fruits and vegetables. Eugene seemed to find this hilarious, because he burst into great chortling guffaws that sounded so downright jolly that even Miss Rutherford had to smile. Peter asked many irritating questions regarding the science behind Ortega's development; Duncan asked if he still knew how to make gorilla noises.

"What do you think?" asked Ortega, bellowing fearsomely.

Everyone — including Miss Rutherford — jumped.

Ortega covered his mouth with his hand and snickered to himself until he noticed Miss Rutherford staring at him.

He stopped snickering.

Miss Rutherford waited a few minutes more, until the children had calmed down as much as could be expected under the circumstances, then quietly told them to take off their blindfolds.

At the sight of Ortega, a fresh jolt of noisy excitement surged through the classroom. Myra and her nose-pinching sidekicks let out four well-rehearsed squeals, then jumped up and flapped to the farthest corner of the room squawking like a flock of self-righteous hens. Eugene dissolved into another fit of infectious chuckles. Peter turned this way and that in his seat, breathlessly telling anyone who'd listen that he'd already spoken to *and* touched the gorilla, while on the other side of the room, Duncan and the boys around him hollered and shoved each other with the kind of exuberance that most great adventures inspire in most boys.

Only Janice was silent. Adjusting the black kerchief — which she was still wearing, pirate-style — she yawned theatrically and put her head down on her desk.

Ortega smiled.

All in all, Miss Rutherford had been right. He *was* surprised by how smoothly his introduction to the class had unfolded.

———

The morning was long, and Ortega found it difficult to work without his usual breaks. Back at the lab, Dr. Susan and the others always went the extra mile to make sure he was enjoying his learning experience. It was Dr. Whitmore's belief that in order to push Ortega to his intellectual limits, handlers had to work around his inherent gorilla limitations, which included stubbornness and a poor attention span. Dr. Susan thought this was a bunch of malarkey, but Ortega had learned to make the most of it, purposely sabotaging even the simplest lessons unless he got frequent tickle breaks and extra-special snacks.

Dr. Susan had warned that things would be different when Miss Rutherford took charge of his education. That was proving to be the understatement of the century. The morning dragged on without even the *hint* of a tickle break, and Miss Rutherford did not appear to be in the habit of *ever* handing out edible reward items to students who managed to answer her questions correctly. Not that Ortega would have gotten one even if she were in the habit — already he was finding the work difficult. For a gorilla, he was considered very smart — a gorilla genius! — but in human terms, he was considered kind of slow. Compared with the average kid, he took longer to understand things, and to remember them, and sometimes he didn't get them at all. It had never really bothered him much before — everyone at the lab had always seemed more interested in what he *could* do than in what he *couldn't* do — but he had the feeling it was going to bother him now. Miss Rutherford didn't celebrate correct answers, she *expected* them. What's more, she insisted that people stand and face the class when giving them.

Being the new kid, Ortega managed to avoid this ordeal for nearly the whole morning. As lunchtime approached, however, he sensed that his luck was about to run out, so he cleverly requested a bathroom pass. By knuckle-walking slowly, resting often and reviewing with great interest the vulgar, poorly spelled comments penned on the walls in the stalls, he was able to make the break last until the bell rang.

By the time he got back to the classroom — having weathered the startled stares and screams of students and teachers from other classes who had been expecting to find a talking gorilla in their midst but who hadn't been expecting to find him today, and who certainly hadn't been expecting him to look quite so *real* — everyone but Miss Rutherford and Peter had already left for lunch.

"Peter has offered to show you to the lunchroom, Ortega, and also to enlighten you regarding the miracle of photosynthesis, which you missed owing to the unusual length of time that you spent in the bathroom," said Miss Rutherford reprovingly.

"Sorry," said Ortega, feeling more hungry than sorry. He grabbed his large, bulky lunch bag and followed Peter out of the classroom.

"You're lucky," whispered Peter, wiping his nose with a tissue. "Duncan wanted you to eat lunch with him and his goons from the basketball team, but I convinced Miss Rutherford you'd be better off with me."

Ortega felt a prickle of annoyance. What right did this skinny little gorilla expert have to make decisions for him? And why on earth would he think that Ortega would be better off with *him* than with the biggest boy in the class? It made no sense at all.

He was still ruminating over this when they finally walked into the cafeteria. At once, children began climbing onto chairs and even tables to catch a glimpse of Ortega; they waved and shouted to try to get his attention. A few of the older kids held up jazzy-colored cellular phones and took pictures and video clips; a few of the more daring younger ones reached out and touched him. Teachers ran to and fro shouting for everyone to just calm down.

Ortega ignored them all.

"Do you like watching movies, Ortega?" asked Peter, guiding him through the noisy crowd like a pint-sized Secret Service agent assigned to a particularly huge and hairy president.

"I'd rather watch TV," Ortega replied, even though this wasn't true.

"I like movies," said Peter. "Movies speak to me."

"I like reality television shows," said Ortega, who'd never seen a reality television show in his life.

"Reality television shows don't speak to a person," smiled Peter.

"They speak to me," said Ortega testily, scratching his itchy backside. "Let's sit here," he said, plopping down next to a tiny child who immediately burst into tears.

"We can't sit *there*," whispered Peter, his voice gruff with embarrassment. "That's the Grade 3 table!"

"Well, we can't just march around forever," said Ortega crossly, standing up again. "For heaven's sake, I'm about half dead from hunger!"

"I doubt that," said Peter as he continued to weave through the crowd. "While it's true that wild gorillas eat up to fifty pounds of vegetation a day, most animal species can survive at least a few days eating little or nothing at all."

Ortega wanted to throw something. Suddenly, he wondered if this pipsqueak was another one of Dr. Whitmore's sick little experiments — a test to see just how far Ortega could be pushed before he *did* start hunting down his protein and eating it raw. Closing his eyes, he took a deep, calming sniff of the contents of his lunch bag, tripped and barreled into Peter, who flew halfway across the nearest table. He slid to a stop almost nose-to-nose with the pirate girl, Janice, who grunted hello without looking up from the notebook in which she was scribbling. Eugene, who was sitting beside her, had a mouthful of food, so instead of saying hello, he waved a powdered doughnut at Ortega and grinned, his eyes crinkling merrily.

"Janice, Eugene and I always sit here, in the back corner," explained Peter, crawling off the table as though nothing had happened. Sliding into the chair across from Janice, he pulled a sandwich from his lunch bag. "Janice likes to keep her back to the wall."

Janice — who was still wearing her black silk scarf — nodded. "I don't like people sneaking up on me," she said in that strange, husky voice of hers.

"Why would people do that?" asked Ortega, fascinated.

"You tell me," she said, returning to her notebook.

Ortega sat down beside Peter and took out his lunch. Sandwiches — three of them: cucumber topped with lettuce and alfalfa sprouts. Celery with cheese spread. Strawberries, apple slices, peaches. A baggy full of raisins. A tub of tapioca pudding for dessert.

"Don't you have anything good to eat?" asked Eugene, licking powdered sugar off his fingers.

"Tapioca is good," said Ortega, peeling back the pudding top and picking up the weird-looking spoon that had been specially designed to accommodate the size of his hand and the odd position of his thumb.

At the suggestion that tapioca was good, Eugene let out a belly laugh that started his whole body jiggling. Peter grinned and took a bite of his tomato sandwich. Janice shook her head and smiled. When Ortega saw her very straight, very pretty white teeth, he smiled, too.

Then the cafeteria door slammed open.

It was Duncan. Good-looking and tall, he stood with his feet apart and his hands on his hips, surveying the room. When he spotted Ortega, he said something over his shoulder to the boys trailing in his wake, then strode confidently in Ortega's direction.

"Oh, great!" huffed Peter. Setting down his sandwich, he carefully wiped the mayonnaise from his fingers and swung around in his chair so that he was hanging over the back of it when Duncan arrived at their table.

"Hey, Harry, what's up?" Duncan asked, fearlessly giving Ortega a pat on the head.

Ortega wasn't used to being patted, and he wasn't sure he liked it. Still. "My name isn't Harry. It's Ortega, remember?"

Duncan and his friends burst out laughing. "I didn't mean Harry — I meant *Hairy*. You know, as in covered with hair. It's a nickname, like Peewee. Right, Peewee?" he said, ruffling Peter's hair.

Peter slapped his hand away. "Get lost, Duncan."

"Easy, Peewee," said Duncan. He slid down into the empty chair on the other side of Ortega. "So, Hairy, how's your day been so far?" he asked pleasantly.

"Fine," said Ortega, wishing the boy would just call him by his proper name.

"Even though you got stuck eating lunch with the runt of the litter?" asked Duncan, jerking his chin in Peter's direction.

Peter craned his head to see past Ortega's vast bulk. "He didn't get *stuck* with me, Duncan," he insisted shrilly. "He *wanted* to eat lunch with me. Isn't that right, Ortega?"

Ortega was tempted to bare his teeth at the smaller boy in order to make it clear to everyone that he wanted nothing to do with the smarty-pants runt of the litter. Instead, he put an apple slice into his mouth and chewed in uncomfortable silence.

Peter looked crushed. Duncan grinned, leaned close to Ortega and whispered, "Do you know what I did on my first day at school?"

Thrilled to be taken into the big boy's confidence, Ortega shook his head.

"I pulled a prank," explained Duncan softly. "You know — I did something clever that made everybody laugh."

"What did you do?" asked Ortega in a hushed voice.

"It doesn't matter," murmured Duncan. "What matters is that this is *your* first day and that everybody is watching you. And do you know why they're watching you, Hairy?"

"Because I'm a talking gorilla?" ventured Ortega, who was pretty sure this wasn't the answer that the boy was looking for.

Duncan made a face. "*No*," he said. "They're watching to see whether you really are the freak result of some mad scientist's sick experiment, or whether you're like me. A regular guy."

Ortega flung his baggy of apple slices down. "I'm a regular guy!" he cried in a passionate voice.

Duncan looked unconvinced. Pushing his lips close to Ortega's ear, he breathed, "Prove it."

"How?" asked Ortega.

"Pull your own prank. Like, see the janitor over by the lunch counter?"

Ortega looked over and saw a lady custodian in faded blue coveralls. He nodded at Duncan.

"Well, if you *really* wanted to prove that you were a regular guy, I *suppose* you could sneak up behind her and do one of those gorilla roars of yours."

Ortega looked back at the thin, dark-haired woman, who was mopping up a spilled bowl of soup. Her shoulders were just a little bit stooped; even from the back, she looked tired.

"I don't know," he said.

"Don't know what?" asked Peter anxiously, looking over at the lady custodian.

"None of your business, Peewee. This is between me and Hairy," snapped Duncan. Then he shrugged at Ortega and said that if he wanted everybody to think he was a freak, that was fine with him.

"I don't want that!" protested Ortega. "It's just that Dr. Whitmore — he's the one in charge of my lab — he says there better not be any funny business while I'm at school."

"Or else what?" asked Duncan contemptuously.

Ortega didn't answer. There were things Dr. Whitmore could do, and he'd do them if he thought his research was being jeopardized. His research meant more to him than anything in the world. Including Ortega.

Suddenly, Duncan shoved his chair back. It scraped across the floor with an angry screech. "You know what?" he said in a disgusted voice. "Just forget it."

"Wait!" pleaded Ortega.

Duncan looked at him expectantly.

"Whatever it is, don't do it," advised Janice, examining her glossy black fingernails.

Ortega ignored her. With a wildly hammering heart, he got to his feet and began to stealthily knuckle-walk toward the oblivious lady custodian. Almost immediately, he heard someone behind him yelp. Looking back, he saw one of the basketball goons sitting on top of Peter, who was flailing his skinny limbs like an insect pinned by a fat thumb. Edging forward again, Ortega got as close to the lady custodian as he could without his smell giving him away, took a deep breath, bent his knees and ...

RRRRRIP!

The seam in his uncomfortable new pants tore without warning. There was a moment of stunned silence, and then the cafeteria exploded with laughter. The lady custodian jumped at the sound of the laughter and then jumped again when she turned and saw Ortega crouched as though preparing to spring. Taking a hasty step backward, she stuck her foot directly into her pail of soapy water. The pail — which was on wheels — lurched to one side, pulling her remaining foot out from under her and dumping its contents in a single, fluid movement.

Both hands splayed awkwardly over his torn seam, Ortega took one look at the shrieking crowd, the soapy mess and the drenched lady custodian, and fled.

He hid in the boys' washroom until Miss Rutherford tracked him down. He tried to make her understand how upsetting it had been for him when the plan to get people to think he was a regular guy had backfired, but she wasn't even a bit sympathetic. After giving him a sound scolding, she ordered him to the classroom to tidy the bookshelves and then marched off in search of Duncan, whom she somehow already knew had been the mastermind behind the plan.

Back in the classroom, Ortega spent the rest of the lunch period lethargically (and sloppily) shoving books onto bookshelves, ruminating over Miss Rutherford's insensitive treatment of him and hoping that Duncan would give him another chance to prove himself.

This hope vanished, however, when Duncan stormed into the classroom just before the start of afternoon classes and — right in front of everybody! — angrily accused Ortega of having ratted him out. Flustered, Ortega tried to explain that he hadn't said anything to Miss Rutherford about whose idea the prank had been, but Duncan called him a "rat freak" and said it wasn't right that the captain of the school basketball team should get a three-game suspension just because some stupid talking monkey couldn't keep his big fat trap shut.

Before anyone — including Ortega — could do or say anything in response to those dreadful words, Miss Rutherford entered the room and, after calling the class to order, launched into a detailed review of long division. Ortega (who was terrible at long division) tried to pay attention, but he was so upset that he couldn't help casting furtive pleading looks across the room at Duncan. The boy ignored him the first three times he looked over; the fourth time, he hit Ortega between the eyes with a very slimy spitball. Peter — who'd been studiously ignoring Ortega since the beginning of class — got the next one, right in the ear. Jabbing Ortega in the back with his pen, he whispered that he hoped Ortega was having fun with his new best friend. Then he picked the spitball from his ear, flicked it at Ortega's head and lapsed back into furious silence.

Ortega spent the rest of the afternoon alone, picking spitballs out of his thick hair and yearning for Dr. Susan, whom he missed more with each passing moment. When the bell finally rang at three-thirty, he slowly packed up his knapsack, all the while mentally fine-tuning the speech he was going to give Dr. Susan the minute he climbed into the back of her Chevette Scooter. So far, his main points were

a) sending a dummy like him to this stupid school had been a stupid idea,
b) he had told her so, and
c) he would come back the day pigs flew out of Dr. Whitmore's rear end.

Feeling somewhat heartened, he threw the knapsack over his shoulder, gave a last, contemptuous glance at his would-be classmates and headed out the door.

When he got downstairs, however, instead of being able to gallop over to Dr. Susan's car in peace, he was confronted by a great mob of people, many of whom were holding signs. Word had gotten out that Ortega had come to school a day early, and protesters and supporters alike had converged on the front lawn of the school. When they spied him standing in the lobby, moodily observing them, they all started shaking their signs and shouting like maniacs. Photographers elbowed their way to the front of the mob, each hoping to be the first to get a shot of the gorilla at school.

Suddenly, a robust woman in an ugly leather jacket and a long, tweed skirt dropped her sign, broke away from the crowd and sailed through the door like a battleship. In the dimness of the lobby, she sniffed this way and that as though picking up a foul scent. When her imperious gaze finally landed on Ortega, she snapped a handkerchief out of her breast pocket and held it to her nostrils.

"I can't believe the town council really went through with it," she said, gesturing toward him with undisguised distaste. "And after I warned them that such goings-on at the school named after my beloved grammy would have her rolling over in her grave."

She paused to cast a wounded look up at the portrait of the lemon-sucking witch.

"Tell me, ma'am," said Ortega gravely, "is your grammy dead, or is the coffin just where she sleeps during the day?"

Behind him, Ortega heard someone stifle a snicker. The woman gasped.

"How ... how *dare* you!" she sputtered, fluttering her handkerchief at him.

"How dare *you*!" he screeched, stamping his foot.

"That's enough, Ortega," interrupted Miss Rutherford, who had just arrived in the lobby, along with Myra and a few others.

"But ..."

"Enough!" said Miss Rutherford sharply.

Ortega said nothing more out loud, but in his mind he muttered some very rude insults at Miss Rutherford and taped a KICK ME sign to the back of her cardigan.

"Mark my words, Cordelia," the woman told Miss Rutherford ominously. "*This*" — she thrust her formidable nose in Ortega's direction — "was a mistake. Come along, Myra," she commanded. Turning away from Ortega and Miss Rutherford, she clamped a bony hand around her daughter's arm and sailed back out the door.

"That wasn't very polite, Ortega," observed Miss Rutherford, after Myra and her mother had gone.

"You can say that again," he agreed sourly. Then he saw Dr. Susan, battling her way to the front door. "Good-bye, Miss

Rutherford," he said, taking a deep breath to prepare himself for the onslaught he was about to face. "I've got to go."

———◦≈◦———

Dr. Susan didn't say much in response to Ortega's speech about pigs flying out of Dr. Whitmore's rear end, but she did take him to the ice-cream parlor for a super-fudge parfait to celebrate his first day of school.

"And my last day," he reminded her, hurriedly trying to lick the parfait glass clean before she could snatch it away from him.

Dr. Susan — who probably *should* have snatched the parfait glass away and then lectured Ortega about his atrocious table manners — just gave him a troubled smile and wiped chocolate sauce off his nose before suggesting they go down to the nearby riverbank and catch frogs for a while before heading home.

Later that night, after tucking him in beside Mr. Doodles, she sat down at the edge of Ortega's bed. Propping her elbow on her knee, she tucked her fist under her chin and regarded him thoughtfully. Ortega looked away, waiting for the pep talk he always got when he was tired of being pushed to be special.

It never came.

Instead, Dr. Susan began to sing his favorite lullaby from when he was small — a song with a low, rocking rhythm that told of butterfly dreams and sunny days. It reminded Ortega of the ocean. He sighed contentedly and scrunched farther down in the soft high-walled nest he'd constructed out of his Spider-Man comforter.

"Tomorrow will be better," she promised, when the lullaby was over.

"Yes, it will," he agreed sleepily, "because I'll be right here with you."

Chapter Three

The next morning, Ortega was wakened by the sound of whispering voices outside his bedroom door.

"Oh, Susan, this is *ridiculous*," muttered Dr. Whitmore in an exasperated voice.

"Dr. Whitmore, please!" whispered Dr. Susan. "If we turn this into a showdown, it'll be bad for everyone and —"

"This is my lab, Susan," he interrupted sternly. "There will be no showdowns — things will be done my way or there will be consequences for those who oppose me."

"Shh!" she hushed him. "I know, I know! I'm sorry, I just meant that ... that I think if we can get him to *cooperate* we'll have a better chance of seeing what he's really capable of."

There was a long pause.

"Fine," sniffed Dr. Whitmore. "We'll do it your way this time, Susan, but I have to tell you, sometimes I wonder whose side you're really on."

Dr. Susan murmured something that Ortega couldn't hear. Then she said, "Okay, now if you'll just lift up the back of your lab coat ... Hold still.... Oops! One got away.... Dr. Whitmore, you have to *hold still*.... Okay, are you ready? Here we go. Shhh!"

Ortega heard the sound of his door opening.

"Ortega? Are you awake?" whispered Dr. Susan as she tiptoed into his room, looking mighty pleased with herself.

Dr. Whitmore shuffled awkwardly in after her, a sour expression on his face.

Ortega sat up and rubbed his eyes. "Do you have to go to the toilet, Dr. Whitmore?" he asked.

"No," he replied peevishly.

Dr. Susan bounded behind her supervisor and jerked up the back of his lab coat. To Ortega's surprise, pink helium balloons decorated with hand-drawn snouts and curly tails started floating across the room.

"Look, Ortega!" cried Dr. Susan, clapping her hands. "Pigs are flying out of Dr. Whitmore's rear end!" She grabbed a balloon with a blue polka-dot bow tie drawn under its porky chin and handed it to him.

"Why, Dr. Whitmore — this pig is wearing the same bow tie you are!" Ortega observed brightly.

"Very funny, Susan," scowled Dr. Whitmore.

Dr. Susan tried to look sorry. "Time to get ready for school, Ortega," she said, tugging his comforter off the bed.

"Hey!" he complained.

"Breakfast is in five minutes. Be dressed," she said briskly, dumping the comforter out of reach and walking out of the room.

Dr. Whitmore looked at Ortega.

"Oink, oink," snorted Ortega, climbing out of bed.

After Dr. Whitmore left, Ortega pulled on his clothes and hurried to feed his pets — Norman, the speckled frog he'd rescued from the neurology lab, Siggy, the white mouse he'd rescued from the endocrinology lab, and the Lancaster-Stone family, a jar of fruit flies he'd rescued from the genetics lab.

"Ortega!" called Dr. Susan from the kitchenette two doors down.

"Coming!" he called back.

Carefully latching the top of Siggy's cage, Ortega knuckled his way down the tiled hall. "You tricked me," he announced as he plopped down into his seat. "I meant *real* pigs."

"Well, next time say what you mean," said Dr. Susan, setting a giant bowl of leafy greens and cut fruit in front of him. "Did you see the look on Dr. Whitmore's face?"

Ortega felt cheered in spite of himself.

Dr. Susan poured him a glass of papaya juice and slid into the chair beside him. "Guess what? You're front-page news," she said, plunking a newspaper down on the table in front of him. "Look, here's a picture of you coming out of school. Don't you look great?"

Ortega thought he looked better than great. He thought he looked fantastic! Next to him, those loudmouthed protesters looked like a bunch of puny little fleas. "I look all right, I guess," he mumbled, taking a slurp of his juice.

"There were also some clips of you on VideoJunkie," she said, frowning. "I'm not at all happy about the fact that the school allowed the children to videotape you, and I've already spoken with the administrators about the need to tighten their policy on cell-phone use in school, for everyone's sake —"

Ortega closed his eyes and slurped his juice as loudly as he could in order to show Dr. Susan that he was rapidly losing interest in the conversation.

"— but those videos are going to astonish our detractors in the scientific community," she continued. Ortega's eyes snapped open. "I mean, they clearly show you doing regular school stuff — walking down the hall with other children, looking for something in your locker. Why, one of them even shows you eating lunch in the cafeteria!"

Ortega waited for her to say something about having seen video footage of his foiled attempt to scare the living crap out of the lady custodian. When she didn't, he breathed a sigh of relief and shoveled a massive clump of organic cauliflower into his mouth.

"Slow down. You're going to choke," clucked Dr. Susan, giving him a poke in the armpit.

He chuckled deeply and shoved another clump of cauliflower into his mouth.

Dr. Susan watched him for a long moment. Then she cleared her throat, looked down at her hands and said, "Listen, Ortega, as interested as I was in those video clips — which I don't think anybody had a right to take — I know in my heart that yesterday wasn't easy for you."

He shrugged noncommittally, but his gaze slid sideways.

"I also understand why you haven't really said much about it," she continued softly. "And why you don't want to go back."

"That's why you are my favorite person in the whole world," he said.

Dr. Susan looked up. "You like me better than the ice-cream man?" she asked in surprise.

"Okay, you're my second favorite person in the whole world," he purred.

Dr. Susan smiled. Then her smile faded.

"I understand all those things, Ortega," she said, reaching out to give his hand a squeeze, "but it doesn't change what has to happen here. You have to go back to school, and then you have to come home and answer my questions so we can get a sense of how you're progressing. It wasn't easy getting Dr. Whitmore to agree to keep trained observers out of the classroom — he only gave in because I convinced him that the benefits of direct data collection didn't outweigh the risk that the presence of observers would be so distracting to you that they'd ruin the experiment altogether."

Ortega — who hadn't realized that having one of Dr. Whitmore's lackeys spying on him all day long had even been an *option* — was horrified. "If you put observers in my classroom, I'll sit at my desk like a drooling imbecile and pretend that I've never even heard of the alphabet!" he screeched, leaning over to lick the fruit juice off his plate.

Dr. Susan snatched the plate away before he could make contact. "Then please — go to school," she said softly, giving his nose a tweak. "And come home and talk to me."

———

Talk to her about what? wondered Ortega morosely, as they bumped and bounced their way down the gravel road on the way to school. *About how I'm a dummy with no friends?* He watched as Dr. Susan rolled down her window and belted out "Feelin' Groovy" to a very surprised Jersey cow, and he knew that she really wouldn't be mad if he was a dummy with no friends.

Somehow that only made it worse.

By the time they reached the school, Ortega had made a decision. Even though Dr. Susan had never said so, he knew from Dr. Whitmore that she needed the data from this next phase of Project Ortega to complete a series of articles she was writing. They were going to be published in one of the most prestigious scientific journals in the field, and although Dr. Susan would never admit it to him, Ortega knew this meant a great deal to her.

And so, since she meant a great deal to him, he vowed to do whatever it took to make sure she got all the data she could possibly need, as quickly as possible — so that he could get out of school and come home to her, once and for all.

———

That morning, after pushing his way past a slightly smaller crowd of protesters and swatting away a lone reporter's microphone, Ortega trudged upstairs to his classroom, slid into his seat and nervously said hello to Peter. The boy immediately turned to Janice and Eugene and invited them to eat lunch with him in his tree fort down by the river. Ortega, who had always *loved* the idea of tree forts, edged a little closer in the hope that he might be invited to join them, but

Peter refused to even look at him, so eventually, feeling foolish, Ortega turned back around in his seat and quietly waited for Miss Rutherford to arrive. While he was waiting, Duncan repeatedly whistled at him, but every time Ortega looked over he got a spitball in the face, so eventually he stopped looking. After that, he kept to himself. He wasn't going to fit in here — that was clear to him now. But it was also beside the point. This wasn't about him anymore. It was about Dr. Susan.

Which is why, when she arrived to pick him up eight hours later, he bounded down to the Chevette Scooter, his face brimming with excitement.

"You had a good day!" she guessed, clasping her soft hands under her chin.

"Did I ever!" he enthused, hopping into the car. He smiled broadly and waved past her at a cluster of students who were looking in the opposite direction.

"Who are you waving to?" asked Dr. Susan, turning quickly.

"Friends, of course!" he laughed, buckling up. "Take me home and I'll tell you everything!"

———⋙⋘———

That night, Dr. Whitmore barged into Ortega's bedroom and told him he'd better knock off the funny business.

"I have no idea what you're talking about," said Ortega, munching romaine lettuce with his mouth open because he knew the sound drove Dr. Whitmore nuts.

Dr. Whitmore twitched. "You told Susan that the class unanimously voted to give you the honorary title of Mr. Popularity."

"You've been eavesdropping on my private conversations with Dr. Susan again, haven't you?" demanded Ortega.

Dr. Whitmore ignored the question. "You said a brawl broke out in the cafeteria because so many of the guys wanted to eat lunch with you, and that a catfight broke out afterward because so many of the girls wanted to kiss you," he continued hotly. "You said your teacher, Miss Rutherford, called you a gifted mathematician and gave you a five-minute standing ovation for your work in the field of the eight-times table."

Ortega leaned back in his purple beanbag chair and peeled a banana. "So?" he said, noisily sucking the entire thing into his mouth.

"So?" snapped Dr. Whitmore. "So, those are *obviously* lies."

With an extremely bored look on his face, Ortega slurped up half the banana peel. The other half dangled out of his mouth as he chewed loudly and scratched his hairy belly.

Dr. Whitmore pursed his lips. "I don't know what you hope to accomplish with this obstinate behavior, Ortega, but if you think I'm going to pull you out of school, think again. I've worked too hard and sacrificed too much to see this experiment fail for want of a little cooperation from you!"

With an exaggerated sigh, Ortega rolled over and poked a tiny piece of carrot through the bars of Siggy's cage. The little white mouse reared up on its hind legs and gave a cautious sniff.

"Has Susan done something to turn you off school?" murmured Dr. Whitmore, almost to himself. "Is that it? Should I have her replaced with a new handler?"

"No!" said Ortega, sitting up in alarm.

"Then cooperate," snapped Dr. Whitmore. "We've learned all we can from observing you in the lab, Ortega. We need real-world experience in order to assess the potential of the technology that you represent. Do you understand?"

Ortega watched Siggy's tiny paws grasp the piece of carrot that had slipped from his own clumsy fingers.

"The advancement of science can be unpleasant for everyone," Dr. Whitmore continued, as Siggy scurried off and began to nibble. "But you must try to remember that

I've always treated you humanely, Ortega. Always. You could have ended up in a zoo — or a circus — or an animal-research laboratory."

"This is an animal-research laboratory," muttered Ortega, rooting around the bottom of his snack bowl for a snow pea.

"You know what I mean," said Dr. Whitmore. "From now on, you will report truthfully on your activities during the day. No more of your ridiculous lies."

Ortega picked up a cluster of green grapes. "What makes you so sure they're lies?" he asked curiously, plucking off grapes with his toes and daintily popping them into his mouth.

Dr. Whitmore grimaced — he hated watching Ortega eat with his feet. It went against everything he was trying to accomplish with Project Ortega.

"Because," he replied tartly, "controlled scientific studies — and my own personal experience — tell me children that age don't react that positively, that quickly, to someone as different as you."

Ortega dropped the grapes back into the snack bowl. "You mean you *knew* they'd be mean to me?" he asked incredulously. "But if you knew, why did you send me?"

Dr. Whitmore started to say something, then stopped. He smiled and wagged his finger at Ortega. "Now, now," he chuckled. "You know I can't tell you that, Ortega. Revealing the full scope of my hypothesis would compromise the study."

In response, Ortega flung the snack bowl at him.

"Ortega!" Dr. Whitmore cried in dismay, as the plastic bowl clattered to the floor.

Ortega leaped up and began pelting Dr. Whitmore with the remnants of his snack.

"Stop it!" ordered Dr. Whitmore, as a tree of broccoli caught him upside the head. "Stop it this instant! Susan!" he shouted, beating a hasty retreat. "Susan! Oh, for Pete's sake. SUSAN!"

Ortega chased him out into the hall. "Did anyone ever vote to give *you* the honorary title of Mr. Popularity?" he hollered, flinging half a red pepper at Dr. Whitmore, who was scampering down the hall to the safety of his office.

"We're not talking about me, Ortega," Dr. Whitmore's voice floated back to him.

"I DIDN'T THINK SO!" Ortega bellowed furiously. Rearing up, he beat on his chest until the *pock-pock-pock* sound echoed up and down the hall. Then he galloped back into his room and slammed his door so hard that the framed baby pictures of him that Dr. Susan had hung up in the hall outside fell to the ground and shattered.

"Good morning, Mr. Popularity," whispered Dr. Susan, gently shaking him awake.

Ortega grunted and huddled farther down in the limp nest of dirty clothes he'd built for himself the previous evening after his confrontation with Dr. Whitmore. He was supposed to sleep in the bed — where he could be easily viewed through the observation window — but whenever he could get away with it, he bedded down in the blind corner behind his beanbag chair.

"Dr. Whitmore isn't very happy," murmured Dr. Susan.

"Dr. Whitmore is a jerk," came the muffled response.

Dr. Susan hesitated. "He's just … focused."

"Yeah. On being a jerk."

"No, on his work."

His jerk work, thought Ortega, snickering to himself.

"What's so funny?" asked Dr. Susan, leaning over to give his ribs a little tickle.

"Nothing," snapped Ortega, sitting up abruptly.

Dirty clothes dripped from his head and shoulders, giving him a comical appearance, but Dr. Susan didn't laugh.

Ortega fixed his small dark eyes on her wide blue ones until she blinked and looked away.

"You're about a billion times smarter than Dr. Whitmore, so if he knew they'd be mean to me, then so did you," he accused, giving her a hard poke in the belly.

Dr. Susan flushed. "Ortega, I —"

"You lied when you said you'd never leave me unless you thought I'd be okay!" he interrupted loudly, flinging a pair of dirty underwear at her head.

"No!" cried Dr. Susan, ducking. "I didn't lie, I just … I wanted you to feel *safe*, Ortega, and … oh, these things are so complicated sometimes! So frustrating! I do everything I can to keep you protected and happy — I *swear* I do — but there's just so much I can't control and —"

Ortega squeezed his eyes shut, stuffed his fingers into his ears and started humming loudly. His plan was to ignore her until she got really, *really* annoyed, and then to lick her across the face before galloping off to empty her purse into the toilet. Unfortunately, she just sat patiently beside him for so long that he finally yanked his fingers out of his ears in irritation and glared at her.

"It would mean a lot to everyone if you'd keep trying," she said with a shrug.

"I don't care about everyone," he snapped. He waited for her to say that it would mean a lot to *her*. When she didn't, he stood up. "*Fine*," he huffed. "I'll try again. Now would you mind leaving my room, please? I'd like a little privacy while I'm getting dressed, if that isn't too much to ask."

The minute Dr. Susan left, Ortega pulled on a fresh pair of ugly, uncomfortable new pants and a stretchy white shirt with a collar. Over the shirt he pulled a green cardigan with very deep pockets. Into one of the pockets he slipped his blue velvet marble bag. And into the marble bag, he slipped his little white mouse, Siggy.

He would try again. But there was no *way* he would try alone.

———

Having Siggy with him at school made all the difference. Ortega wasn't nervous anymore when Miss Rutherford asked him to stand and answer questions, because he knew he wasn't standing alone. And when no one wanted to be his partner in gym or share paints with him in art class or sit beside him in the cafeteria, it didn't bother him a bit. What did he care if those jerk kids didn't want to be his friends? He didn't need them. He already had a friend — a friend *and* a secret. It didn't get better than that.

The mouse-in-the-pocket strategy worked beautifully for exactly two days.

Then, at high noon on Friday, disaster struck.

———

In hindsight, Ortega decided that he, of all people, should have anticipated Siggy's reaction to being cooped up in a marble bag all day. Though the little mouse was frequently slipped bits of carrot and cracker and taken to the bathroom stall for fresh air, chin tickles and clean toilet water from a juice bottle cap, Siggy clearly longed for freedom. In fact, when Ortega thought about it afterward, the only thing that surprised him was how long it had taken his little friend to decide to chew his way out of his blue velvet prison.

But none of this occurred to Ortega until after it was all over, so it shook him badly when he reached into the pocket of his cardigan that day to slip Siggy a lunchtime treat and discovered him missing. Heart pounding, Ortega dug around his pocket more carefully, hoping that somehow his clumsy fingers had simply failed to detect the presence of a live rodent in five square inches of fuzzy darkness. When he still felt nothing, Ortega pulled out the marble bag. Empty! He examined it furtively. Chewed! Oh no! Siggy was gone!

Before he could succumb to a full-blown panic attack, Ortega heard a tiny squeak in his left ear. Looking down, he saw Siggy perched comfortably on his massive shoulder, surveying the wide world around him with keen interest.

"There you are!" Ortega whispered fondly. He resisted the urge to grab the little mouse and hurry him back to the safety of the cardigan pocket. He didn't want to frighten him, and besides, any sudden move could inspire Siggy to jump and run. And if *that* was to happen, Ortega knew he'd never be able to catch him without making a scene. "You frightened me," continued Ortega in a soft whisper, nudging a tiny piece of celery toward Siggy. "I guess I didn't feel you climbing up my sweater."

The mouse clutched the proffered treat, and as he began to nibble away at it, Ortega slowly reached out for him. Just before his large, leathery hand could close around his little friend, however, another hand darted in, scooped up Siggy and whisked him away.

"Got it!" whooped the voice that belonged to the hand.

Ortega spun in his seat to see Duncan dangling Siggy by the tail. The little mouse was squeaking pitifully; his tiny paws clawed the air in terror.

"WHAT ARE YOU DOING!" shrieked Ortega, springing to his feet.

Startled by the suddenness of Ortega's movement, Duncan flung the mouse aside. Ortega watched in horror as Siggy flew slow somersaults in the air before landing hard.

On Peter's head.

Instinctively, Peter's hand flew up and closed around the limp little body. The feel of the squeezing hand revived the stunned mouse in the most spectacular way. With a heroic squeak, Siggy began to squirm. The feel of the squirming furry thing caused Peter to panic. Snatching his hand away, he jumped up, screaming, and began to shake his head furiously. The noise and movement spurred Siggy to even greater heights. With renewed vigor, he scrabbled and clawed his way through the boy's thick hair. Upon reaching the forward hairline, Siggy paused for the merest instant before leaping into the abyss before him. He landed with a *plop* on Peter's tomato sandwich, skidded on a stray droplet of mayonnaise and proceeded to scurry across the table, his hindquarters wiggling hard, his tail lashing from side to side.

Peter — who was clearly caught in the grips of a major case of the willies — continued to scream, but his screams were soon drowned out by the cries of "Mouse! Mouse!" that echoed up and down the lunchroom. Hysterical children leaped onto tables, squashing sandwiches and kicking over drink boxes; someone across the room started a food fight. Spurred on by the chaos he'd created, Siggy scurried faster — under pieces of smeared wax paper and across torn foil wrappers — until he skidded to a halt at the far edge of the table. Now began shrieks of "Catch it! Catch it!" which clearly resonated deep within the little mouse, triggering an even more profound self-preservation instinct. Hurting, terrified and out of breath, Siggy recklessly flung himself at the nearest student, scurried down the stomping child's pant leg and took off across the lunchroom floor.

By this point, Ortega was half mad with fear. The place was like a mouse minefield — careless, trampling feet were everywhere!

"Careful!" he cried as he tiptoed in the direction he'd last seen his friend. "Please, watch where you're stepping!"

Dropping to his knuckles, he frantically scanned the floor. When he stood up, he noticed a heightened commotion a few tables down. The self-righteous hens were perched on their chairs squealing like a trio of tone-deaf alley cats.

And on the floor in front of them, pinch-faced Myra was stomping with a deliberateness that made Ortega's blood run cold.

The sight triggered in him the instinct that all too frequently resulted in the death of the dominant silverback male gorilla when poachers threatened the safety of the wild family group.

It was the instinct to protect.

There was nothing human in the scream Ortega made when he saw Myra's foot come down again.

And no bluff in the charge that followed.

And deep within his heart, Ortega knew that the only thing that saved Myra from ... well, from *him* ... was the fact that Janice beat him to her.

Brandishing her notebook in one hand and a thermos cup in the other, the pirate girl leaped from table to table before swooping down lightly and shoving Myra just hard enough to knock her off balance. Dropping to her knees, Janice disappeared from sight. Half a second later, when Ortega skidded to a halt before her, she was holding the thermos cup carefully over Siggy, whose quivering white tail protruded pathetically from the crack between the cup and the notebook.

Ortega bared his teeth at Myra, but there was no real heart in it. The fever had passed. Siggy was safe.

"Out of my way," a quavery but commanding voice rang out. "Out. Of. My. Way."

Behind him, Ortega heard the sound of sensible shoes, and a moment later Miss Rutherford appeared. A single, sweeping glance was all she needed to identify this as the epicenter of the tempest. Her gaze came to a rest on the overturned thermos cup. "What is that?" she asked Janice sharply.

"It's my mouse," blurted Ortega. "Duncan kidnapped him and Myra tried to murder him!"

"Exterminating vermin is not *murder*," sneered Myra.

"SIGGY IS NOT VERMIN," bellowed Ortega.

Everyone in the cafeteria fell silent — so silent that Ortega could hear the sound of raindrops splattering against the grimy windows high above. Suddenly, he felt as if he was suffocating. In his mind, he pictured himself throwing back his head and bellowing again — not words, this time, but pure feeling, raw and wild and *free*.

"Get your mouse and come with me, Ortega," said Miss Rutherford quietly.

For a moment, he just stood where he was, tense with indecision. Then Janice flipped over the thermos cup and held it out to him. Siggy blinked and peered anxiously over the sides of the cup like someone clinging to a swaying life raft in stormy seas. Ortega made a series of low, comforting noises in his throat and gently drew the cup to his massive chest. Here, the little mouse — thoroughly exhausted by his harrowing adventure — promptly curled up and fell asleep.

If Ortega had caused such an incident at the lab, Dr. Whitmore would probably have locked him up and thrown away the key. But Miss Rutherford didn't lock up Ortega, or even threaten to do so. Instead, she admonished him for bringing his pet to school, found him a box in which to store Siggy for the afternoon and told him to wait quietly in the classroom until the bell rang.

Ortega supposed he should have felt grateful for getting off so easily, but he didn't. He reeked of fear, his stomach was churning and the walls felt as if they were closing in on him. After Miss Rutherford left the room, he tried to calm himself by counting to one hundred, but by the time he reached seventeen, he was hooting at the top of his lungs and slapping the palms of his hands down on the desktop with such force that he created a breeze that reached all the way across the aisle to Eugene's desk. Here, it nudged a folded note at the edge of the desktop, causing it to flutter to the ground.

Ortega stopped beating his desk at once. He stared at the note. He'd watched it being passed around the room that morning — stealthily, so that Miss Rutherford wouldn't notice. Then, just before the lunch bell rang, it had been passed to Peter, who sat right behind Ortega. There'd been a minute of silence, then Ortega had been *shocked* to hear the boy whisper, "Psst!" Heart hammering with excitement, Ortega had reached his long arm back and waited for the feel of the mysterious note being furtively pressed into his waiting hand.

But it had never come, because instead of passing the note to Ortega, Peter had passed it right under Ortega's nose, to Eugene.

Ortega had felt like a fool.

Leaning over now, he picked up the note. Without thinking, he gave it a cautious sniff. It smelled like dirty fingers. Intrigued, Ortega stuck out his tongue and licked it. Then — as though suddenly remembering where he was — he snorted self-consciously, looked around to make sure no one had seen what he'd done and hastily unfolded the note, eager to be let in on the secret.

Only it wasn't a secret. It was a poorly drawn cartoon of an ugly, hulking, cross-eyed gorilla with a long rat tail. He had several tiny, terrified stick children stuffed into his mouth and a speech bubble over his head that said, "I'M A RAT FREAK. WILL YOU BE MY FRIEND???"

Ortega stared at the cartoon.

"But I'm a vegetarian," he whispered in a tremulous voice.

On a shelf near the window, Siggy clawed noisily at the sides of his small, unfamiliar box, hungry to be free.

Feeling dazed, Ortega let the note slip from between his fingers. Slowly, he stood up, knuckle-walked over to the shelf and lifted Siggy out of the box. For a long moment he just stood there, nuzzling the mouse's warm, furry body against his leathery cheek and looking out the window into the wet gray day beyond. Then, almost without thinking about what he was doing, he slipped Siggy into his pocket, turned on one heel and abruptly left the room.

Five minutes later, Ortega slipped out the front doors of the school and into the driving rain. It felt wonderful to be able to breathe again, but he hardly noticed. He needed to find somewhere to hide, and fast, before anybody noticed he was missing. Surveying the barren landscape, he was momentarily discouraged. Then he spotted the dilapidated factory on the hill in the distance. Going inside was out of the question, of course, but it was surrounded by trees, and if he could make it to them without being spotted, he just might be okay.

Dropping both fists to the ground, Ortega galloped as fast as he could across the open field, taking care not to joggle Siggy too much and snatching glances over his shoulder every few seconds, fearful that he would discover that he was being pursued. When he finally barreled into the shelter of the trees, he was gasping for air and had a painful stitch in his side, but without stopping or even slowing down he picked out the sturdiest tree and began climbing to the highest branch that looked capable of supporting his weight.

When he reached it, he was surprised to discover that a muddy-looking river ran behind the factory. He stared at it, wondering what it would be like to float down that river and discover a place full of gorilla people just like him. Then he bowed his head and huddled against the trunk of the tree. He listened to the sound of the chill wind in the leaves, and watched his hot breath mist the air around him. With a thick finger he slowly traced the path of a stray raindrop that had landed near the corner of his eye and trickled down his cheek. And he thought to himself that it was probably a very *good* thing that gorillas didn't know how to cry. Because at that moment, if he'd been able to start, Ortega wasn't sure he'd ever have been able to stop.

Chapter Four

About an hour later, Ortega watched without much surprise as Dr. Susan's rusty old Chevette Scooter turned sharply onto the overgrown road that led up to the abandoned factory and skidded to a bumpy halt not far from the tree in which he sat. Miss Rutherford must have called to let her know he'd bolted, and knowing what a nature lover he was, Dr. Susan must have decided that the nearest big tree was as good a place as any to start looking for him.

The car door opened and Dr. Susan stepped out. "Ortega?" she called.

He stared down at the top of her frizzy head with a lump in his throat, resisting the urge to call out to her.

"I've got Mr. Doodles in the backseat," she said. "He insisted on coming along to help look for you, and even snuck into Dr. Whitmore's office and used his last three packets of specialty cocoa mix to make a nice big thermos of hot chocolate for you. I don't think I have to tell you how upset Dr. Whitmore is going to be when he discovers what Mr. Doodles has done."

Ortega smiled in spite of himself. He longed to take a deep sniff of his ratty old stuffed bear, and his mouth watered for cocoa.

"Come down, Ortega," she coaxed. "Let's talk about what happened."

"I'M SICK OF TALKING!" he shouted suddenly, shaking a nearby branch so hard it broke off with a satisfying *snap*. "TALKING IS WHAT GOT ME INTO THIS STUPID MESS IN THE FIRST PLACE!"

He bellowed and hurled the broken branch downward. As planned, it landed well clear of Dr. Susan.

"Then don't talk," she said softly. "Just come down. Come home with Mr. Doodles and me."

Ortega's heart leaped. "Come home with you? Really?" he asked.

Squinting up into the rain, Dr. Susan nodded.

"But what about school?" he asked. "Dr. Whitmore will kill me if I mess up his experiment."

"He won't *kill* you, Ortega."

"You're right," he agreed sourly. "He'll do worse than that. He'll dress me up in a tutu and sell me to a circus and I'll spend the rest of my life performing humiliating dance routines for cheering morons with candy apple caught between their teeth."

Dr. Susan sneezed twice. "Let me worry about Dr. Whitmore," she said. "Just get down here, will you? I'm getting soaked."

Ortega hesitated. "I'll come down on one condition."

"What is that?" asked Dr. Susan.

"Tonight, I want to eat dinner at Pizza Pizzazz."

"Fine," she agreed.

"Then I want us to spend the evening together eating popcorn and watching gruesome horror movies, and then I want you to sleep over in case I wake up with nightmares," said Ortega as he began to climb down the tree.

"You said one condition."

"I know, but you gave in to that one so easily that I changed my mind," he explained, continuing his downward climb.

"I'll think about it."

"I want an answer now!" he demanded as he launched himself out of the tree in a flurry of snapped twigs and torn leaves.

"Fine," said Dr. Susan, as Ortega landed in a huge, hairy lump at her feet. "Then the answer is no."

"Okay, you think about it," he murmured agreeably, reaching up to give her a wet chin tickle. "Did you really steal Dr. Whitmore's last three packets of specialty cocoa mix to make hot chocolate for me?" he asked.

"Of course not," she replied, avoiding his gaze. "Like I said, it was Mr. Doodles."

Ortega smiled and reached for her hand. "That's what I thought," he sighed.

Luckily, Dr. Whitmore was in a meeting when they got back to the lab, so Ortega was able to return Siggy to his cage, change into dry clothes and escape to Pizza Pizzazz without being reprimanded or, worse, being subjected to another ridiculous speech about how progress was just as hard for the famous scientist as it was for the miserable test subject.

"Because it isn't, you know," he insisted, in between shoveling thick slices of vegetarian pizza into his mouth. "How can it be? He can do whatever he wants to me and I can't do anything to him."

"What about the time you put in a work order to have the hard drive on his laptop wiped clean?" asked Dr. Susan, leaning over to wipe sauce off his wrinkled nose.

Ortega chuckled deeply, remembering with pleasure the reaction he'd received when he'd helpfully suggested to a panicked Dr. Whitmore that he might want to back up his data next time. Then he suddenly stopped chuckling and smacked Dr. Susan's hand away. "How can you compare *anything* I've done to him with what he's done to me?" he demanded, so loudly that everyone in the restaurant jumped.

Dr. Susan turned red with embarrassment. "I'm sorry," she murmured. "I didn't realize we were having a serious conversation."

Ortega snorted rudely.

"I *said* I was sorry," repeated Dr. Susan, a little louder. "I would never try to minimize what you've been through, Ortega, but ... but has it ever occurred to you that maybe your life hasn't been all bad?"

"No."

"Come on," she coaxed. "You've always eaten well, you've always had a safe, warm place to sleep; you've traveled, you've been on TV, you've learned to read and write and talk. You've accomplished things that no other gorilla on the planet has even come close to accomplishing!"

"So?" yawned Ortega as he casually fingered the greasy paper that lined the empty garlic-bread basket.

"So?" said Dr. Susan, trying hard to keep the frustration out of her voice. "So doesn't that mean *anything* to you? Doesn't it make up for anything that you've gone through?"

"Not really," he shrugged, suddenly bored by the conversation. "Can I ask the waitress for another basket of garlic toast?"

Dr. Susan took a deep breath, exhaled loudly and drew her lips back in a big fake smile that Ortega found very hilarious. "No more garlic toast," she said, snatching the greasy paper basket liner away a split second before he could cram it into his mouth. "We've got to get going. I have a surprise for you."

The surprise wasn't popcorn and a movie with Dr. Susan. It was something even better.

"IT'S ME, GRANDMA, I'M HERE!" Ortega hollered excitedly, dumping Mr. Doodles on his head in the front foyer before barreling down the hall toward the kitchen. She emerged unexpectedly — a dusting of flour across the bridge of her nose and a spatula held high in one plump hand — and they collided in a tangle of long, hairy arms and frilly apron strings.

"Slow *down*, Ortega," said Dr. Susan, cringing as she set down his overnight bag.

"Oh, that's fine," laughed Grandma indulgently, giving Ortega a hug.

"No, it isn't, Mom. I've tried to explain to him that he's too big to —"

"What are you making, Grandma?" interrupted Ortega, sniffing deeply at the intoxicating smells wafting his way.

"Go and see," she whispered, her eyes crinkling merrily.

"Say good-bye to me first," said Dr. Susan.

"Good-bye," he said, heading for the kitchen.

"Thanks for taking him tonight, Mom," Ortega heard her murmur as he gave a bowl of cookie dough an exploratory poke with his finger.

"No problem at all. You have a nice time on your date, honey," he heard Grandma reply.

Startled, Ortega hustled back into the hallway. "You have a *date*?" he exclaimed indignantly. "With who?"

"None of your business," said Dr. Susan, checking her makeup in a compact mirror.

"It's not Mohammed from the physiology lab, is it?" asked Ortega, stealthily reaching out to untie her shoelaces. "Because he and I haven't gotten along very well ever since I tried to save his miserable test subjects."

"They were rats, Ortega, and you set Mohammed back six months by releasing them into the ventilation system," said Dr. Susan, bending down to retie her laces.

"Still. You should know that he's going to have a very hard time trying to worm his way back into my affections," he advised.

"It's not Mohammed," smiled Dr. Susan, standing up again. "But the next time I see him, I'll let him know that he's got his work cut out for him."

———◦◦◦◦———

As soon as Dr. Susan left, Ortega changed into the gray tracksuit that Grandma kept for him in the cedar chest in the spare bedroom. Then he raced out of the room and began galloping around the house as fast as he could, bashing into walls and hooting at the top of his lungs.

Ortega loved Grandma's house. From the quiet front room with the dusty, overstuffed parlor chairs, to the big yellow kitchen with its burbling pots and painted canisters, to the apple tree whose blossoms played at the open window of the spare bedroom on breezy spring mornings, this was Ortega's favorite place on earth. He was so happy here that a few years back, Dr. Susan had suggested to Dr. Whitmore that she and Ortega move in on a permanent basis. When Dr. Whitmore had refused on the grounds that he would lose the environmental control that the laboratory afforded, Grandma had hit the roof, and when he'd pointed out in his fuddy-duddy way that Ortega belonged to the company and that technically she wasn't even related to Ortega, Grandma had very nearly *clobbered* him. In response, Dr. Whitmore had said that she wouldn't see Ortega again unless she apologized and agreed to respect his absolute authority over the young ape. Before Grandma could punch him right in the nose, Dr. Susan had stepped between them and hastily expressed to Dr. Whitmore her concern that separating Ortega from someone he loved might cause him to become even more uncooperative than usual. In response, Dr. Whitmore had angrily accused Dr. Susan of putting her own personal agenda before what was best for Project Ortega. Then he'd sent her home for a week without pay. The whole situation had so upset Ortega that in the end, Grandma and Dr. Susan had both done whatever it took to get back into Dr. Whitmore's good books.

"OKAY, I'M READY TO SETTLE DOWN NOW!" Ortega bellowed as he burst into the kitchen and barreled up to Grandma with a speed and force that would have made grown men dive for cover.

"Don't settle down on my account," she replied mildly, holding up a heaping plate of still-warm oatmeal-raisin cookies.

Grinning broadly, Ortega took the biggest one he could find and bit into it with gusto.

"Just one?" said Grandma in mock dismay. "But Ortega, I was hoping you'd eat them all. And when you were done, I was hoping you'd help me make caramel popcorn so we'd have something to nibble on while we watched *The Thing That Went Bump in the Night*."

"Don't worry, Grandma!" he cried, hastily shoving two more cookies into his mouth before deciding it would probably be more helpful to just take the entire plate from her. "You can count on me!"

It was a wonderful evening. The movie was deliciously terrifying, and Ortega ate so much caramel popcorn that he got a stomachache, which Grandma miraculously cured by serving him a large, extra-thick, banana-chocolate milkshake. He went to bed feeling sleepy and contented, but woke repeatedly hollering for Grandma, convinced that he'd heard something go bump in the night *right under his very own bed*! Dr. Susan usually gave him a cranky lecture about controlling his imagination when this sort of thing happened at the lab, but Grandma bravely searched every inch of the room to ensure that there were no hideous monsters waiting to do gruesome things to innocent gorillas, then sat at the edge of Ortega's bed, humming softly and smoothing the hair at his temples, until he drifted off to sleep once more.

———

The next day, Dr. Susan walked into the kitchen while Ortega was in the middle of breakfast. Her eyes bugged out at the sight of the feast that Grandma had prepared — pancakes with maple syrup, raisin muffins and jelly doughnuts, porridge with brown sugar, another milkshake (this time with whipped cream and sprinkles on top) and, of course, the leftover caramel popcorn from the night before.

"Mom!" cried Dr. Susan, snatching Ortega's fourth jelly doughnut right out of his hand. "How many times do I have to ask you not to feed him so much junk food?"

"Don't lecture me, Susan," replied Grandma smoothly. "He's my grandson. I can spoil him if I want to, can't I, Ortega?"

"You better believe it," he agreed in a sticky voice, wondering how on earth a woman as perfect as Grandma had ended up with a daughter as chintzy with the treats as Dr. Susan.

Grandma smiled warmly at Ortega, who smiled back at her just as warmly.

Dr. Susan shook her head. "Oh, you two are just *impossible*. Go get ready, you," she said, giving Ortega a little nudge. She hesitated before adding, "Dr. Whitmore called me at home this morning to let me know he wasn't pleased that I took you to Grandma's without his permission. He said I'm to bring you back to the lab at once."

———

Annoyed that his beautiful breakfast with Grandma had been cut short, Ortega got dressed as slowly as he possibly could. When he finally knuckled moodily out into the dazzling morning sunshine, Dr. Susan was already waiting by the car. Grandma was beside her, talking and gesturing about something that was clearly making Dr. Susan agitated. Ortega tiptoed down the porch steps in the hope of sneaking up on them and hearing what they were saying. Unfortunately, it is extremely difficult for a two-hundred-pound gorilla to sneak up on anyone in broad daylight, so all he managed to hear before the two of them clammed up was Dr. Susan heatedly telling Grandma that she was caught between a rock and a hard place and Grandma calmly insisting that she had to keep doing all she could.

"I think Grandma makes an excellent point," announced Ortega.

"You don't even know what we were talking about," grumped Dr. Susan.

"I don't need to know," purred Ortega, flinging his long, hairy arms around Grandma and grunting with pleasure as she rained kisses down on top of his head. "Grandma is a genius!"

"Actually, Ortega, Susan is the genius," confided Grandma.

"Actually, Grandma, I am the genius," Ortega confided back.

Grandma threw back her head and laughed. Dr. Susan rolled her eyes, gave her mother a kiss on the cheek and got into the car.

Grandma gave Ortega one last hug. "Be a good boy, okay?" she whispered. "Don't make things harder on yourself than they already are."

"I'm not making any promises," he replied.

When the car pulled up to the lab building fifteen minutes later, Dr. Whitmore was waiting on the front step next to the patch of tulips Ortega had mangled on his first day of school.

His arms were folded across his thin chest, but he didn't look angry. In fact, he was smiling.

It was a bad sign.

"Good morning, Ortega," he called.

Ortega, who had been slowly knuckle-walking across the dewy lawn in an effort to get the cuffs of his pants as wet and dirty as possible, slowed down even further.

"I hope you had a nice evening," continued Dr. Whitmore, "because we have a busy weekend ahead of us."

Ortega stopped dead in his tracks. "Not one of your boring scientific conferences, I hope," he said, looking anxiously at Dr. Susan, who usually gave him plenty of warning about these things.

Dr. Whitmore chuckled. "No, no, nothing like that," he said. "Rather, I've decided it's time to undertake a full reassessment of your language skills. Vocabulary, grammar, comprehension, humor, sarcasm ..."

"OH, WOW! THAT IS TOTALLY AWESOME!" cried Ortega, pushing himself upright and clapping his hands together in mock ecstasy.

Dr. Whitmore pursed his lips. Dr. Susan cringed. Ortega was tempted to fart, but decided not to push his luck until he found out exactly how angry Dr. Whitmore was with him for having bolted from school the day before.

"Just kidding," he muttered. Dropping to his knuckles, he started past Dr. Whitmore. "Come on, Dr. Susan. Let's get this over with."

"Oh, no," said Dr. Whitmore with a small smile. "You'll be undertaking the reassessment with me, Ortega. I'm giving Susan the weekend off."

"What?" she blurted. "Oh, Dr. Whitmore, that's all right. I don't need —"

"I insist," he snapped, tugging Ortega's overnight bag from her hand. "Good-bye, Susan."

That day was the longest of Ortega's life. He did flash-card tests, IQ tests and word-association tests. He was observed, tape-recorded and videotaped. When he complained of being tired, Dr. Whitmore promised to send him to bed early, then hustled him down the hall to the phonics lab. When he complained of being hungry, Dr. Whitmore told him when his next meal would be served, then subjected him to another articulation drill. It was tedious and annoying, and if Ortega had been working with anyone but Dr. Whitmore, he would almost certainly have started sabotaging the tests. Over the years, he'd come up with many clever ways to do this — pointing to the wrong answer on a flash card while looking at the right one, for example, or responding to every question posed to him by asking an embarrassing question about the tester's personal life.

But Dr. Whitmore was different. While it was enormously satisfying to provoke him when Dr. Susan was around, when she wasn't, it sometimes felt to Ortega as if he were poking sticks at a grizzly bear.

Besides, although Dr. Whitmore never once brought up the subject of how Ortega had behaved at school on Friday or what it might mean to his precious research, all weekend long it hung between them, as grim and foreboding as anything that ever went bump in the night.

Sunday morning, Ortega slept until almost ten o'clock. When he first noticed the time and realized he hadn't been wakened early for another day of stupid tests, he wrapped his long arms around himself and chuckled deeply, unable to believe his good fortune. After a few minutes, however, his stomach began to growl and he realized he was hungry.

Feeling neglected, he moodily kicked aside the limp-walled nest he'd fashioned the night before out of his comforter and rolled out of bed. Pulling on his tattered blue terry-cloth robe, he padded over to the bedroom door, jerked it open and poked his head into the hallway.

"Hello?" he called.

No response.

Sucking his lips in annoyance, Ortega knuckle-walked down the hallway toward the little kitchenette. He didn't know what Dr. Susan had been thinking, letting him sleep so late. Even if she couldn't be here, she could at least have called to make sure that *someone* was here, and that that someone woke him up in time for breakfast. She knew how hungry he always was in the morning. Ortega shook his head in disgust. First she abandons him for the entire weekend, then she practically lets him starve to death? Wasn't she at all concerned for his well-being?

Upon reaching the kitchenette and discovering that no one had even bothered to lay out anything for him to eat, Ortega decided to wreak havoc in order to demonstrate to Dr. Susan how unhappy he was with her behavior. Hurrying over to the fridge (which was always a good place to start, since it was full of wet, goopy things that made the most delightful messes), he yanked open the door and then froze.

There, on the top shelf, sat an enormous fruit platter, carefully covered in plastic wrap and brimming with all the best kinds of fruit — fresh pineapple and honeydew-melon wedges, succulent cherries and cantaloupe curls, bunches of seedless grapes and heaping mounds of juicy blackberries.

Mouth watering copiously, Ortega clasped his hands beneath his chin in rapture. His squashy nose quivered as he silently but fervently apologized to the absent Dr. Susan for ever having planned to fill the pockets of her best lab coat with blueberry yogurt. Then, with the utmost care, he took the beautiful platter in his arms, reverently carried it over to the table, pulled off the plastic wrap and dug in.

Fifteen minutes later, his favorite part-time handler wandered into the kitchenette.

"Sorry I'm late," yawned Glen, taking a large sip from his coffee-filled travel mug before slumping into the chair across from Ortega. "Susan made me promise to be here early so you wouldn't wake up alone, but once again, I got attacked by an Ortegasaurus on the way over." He shook his head ruefully. "Biggest, smartest, most handsome one I've seen yet."

In addition to smiling way too much whenever he was around Dr. Susan, Glen was working toward his doctorate in paleontology. Normally, Ortega would have asked him to describe every detail of his latest encounter with the most fearsome herbivore that ever roamed the earth, but he was so busy eating that he merely grunted and pulled the fruit platter closer to him.

Yawning again, Glen raked his hand through his disheveled, sandy blond hair, then picked up a note that Ortega had noticed stuck to the plastic wrap but hadn't bothered reading. "'Do not touch. Fruit to be served at the faculty meeting.' What do you think that means?" asked Glen, looking pointedly at the nearly empty platter.

"Search me," mumbled Ortega, stuffing the last wedge of pineapple into his mouth and smacking his lips.

Glen chuckled and took another sip of coffee. "Search me, too," he said, balling up the note and tossing it into the garbage can on the other side of the room. "Come on. Let's go play checkers."

They played for almost two hours. Ortega won every game and celebrated by charging around the room hooting and whacking at Glen with his hands. When they were done playing, Glen made Ortega lunch before heading back to his own lab to continue his analysis of a fossilized bone fragment he'd personally discovered during a dig in the badlands of Alberta the previous summer. Shortly after Glen left, Ortega overheard Dr. Whitmore order one of his lackeys to call Dr. Susan to the lab for an emergency meeting. Elated, Ortega galloped to the locked glass doors at the front of the lab where he waited impatiently for her to arrive so that he could complain to her about his boring weekend and also pester her to take him for ice cream. Unfortunately, when she got to the lab she barely had time to give him a hug, a kiss and a scolding (for eating the fruit platter) before Dr. Whitmore whisked her back out of the lab to go to their mysterious emergency meeting.

Unsettled by the fact that Dr. Susan's day did not appear to be revolving around him, Ortega kept to his room for most of the afternoon. By early evening, however, he was so bored that he decided to sneak into Dr. Whitmore's office. Now that Dr. Susan was back in the picture, it was time to deliver a little payback to Dr. Smarty Pants for being such a jerk the day before.

As he tiptoed up to the closed office door, however, he heard the sound of Dr. Whitmore and Dr. Susan arguing.

"… going back whether he likes it or not," said Dr. Whitmore.

"I understand —"

"I'm not sure that you do," interrupted Dr. Whitmore tersely. "If you did, you wouldn't have rewarded him for running away from school and hiding in a tree like some kind of *animal*."

"I wasn't rewarding him! I-I was trying to calm him down because … because I didn't feel it would be advantageous to the project to have a traumatized, uh, test subject."

Upon hearing himself referred to as a test subject, Ortega pranced around the hallway, grimacing and flapping his arms in silent protest. Then he hurried back to his position by the door so that he could continue eavesdropping.

"I see," said Dr. Whitmore. "Well, just so long as you've made it perfectly clear to him that he will be returning to school tomorrow."

In your dreams! screeched Ortega, in his mind.

"I haven't talked to him about that yet," admitted Dr. Susan reluctantly. "You sent me home yesterday, remember? Besides, I thought it would be best to wait until he was in a more receptive mood before trying to —"

"We can't afford to wait for *anything*, much less that overindulged, preteen primate's so-called cooperation!" exploded Dr. Whitmore. "You heard what that lawyer said this afternoon, Susan — the town council is going to hold us to the contract no matter what. Do you understand what that means?"

"Yes, I —"

"It means we will be obligated to pay them their money even if he never sets foot in that school again," snapped Dr. Whitmore. "If that was to happen, we'd never be able to collect the data we need in order to be able to publish further articles. The project would stall and we'd begin to suffer funding cuts. And do you know what would happen next, Susan? Do you?"

Ortega was dying to know what would happen next. He hoped it had something to do with Dr. Whitmore getting fired and possibly being publicly ridiculed. Unfortunately, before he could find out if it did, he heard the sudden sound of Dr. Whitmore's footsteps approaching the door, and so, with a startled screech, he turned and fled back to his room.

———

That night while he was eating his before-bed snack, Ortega casually brought up the subject with Dr. Susan.

"TELL ME WHAT HAPPENS IF YOUR FUNDING IS CUT!" he bellowed, pounding both fists on the table.

Dr. Susan was so startled that she accidentally knocked over his glass of milk. Ortega laughed loudly and clapped his hands. Then he coughed into his fist.

"Sorry," he said primly. "Can I have another gingersnap?"

"No," she replied, as she wiped up the spill. "You've already eaten six, not including the four you swiped while I was over at the fridge getting the milk for dunking."

"Then tell me what happens if your funding is cut!" he demanded, returning to his original line of questioning.

Dr. Susan looked away for a long moment before turning to face him. "It's ... well, it's hard to say exactly what would happen, Ortega," she said softly.

"Try," he suggested, looking deeply into her eyes as his hand stealthily crept toward the open bag of gingersnaps.

Dr. Susan looked deeply into *his* eyes as she inched the bag of gingersnaps away from his creeping hand. When it was safely out of his reach, she leaned forward in her chair, put her small, soft hand over his large, hairy one and opened her mouth to speak.

Before she could say anything, however, the intercom on the wall buzzed. It was the security guard from downstairs. In a crackly voice, he announced that there were two people from school here to see Ortega and asked Dr. Susan if he should send them up.

With a puzzled expression on her face, Dr. Susan looked over at Ortega. He was tempted to take this opportunity to inform her that he'd go back to school the day *real* pigs flew out of Dr. Whitmore's rear end. However, he was so curious about who the unexpected visitors might be, and so excited by the possibility that he'd be able to stay up past his bedtime in order to entertain them, that he nodded eagerly at her.

The instant Dr. Susan let go of the Talk button on the intercom, Ortega leaped out of his chair and began charging around the room, knocking things over for the sheer joy of hearing them clatter to the floor. When he was done, he grabbed Dr. Susan by one arm and galloped her to the main doors of the lab, where he poked her repeatedly in order to get her to hurry up and swipe her personal security pass through the high-tech lock on the door so that his visitors would be able to walk right in when they arrived.

She had just finished giving him a lecture about being rude and overbearing, and was turning to comply with his demand that she open the door, when Ortega caught a glimpse of one of his visitors as she stepped off the elevator.

It was the lady custodian!

Instantly, he realized why she'd come: to tell Dr. Susan and Dr. Whitmore how he'd sneaked up behind her in the cafeteria. Never mind that his seam had ripped and he'd been laughed at by the entire school — he just knew she was going to focus on the fact that she'd tripped over her stupid pail of soapy water because of him.

Thinking fast, he clamped his arm around Dr. Susan's belly and dragged her away from the door.

"Ortega!" she grunted. "What in the world are you doing?"

Holding his shirt up over his nose — as though this might prevent the lady custodian from recognizing him — Ortega hurriedly explained that the woman was a dangerous psychopath who had been stalking him for some time now.

On the other side of the glass lab doors, the lady custodian smiled pleasantly and gave Ortega a little wave.

"I'm not kidding," he whispered. "She's completely nuts."

Muttering in annoyance, Dr. Susan peeled Ortega's long, hairy arm away from her stomach, marched over to the door, swiped her security pass through the lock and politely invited the lady custodian inside.

In a panic, Ortega dropped to his knuckles. His head swiveled this way and that as he tried to determine the most promising escape route.

Then the lady custodian stepped to one side, revealing a second visitor — one who looked even less excited to see Ortega than he was to see the lady custodian.

It was Peter, the pint-sized gorilla expert.

Ortega was so surprised to see him that he forgot all about bolting. Instead, he pushed himself up into a standing position, scratched his head in puzzlement and said, "What in the world are *you* doing here?"

Chapter Five

Instead of answering, Peter folded his arms across his chest. The lady custodian leaned over and impatiently whispered something into his ear. He scowled. She gave him a nudge. He sighed moodily and dragged the toe of his sneaker back and forth along a scratch in the floor.

Utterly fascinated, Ortega watched the exchange in silence for as long as he could. Then he fixed his eyes on the boy and, in a low voice, asked, "Did your mom give that lady permission to hassle you?"

"She didn't have to," muttered Peter. "That lady *is* my mom."

Ortega's mouth formed a small O of surprise.

The lady custodian smiled and held her hand out to Dr. Susan. "My name is Laverne Rockwell. I'm the custodian at the school, and this is my son, Peter," she said. "Miss Rutherford told me about the note she found on the floor by Ortega's desk, and this evening during dinner, when I happened to mention it to Peter, I am sad to say that he admitted to his involvement in the bullying."

"I did not!" interjected Peter hotly. "I specifically said that I *wasn't* involved. I didn't have anything to do with drawing that idiotic cartoon — the first I knew about it was when someone handed it to me. All I did was to pass the note to Eugene!"

"You could have ripped up the note, or even confronted the others about their unkind behavior, but you didn't," retorted his mother. "You went along with the crowd, as though being popular with them was more important than sticking up for someone who clearly needed a friend."

Peter's eyes bulged. "How can you *say* that?" he squeaked in outrage as he jabbed a skinny index finger in Ortega's direction. "I *tried* to be his friend. I spent *weeks* studying gorillas just so that his differences wouldn't seem so ... so *different* when I finally met him. *He* was the one who —"

"I didn't run away from school because of any silly note," interrupted Ortega hastily, before Peter could blurt out the truth about the nasty trick Ortega had tried to play on his mother.

"You didn't?" said Dr. Susan and Mrs. Rockwell in surprise.

Ortega gave a big belly laugh. "Of course not! I thought it was funny, and besides, I knew Peter would never do anything to be mean to me. He *did* try to be my friend — he even invited me to eat lunch with him and his friends on my first day. Remember, Peter?" he asked hopefully.

Slowly, Peter nodded his head. "Uh-huh," he said uncertainly.

Mrs. Rockwell looked perplexed. "But if your feelings weren't hurt by the note, Ortega, why did you run away?"

"I was bored," he admitted. "I thought school was going to be a challenge, but the work was so easy I almost puked."

Dr. Susan narrowed her eyes at him. She knew something was up, she just didn't know what it was. "So what you're telling me, Ortega," she said, "is that you and Peter are friends?"

Ortega looked at Peter. Peter looked at him.

They both nodded — hesitantly at first, then with more enthusiasm. Ortega tried hard to play it cool, but he was so exhilarated by the fact that, for the first time in his life, someone had actually referred to him as a friend that he had to suck in his cheeks to keep himself from grinning. He looked so funny that Peter started to giggle and gave him a tentative poke. Peter sounded so funny that Ortega started to giggle and gave him a careful push. Still giggling, Peter boldly placed both hands on Ortega's huge, hairy shoulder and pushed back. Ortega didn't budge an inch, but he *did* clamp one arm around the boy's skinny rib cage, hoist him into the air and gallop in tiny circles until he was dizzy. With a mighty roar, he crashed backward to the ground with Peter tucked protectively against his big, hairy belly. There was an instant of stunned silence in the bright, antiseptic laboratory hallway. Then — at the exact same moment! — the two youngsters noticed the near-panicked expressions on the faces of the women and promptly dissolved into howls of laughter.

Mrs. Rockwell smiled shakily at Dr. Susan in an attempt to pretend that she hadn't just about had a heart attack when Ortega had started tossing her son around like a rag doll. Dr. Susan gave her arm a sympathetic squeeze and asked if she could use a cup of coffee. When Mrs. Rockwell nodded, Dr. Susan bent low over Ortega, who was now lying flat on his hairy back making silly faces at the adults and hiccuping as loudly as he possibly could.

"If you ever manage to regain control of your senses," she said, giving him a poke that caused him to grunt mid-hiccup, "you might want to show Peter around."

Ortega lay on the floor until the two women disappeared down the hall toward the kitchenette. Then he jumped up and did an imitation of a drooling Dr. Susan lurching off in search of her precious coffee. Peter thought it was extremely hilarious and jumped up and did an imitation of his mother crying her eyeballs out about his having passed that stupid note to Eugene. Ortega laughed heartily until he remembered how hurt his feelings had been when he'd seen the cartoon. Then his laughter died away, and a thick, awkward silence filled the air.

"Look, I'm sorry," said Peter suddenly, after a long moment. "I guess I did act like kind of a jerk."

Ortega blinked in surprise. "Oh. Well … I think maybe I acted like a bigger jerk," he replied, squirming slightly as he recalled how he'd treated this boy who'd tried so hard to befriend him.

"You *definitely* acted like a bigger jerk," said Peter. "But you also covered for me in front of my mom just now, so I'm willing to let bygones be bygones if you are."

"I am. I definitely am," said Ortega fervently. "What's a bygone?"

Peter laughed. "You're funny," he said. "I never knew gorillas could be funny."

"I never knew boys could be funny," replied Ortega.

"Boys can be lots of things," said Peter.

"So can gorillas," said Ortega, slapping his open hand lightly against his chest. "Come on. I'll show you my room."

Ortega led Peter across the lab to his bedroom. He showed him his rumpled bed, his cluttered closet and his disorganized desk. He showed him the tape recorder he'd used to record the rude noises he'd played during Dr. Whitmore's last faculty meeting, and also the secret hole in his beanbag chair where he stuffed wrappers from candies pilfered from inattentive handlers. Peter agreed that the two-way mirror was totally creepy, and for a while, the two of them acted as demented as possible just in case anyone was observing them. Then Ortega introduced Peter to his pets.

"This is the Lancaster-Stone family," he explained in a hushed voice as he gently shook the jar of fruit flies in front of Peter's face. "I rescued them after I learned they were all going to be *gassed* so that some third-year bonehead could count how many of them had red eyes."

Peter's mouth dropped open.

"And this is Norman," continued Ortega, pointing to a fat, speckled frog dozing on an aquarium rock. "They wanted to cut his head off just above the brainstem in order to show a class of first-year students that his body would keep swimming even without a head."

"That is sick," murmured Peter, leaning over to take a closer look at Norman.

"If you think *that* is sick," said Ortega as he unlatched the door of the mouse cage and scooped up Siggy, "you don't even want to *know* what they were going to do to this little guy."

Peter turned to see which pet Ortega was talking about. When he found himself almost nose to nose with Siggy, he jumped backward so fast that he nearly tripped over his own feet.

"Don't worry," said Ortega hastily. "He won't bite. I promise!"

"I believe you," stammered Peter. "It's just that ... well ... I'm kind of ... I don't like mice very much."

"I don't like snakes very much," admitted Ortega, as he gently lowered Siggy back into his cage. "They give me the shivers. Do you want to see Dr. Whitmore's office?" he asked.

"Okay," said Peter. "Who is Dr. Whitmore?"

"He's the evil scientist who performs experiments on *me*," explained Ortega. "He wears the ugliest bow ties I've ever seen in my life."

"Bow ties give me the shivers," said Peter.

Ortega showed Peter where Dr. Whitmore hid the extra key to his office, then how to jiggle the door handle so that the finicky lock released. Once inside, he showed Peter the secret drawer where Dr. Whitmore kept his wallet, his keys and his personal stash of specialty cocoa. Then he farted on a picture of Dr. Whitmore's nephew, Rupert, shredded several important-looking letters, ate twelve mints out of the fancy crystal dish on Dr. Whitmore's desk and licked every letter on his computer keyboard.

"You can lick his pens and pencils if you want," offered Ortega generously.

"Okay," said Peter.

When they were done in Dr. Whitmore's office, they carefully relocked the door and returned the key to its hiding spot. Then they went down the hall to the language lab, where Peter crowed with delight at the sight of all the high-tech audiovisual equipment that Dr. Whitmore used to record and analyze Ortega's linguistic development.

"You're *so* lucky," Peter breathed, running his hands lovingly over the cameras and tripods and spotlights.

Ortega was about to ask what was so lucky about being the star of the longest, most boring movie ever made when Mrs. Rockwell poked her head into the room and told Peter it was time to go. Groaning and complaining, Peter followed her to the main doors of the lab. Ortega trailed behind them, feeling a strange tightness in his broad chest.

"Well, see you around," said Peter.

Ortega cleared his throat. "Sure," he said. "Uh ... thanks for coming."

"Like I had a *choice*," whispered Peter, making a face behind his mother's back.

They both guffawed at this, then Dr. Susan swiped her security pass through the lock, and Mrs. Rockwell led Peter over to the elevator. Slowly, Ortega knuckle-walked forward so that he'd have a better view of his departing friend.

Suddenly, Peter broke away from his mother, ran back and hammered on the glass door. "Ortega, are you coming to school tomorrow?" he shouted, his voice sounding funny through the thick, shatterproof glass.

Ortega jumped as though someone had just poked him in the backside with a pitchfork.

"I hope you are," continued Peter loudly, as his exasperated mother dragged him back to the waiting elevator, "because there's something I'd like to talk to you about."

"What is it?" blurted Ortega, pressing his nose and both hands against the glass.

"Tomorrow," came Peter's voice thinly as the elevator doors closed. "I'll tell you tomorrow."

———

After Peter and his mother left, Ortega fully expected Dr. Susan to finally break the news to him that he was, in fact, going to be going to school the next day. To his surprise, however, she simply yawned and told him to get ready for bed.

He brushed his teeth for just long enough to give his mouth the minty fresh smell Dr. Susan would check for, then pulled off a long string of dental floss and draped it over the faucet to make it appear as though it had been carelessly discarded after use. Then he raced down the hall to his bedroom, burst through the door like a force of nature and jumped up and down on the bed with all his might until he heard an ominous crack from somewhere beneath him. At that point, he carefully slid under his covers and planned a short speech concerning shoddy furniture construction that he could deliver in the event that his bed suddenly broke in half while Dr. Susan was kissing him good-night.

But it didn't break in half, and after Dr. Susan turned out the lights and left the room — again, without once mentioning school — Ortega lay in the darkness for a long while, wondering what Peter wanted to talk to him about and what he was going to do about school.

———

The next morning Ortega awoke with a start. Sitting bolt upright in bed, he checked his glow-in-the-dark clock radio and was relieved to see that it was still early. Sliding out of bed, he kicked his way across the messy floor, flung open the bedroom door and bellowed for Dr. Susan at the top of his lungs. Almost immediately, she poked her head out of the kitchenette down the hall.

"Shhh!" she said, putting her finger to her lips.

"Quit shushing me," he complained as he loped over to where she was standing. "You know how I hate to be shushed. What's for breakfast?"

"Blueberry pancakes with sliced bananas," she replied.

"My favorite," he said, plopping down in his chair. "Are you trying to butter me up or something?"

"Why on *earth* would I be trying to do that?" she asked innocently.

Instead of pointing out the obvious — that she was trying to bribe him into going back to school — Ortega snorted at her, then turned his attention to the steaming stack of syrupy pancakes before him. They were delicious, and Dr. Susan had just finished complimenting him on the fact that for once he was chewing with his mouth closed, when Dr. Whitmore strode into the room.

Ortega smiled and took another bite of pancake. Dr. Whitmore ignored him.

"I found this on the counter by the main door of the lab," he said, holding Dr. Susan's security pass out to her.

"Oopsy," she said, reaching for it. "I guess I put it down after saying good-bye to our guests last night."

Dr. Whitmore pulled the pass back. "I have warned you about this before, Susan," he admonished, twitching slightly as slobbery chunks of chewed pancake sprayed out of Ortega's now-gaping mouth. "There are people out there who disapprove of my research and who would go to any length to sabotage it. Need I remind you that a security breach could have catastrophic implications for us all?" he asked, with a significant glance at Ortega.

"No, of course not," murmured Dr. Susan hastily. "I'm sorry, Dr. Whitmore. I won't let it happen again."

"See that you don't," he said, handing her the pass. "By the way, have you seen that letter from the Nexus Foundation anywhere? I was certain I'd left it on my desk but now I can't seem to find it."

Ortega covered his sticky mouth with both hands and snickered as he recalled the letters he'd fed into the paper shredder the night before.

Dr. Whitmore looked over at him. "Do *you* know what happened to my letter?" he asked.

Instead of answering, Ortega started whistling like a bluebird.

Dr. Whitmore stared down at him for a moment, then said, "You're going to school today."

Ortega bristled and glared. "No, I'm not," he snapped.

"Yes, you are," said Dr. Whitmore.

"You can't make me," hollered Ortega, leaping to his feet.

"I most certainly can," said Dr. Whitmore, taking a hasty step back.

"Can't!"

"Can!"

"Dr. Whitmore, *please*," Dr. Susan broke in.

"Don't interfere, Susan!" he thundered. "Ortega needs to be reminded who is in charge around here!"

"NOT YOU!" bellowed Ortega, swaggering back and forth in front of him.

"Ortega!" shouted Dr. Susan, grabbing him by both shoulders and pulling him toward her. "Listen to me: if you don't go to school, that's fine, but you'll be spending the day in the language lab with Dr. Whitmore."

Dr. Whitmore looked outraged. "Susan, I told you to let me handle this! You have no right to —"

"Dr. Whitmore is being considered as an alternate presenter at the Tenth Annual Conference of Language Development Specialists next month, Ortega," continued Dr. Susan doggedly. "He'll almost certainly be selected, and when he is, he'll need to be able to give conference delegates as accurate a picture of your current abilities as possible."

Ortega planted his knuckles firmly in front of him, stuck his juicy tongue between his lips and blew a very loud raspberry at her. If she thought for one *second* that he was going to spend the day in the hot, stuffy language lab being ordered to do the same boring tasks over and over again while Dr. Smarty Pants tried to get the video camera working properly, she was sadly mistaken.

"I'd rather have my hands and head chopped off and sold to the highest bidder!" he screeched.

Dr. Susan winced at this reference to the fate so often suffered by gorillas in the wild. Then she put her hands on his cheeks and stared straight into his eyes. "All I'm trying to say is that you can go to school, or you can work with Dr. Whitmore," she said. "It's your choice."

"It is *not* his choice!" interjected Dr. Whitmore hotly.

Dr. Susan ignored him, and so did Ortega. He couldn't remember ever having been given such an important decision to make, and he was so overcome at the prospect that he wanted to upend the table, kick over the chairs and gallop around the room hooting at the top of his lungs. Instead, he took a deep breath and said:

"I'll go to school."

Dr. Susan heaved a sigh of relief. "Good choice," she murmured, leaning forward to tickle his nose with her frizzy hair. "It's nice when things work out the way everybody was hoping they'd work out, isn't it, Dr. Whitmore?"

But Dr. Whitmore was gone.

After breakfast, Ortega got dressed as fast as he could. He brushed his teeth — for real, this time — said good-bye to Siggy and the others, grabbed his knapsack and was waiting for Dr. Susan at the main doors of the lab when she walked out of the kitchenette twenty minutes later, carrying his lunch and calling for him to hurry up or he'd be late. She laughed when she saw him, then kissed him on the top of his hairy head, swiped her security pass through the lock and pushed open the door.

Ortega didn't say much on the drive to school, and neither did Dr. Susan. By the time they arrived, Ortega's stomach was churning, but he rolled his eyes when Dr. Susan asked if he was nervous.

"I'm not a baby, you know," he complained, making no effort to get out of the car.

"You'll always be my baby," said Dr. Susan with a fond smile.

Ortega rolled his eyes again, then turned and scanned the schoolyard for protesters. There were none in sight. While it was possible they'd gotten tired of shouting about how his existence was a sign that the end of the world was near, Ortega thought it was more likely that when they'd found out that he'd run away from school on Friday, they'd figured they'd gotten rid of him. Based on his experiences at conferences and other public appearances, Ortega knew that certain kinds of people hardly ever got tired of being outraged.

Relieved to see that he at least had a hassle-free path to the door of the school, Ortega stepped out of the car.

"Good luck," called Dr. Susan through the open window.

Ortega gave his chest a one-fisted thump. Dr. Susan laughed, blew him a kiss and, with a toss of her head, hit the gas and peeled off down the road.

And just like that, he was on his own.

Kids stared as he headed upstairs, but they didn't stare quite as hard as they had the week before. A few held up phones and took pictures or videos, but not many. When he walked into the classroom, Myra's mouth cinched into a tight little knot, but Peter's face lit up like a Christmas tree. Smiling as bashfully as a two-hundred-pound gorilla with fanglike canine teeth could possibly smile, Ortega hurried over to his seat. As he walked past Miss Rutherford's desk, she nodded at him respectfully, as though he were a high-altitude mountain climber who'd just clawed his way out of a crevasse in order to renew his bid for the summit.

Ortega didn't get a chance to talk to Peter or anyone else before class began, but later that morning, during math class, Eugene wordlessly slipped him half a coconut sponge cake. Thrilled, Ortega tried to return the favor by passing Eugene a handful of pitted prunes. Unfortunately, Eugene found this trade so hilarious that he couldn't stop chortling, and the two of them ended up getting an extra page of math homework as a consequence. The minute Miss Rutherford's back was turned, Ortega whispered an anxious apology to Eugene for getting him into trouble, but Eugene just grinned, looked down at the little brown pile of pitted prunes on his desk and clapped his hand over his mouth to keep from starting to giggle again.

Ortega — who wasn't exactly sure what was so funny, but who was sure it wasn't him — happily did the same.

Then, just when he thought things couldn't get any better, the lunch bell rang and Peter invited him to come eat with him and Janice and Eugene in his tree fort.

"Oh!" cried Ortega, clasping his hands beneath his chin. "I would *love* to!"

"Great," smiled Peter. "Let's go."

After Ortega used Eugene's cell phone to call Dr. Susan and let her know he was going to Peter's for lunch, they all hurried out of the school, across the field and past the dilapidated factory to the very end of a tired street lined with small houses ringed by peeling picket fences. Here, set well apart from the houses, sat a small trailer. The area behind the trailer was wooded and appeared to back onto the river. When Ortega caught sight of the fort half hidden among the trees, his heart gave a wild thump of excitement.

"You guys go ahead," Peter told him and the others, waving them in the direction of the fort. "I'll get the sandwiches from my mom. Her lunch break started twenty minutes ago, so she should be finished making them."

Eagerly, Ortega followed Eugene and Janice into the woods. When they got to the fort, the two children scrambled up a wooden ladder and disappeared inside. Ortega knuckle-walked slowly around the base of the tree, pausing often to squint up at the little house nestled among the sun-dappled leaves. Then, with a hoot of pure delight, he swung himself up branch by branch, squashed his shoulders together so he could fit through the door and stepped inside.

It was bigger than it looked from the outside, and sturdier, too, so Ortega didn't think he had to worry about crashing through the floor. There were binoculars and life jackets and nets and slingshots and lengths of rope hung up on nails along one wall; another wall was covered in photographs. When Ortega looked more closely, he saw that the same good-looking man was in every picture — sometimes by himself, sometimes with other good-looking people. In a couple of shots, he was even standing with Peter.

"Who is that man?" Ortega asked Janice, who was sitting nearby, on an overturned wooden crate.

Janice — who was still wearing the gold hoop earrings and the pirate kerchief from the week before — shrugged and continued reading.

Eugene assured Ortega that this was perfectly normal.

"She's the strong, silent type," he explained in a loud whisper.

"I heard that," she said without looking up from her book.

"She also has excellent hearing," added Eugene in an even louder whisper.

At this, Janice shook her head and smiled. Ortega smiled too, and tried to think of something clever to say, but before he could, Peter shouted up from the bottom of the tree, "Send down the elevator!"

Eugene jumped up and trundled over to the little porch, where he slowly lowered another wooden crate attached to a rope. The rope was thrown over a pulley, which was attached to a nearby tree branch, so it really was just like a little elevator. Ortega thought it was probably the neatest thing he'd ever seen in his life.

"I hope you like peanut butter and jelly, Ortega," said Peter a few moments later, as he unloaded a big platter of sandwiches and a thermos full of cold milk from the crate.

"They're my *favorite*," said Ortega, who hadn't until that very moment realized how passionately he loved peanut-butter-and-jelly sandwiches.

Eugene gave a grunt of heartfelt agreement and then they all dug in. It wasn't until the platter was almost empty that Peter said, "Ortega, last night I said there was something I wanted to talk to you about. But before I tell you what it is, I need to know if you can keep a secret."

Ortega nodded eagerly as he licked a blob of jelly off his finger.

"Are you sure?" pressed Peter, his mouth full of half-chewed sandwich. "You'd never talk, not even if you were being tortured?"

"I'm not sure," admitted Ortega. "I've never been tortured before, unless you count the time Dr. Whitmore made me sit through a two-hour slide show of his trip to the family hog farm in Saskatchewan."

At this, Eugene began to chortle so infectiously that even Janice joined in. Elated, Ortega pretended to gouge out his own eyes in order to avoid seeing another slide of hogs cavorting in mud puddles. Eugene and Janice laughed harder.

"You're a born entertainer, Ortega," said Peter. "And that's my professional opinion, by the way."

"What do you mean?" asked Ortega, who was still mugging for the others.

Peter leaned forward and dropped his voice a notch. "Three years ago, my dad sent me a video camera for my birthday, and ever since I've been making movies in my spare time. Someday I'm going to move to Hollywood and live with him and become a director and win an Academy Award. At the moment, however, I'm about to start production on my most important film to date."

"Why is it your most important film to date?" asked Ortega in a hushed voice.

"Because my dad is about to start work on a movie with Derek Blackheart —"

"The famous horror film director?" blurted Ortega, his eyes bugging out in surprise.

"That's right. My dad is an actor," Peter explained, gesturing to the photos of the good-looking man. "I always send him copies of my films — you know, to show him that I'm serious about following him into the business — and he always says they're great. I figured it was just one of those things that good dads say, but then a couple of weeks ago, when he called to tell me about the Derek Blackheart gig, he said he was going to tell Derek to watch one of *my* films if he wanted to see what a *really* talented director could do."

"No *way*," breathed Ortega.

"*So* way," said Peter. "Anyway, right then and there I decided to do a new film — my best film ever. And that's where you come in, Ortega."

"You mean ... because I'm a talking gorilla?" asked Ortega hesitantly.

"No. Oh, don't get me wrong — making you the star of the movie seemed like a great idea at first," admitted Peter. "Kind of like special effects without the special effects. But then I thought ... it felt kind of gimmicky, you know? Building a whole story around a talking gorilla? I mean, how does that showcase my talents as a moviemaker?"

"It doesn't, I guess," said Ortega uncertainly.

"Exactly," said Peter. "The other thing is that Derek Blackheart is a horror movie director, so if I wanted to catch his attention, I needed to make a *horror* movie and no offense or anything, Ortega, but the more I get to know you, the less horrifying you seem."

Eugene bobbed his head agreement.

Ortega shrugged, embarrassed but pleased. "So, if you don't want me in your film, where do I come in?" he asked, reaching for another sandwich.

"I didn't say I didn't want you in the film, Ortega, I just said that the film won't be about you. As far as where you come in — well, for one thing, after you told me about the gruesome experiments the evil scientists in your laboratory perform, it got me thinking that it would be a great place to shoot the spine-tingling opening scene of my movie. You know — because the place has all those creepy two-way mirrors and locked doors and is full of the spirits of murdered animals."

"Oh," said Ortega, who'd never thought of his home in quite that way.

"I also thought you could play the giant bloodthirsty zombie monster who hunts humans for food and eventually rips his way into a haunted factory in order to fight a battle to the death with the ultra-tough, time-traveling zombie killer ..."

"That would be me," said Janice without looking up.

"... and her horribly mutilated, cowering companion," concluded Peter.

Eugene gave a jolly grin and pointed to himself.

Ortega looked from one kid to the next.

"That sounds great," he finally said, shifting his great bulk in an effort to get more comfortable. "Except that Dr. Whitmore would have a conniption fit if I was caught on film trying to eat people."

"You wouldn't *actually* be eating anyone, Ortega," said Peter, rolling his eyes. "You'd be acting."

"Yeah, but if I'm a born entertainer like you say, it wouldn't look like acting," said Ortega. "It would look like eating!"

"Maybe, but everyone knows gorillas are mostly herbivores, so what's the difference?" said Peter.

Ortega knew that there was a difference, but since he couldn't quite put his finger on what it was, he said, "The other problem is that I'm pretty sure Dr. Whitmore won't give you permission to shoot a scene at the lab."

"That's why I had to swear you to secrecy," explained Peter. "Because I knew you were going to have to break some rules to be part of the team." He reached out and laid a small hand on Ortega's big shoulder. "Listen, if it makes you feel any better, we'll all be in the same boat, so to speak. Both of the other locations I'm considering for filming are also off limits."

"What are they?" asked Ortega.

"The river and *maybe* the haunted factory," mumbled Eugene as he munched away on one of Janice's discarded crusts.

"What haunted factory?" asked Ortega.

Without warning, Janice slapped her book closed and fixed him with her startling blue eyes. "The one on the hill across the field," she said in her husky voice. "You know Myra, the girl who tried to off your mouse?"

Ortega nodded.

"Well, her family used to own that factory. In its day, it was the biggest, busiest tannery in these parts."

"Neat," said Ortega. "What's a tannery?"

"It's a place where fresh animal skins are turned into leather," said Janice.

Ortega shuddered.

"Anyway," she continued. "Late one stormy night, a drifter showed up at the backdoor of the tannery looking for a hot meal and a place to sleep in exchange for a few hours of work. Myra's mother was alone in the building, finishing up some paperwork. Normally, she wasn't the kind to lend a helping hand — you've met her, you know what I'm talking about — but on this particular night, for some strange reason, she decided to let him in. She told him she needed the tanks of tanning chemicals drained and cleaned by morning."

"That doesn't sound like the kind of thing you'd ask an untrained person to do," frowned Ortega.

"Exactly," hissed Janice. "Those chemicals would peel the flesh right off your bones. That's what made what happened next so suspicious."

"What happened next?" breathed Ortega.

"Somehow, the drifter ended up in one of those bubbling tanks ..." began Janice.

"... and was never seen again," guessed Ortega with a shiver.

"Wrong," said Janice. "They say that every year, on the anniversary of his death, the drifter returns — climbs out of the tank where he sizzled to death and wanders through the tannery, searching for Myra's mother and his promised reward for a job well done."

Ortega tried to say something but discovered that he was unable to move — or even feel — his lips.

"And that's not even the worst of it," whispered Janice, leaning so close to Ortega that he could feel her warm, peanut-buttery breath against his leathery nose. "Do you know that ugly coat Myra's mother always wears? The one with the ratty fur trim? They say she got the leather from the very tank where the drifter met his untimely end."

Ortega had to lean against the wall to keep from toppling over. "I think I'm going to throw up," he bleated.

Janice sat back with a satisfied look on her face. "Filming the final battle scene there is going to be the most fun *ever*, don't you think?" she asked.

Ortega wondered if he was the only one who thought she was insane, but before he could find out, Peter cleared his throat and asked, "So, Ortega, are you in or not?"

Ortega thought about what Dr. Whitmore would do if he caught Ortega sneaking around behind his back, what the ghostly drifter would do if he stumbled upon a gorilla zombie lurching past his final resting place and how utterly frazzled Dr. Susan would feel about the entire situation. Then he thought about how empty the fourth corner of the tree fort would look without him in it, and realized that none of the rest of it mattered.

"I'm in," he said. "When do we start?"

Chapter Six

That afternoon went even better than the morning. Miss Rutherford asked Ortega to take the attendance sheet to the office, so he got to miss the first part of the spelling lesson. Then, during art class, a girl he'd never spoken to shyly complimented him on the self-portrait he'd painted, even though it looked like a blob with no face and five legs. Best of all, he got picked first in gym class — by Duncan, who promised never to shoot spitballs at him again if he body-slammed Peter into the crash mat during the floor hockey game. Ortega pretended to reluctantly agree, then waited until Duncan was winding up for the game-winning slap shot to sneak up behind him and roar as loud as he could. Duncan was so startled that he hollered and dropped his hockey stick. This allowed Peter to dash over, steal the ball and get in a shot before the final buzzer. The shot went wide, but whether this was because Peter was uncoordinated or because he was laughing hard enough to rupture a major organ was hard to say.

The only real trouble came at the end of the day. Class had already been dismissed when Myra Harding's mother swept into the classroom wearing the hideous coat she'd made out of leather plucked from the doomed drifter's tank of chemicals. Ortega was at the back of the room in the reading corner, looking for a new home-reading book. He was so absorbed in a collection of ghost stories that he didn't even notice Mrs. Harding gliding toward him until she was right behind him.

"You," she breathed.

Ortega practically leaped out of his skin. Dropping to one knuckle, he hastily pivoted around and nearly screamed when he saw her looming over him.

"I thought we'd gotten rid of you," she continued, jabbing a bony finger at him.

"I-I came back," he stammered, hoping he'd be able to escape before she transformed into a shrieking swarm of blood-sucking vampire bats.

"Not for lack of decent people trying to do the right thing," she said tightly as she took another step toward him. "Children being taught in the same classroom as animals — as though they were no better than animals," she spat. "All to satisfy the sick, twisted minds of those who care nothing for the consequences of their reckless, thoughtless pursuit of what is possible. You think you have won? You have not. As God is my witness, I promise that one of these days I will get rid of you — for *good*."

Her words clutched at Ortega's heart like an icy fist. Flinging his book of ghost stories to one side, he dropped to both knuckles and tried to gallop past her. But she was blocking almost the entire path out of the book corner, and when he brushed by her, the clasp on her purse somehow became tangled with the strap of his knapsack. In his terror, Ortega didn't realize this, however, so when he felt a sharp tug from behind, he assumed that she was trying to drag him backward in order to finish him off. With a scream, he veered sharply to the right, wrenching his knapsack away from her as he galloped to the nearest bookshelf and scrambled upward, hoping to climb over it and flee before she could pounce on him. Unfortunately, just as he reached the summit, the shelf gave way beneath him and he crashed to the ground in a pile of splintered wood and scattered books.

After the dust settled, it took Miss Rutherford quite a while to convince Mrs. Harding that Ortega had not been trying to snatch her purse and even longer to usher her and Myra out of the classroom. When they were finally gone, Miss Rutherford strode briskly over to where Ortega was still lying flat on his back.

"You have some very spindly furniture in this school," he declared as he waved a piece of the destroyed bookshelf at her.

Pursing her lips at him, Miss Rutherford placed her hands on her hips and said, "That was quite the little performance you put on, Ortega."

"Thank you," he replied.

"I was being sarcastic," she said severely.

"Oh."

"You would do well not to antagonize Mrs. Harding," she advised as she hauled him to his feet and set him to work cleaning up the mess he'd made.

"She would do well not to antagonize *me*," he retorted sourly.

"Let us think on this for a moment, shall we?" suggested Miss Rutherford. "She still has a great deal of power in this town and could cause you considerable trouble. What could you possibly do to her?"

"I could eat her," said Ortega, smacking his lips together.

"Don't be ridiculous," clucked Miss Rutherford. "Avoid trouble where you can, Ortega."

Ortega flung a piece of the ruined bookcase to one side. "Why are people always telling me things like that?" he demanded loudly, thumping an open hand against his chest. "Why should *I* have to avoid trouble? Why should *I* have to worry about not making things harder on myself? I didn't ask to be turned into the world's most amazing gorilla — I didn't ask for any of this!"

"That's true," agreed Miss Rutherford swiftly.

"She should be yelling at Dr. Whitmore, not me," he added, jabbing his finger aggressively in the direction Mrs. Harding had gone.

"What about Dr. Susan?"

"What about her? This isn't about her," said Ortega, flapping his arms in agitation. "This is about *you* telling me to watch my back after that murdering maniac with the roadkill breath said mean things to me for no good reason at all. Does that sound fair to you? Does it?"

"No, it doesn't," said Miss Rutherford, acting as if she hadn't heard his less-than-flattering description of Mrs. Harding. "Unfortunately, life isn't always about what is fair. I didn't say she was right, Ortega; I said she was powerful. In a perfect world, no one would ever say unkind things to you. People would accept you as an intelligent, sensitive being who has the same rights as everyone else — the right to be treated with dignity and respect; the right to have certain freedoms and responsibilities; the right to be looked upon as equal but different."

The idea had never even occurred to Ortega. Something in his chest started aching at the thought of it now.

"But we don't live in a perfect world," continued Miss Rutherford. "We live in a very imperfect world, I'm afraid — a world where someone like you needs to be careful around someone like her. You are a pioneer, Ortega, and like any pioneer, your place in society is somewhat unclear. You are neither fully a part of the world into which you were born nor fully a part of the world you have come to live in. It is unquestionably an extraordinary adventure, but one that is fraught with challenges and difficulties. And so I say: keep your chin up, keep your heart strong and avoid trouble where you can."

Ortega carefully considered everything Miss Rutherford had just said. Then he muttered, "I still think it would be easier just to eat her."

"What was that?" asked Miss Rutherford sharply.

"Nothing," said Ortega loudly.

After dinner that night, Dr. Susan got ready to go out to a movie with friends while Ortega sat on the edge of his bed, eating a snack and telling her and her tape recorder all about his day at school.

"I had a great time hanging out with my friends," he said as he munched away on a fat piece of cucumber. "Peter is nothing like I thought he was when I first met him. He's really interesting, and even kind of cool. Eugene likes food almost as much as I do, and Janice is … well, it's hard to describe Janice. Anyway, the four of us have some big, BIG plans, but I'm not allowed to tell you what they are, not even if you torture me."

"So I guess that means there's no point in stringing you up by your toes and trying to tickle the information out of you?" asked Dr. Susan as she struggled to pull her frizzy hair into a ponytail.

"Exactly," said Ortega. "So let's just move on. Did I mention that Myra Harding's mother threatened to kill me?"

"What!"

"Uh-huh," he nodded, wondering if Dr. Susan realized her hair looked like the business end of a broom. "She'd probably do it, too, if she got the chance. She's killed before, you know."

"Oh, come on," chuckled Dr. Susan, adjusting the volume on the tape recorder.

"That kind of attitude is probably the reason she's not in jail right now," complained Ortega, shaking a stalk of celery at her. "Because no one would believe that someone like her could do something like that. Especially since she got rid of all the evidence."

"And just how do you know all of this?" asked Dr. Susan, as she rummaged through her purse in search of a lipstick.

"I have my sources," he replied mysteriously. "Miss Rutherford says I'm a pioneer."

"She does?" said Dr. Susan, looking up.

Ortega nodded as he squashed half a banana into his mouth, peel and all. "She says that in a perfect world I'd have rights and freedoms." Pausing, he cocked his head and got a dreamy look in his eyes. "She says that people would think of me as equal, only much stronger and more handsome."

"She said that?"

"More or less," he shrugged. "Do you think of me as an equal?"

Dr. Susan blinked in surprise. "I-I've never really thought about it."

"Think about it now."

Dr. Susan's mouth opened and closed several times.

Abruptly Ortega banged his snack bowl down on the desk hard. Cut-up fruits and vegetables went flying in all directions. "I don't believe it!" he screeched, flinging the bowl across the room. "You don't think of me as an equal, do you?"

"Ortega —"

He leaped onto the bed, snatched up his pillow and flung it at her.

She ducked. Then she grabbed his arm. He could easily have pulled away — he could easily have thrown her half-way across the room! — but instead, he froze.

"I fell in love with you the first time I held you in my arms, and I have loved you ever since," said Dr. Susan, fixing him with a steady gaze. "I want you to be happy, and I would do anything in my power to protect you."

"Does that mean you think of me as an equal?" asked Ortega, who wanted to be thought of as an equal, but who wasn't exactly sure what that meant.

"I don't know," admitted Dr. Susan, shrugging helplessly. "But ... I think if I had a child of my own, I would probably feel the same way about him."

For the second time that day, Ortega felt a strange ache in his chest.

"Okay," he murmured, shaking his arm free of her hand so that he could lean over and give her a chin tickle.

Dr. Susan patted his cheek in return. They sat like that for a long, contented moment. Then Ortega decided to collect the scattered remains of his snack, so Dr. Susan returned to rummaging around in her purse. Almost immediately, she gave a triumphant little cry and pulled out a battered tube of lipstick. Carefully, she applied the hideous orange color to her lips and then turned to Ortega.

"What do you think?" she asked, making a kissy face at him.

"You're beautiful on the inside," he shuddered.

Dr. Susan wiped the lipstick off with a tissue.

"Better," he said. "Can I have my friends over on Saturday?"

"Will it make you happy?" she asked.

"Not as happy as ice cream and chocolate cake," he admitted. "But pretty happy."

"Pretty happy is pretty good," she smiled.

The minute Dr. Susan left, Ortega checked to make sure Dr. Whitmore wasn't lurking nearby. Then he scampered over to the nearest phone to call Glen, the paleontologist who had nearly got his heart ripped out by a rampaging Ortegasaurus the last time he went to the doughnut shop. Ortega misdialed twice because his thick fingers had a hard time punching the ridiculously tiny buttons on the phone. On his third try, the call went through.

"I need a favor," he blurted, the minute Glen answered the phone.

"Who is this?" asked Glen.

"It's me," said Ortega hurriedly. "Listen, I need you to come over this Saturday and keep Dr. Susan occupied in her office for an hour."

"Ortega?"

"What?" he said impatiently.

There was a small pause. Then Glen said, "I didn't realize you'd been given back your telephone privileges after losing them for calling a tow truck to remove Dr. Whitmore's car from the parking lot."

Ortega chuckled deeply at the memory of Dr. Whitmore frantically chasing the tow truck down the street, his spindly arms flailing and his lab coat flapping behind him. Then he cleared his throat and said, "Well, now you know. So, can you come over this Saturday and keep her busy for me? I'd ask Dr. Whitmore, but he's taking his nephew, Rupert, to the circus, and plus I'd rather rip out my own eyeballs and play Ping-Pong with them than ask that jerk for a favor."

"Interesting," said Glen. "Why is it so important that she be kept busy?"

Ortega took a deep breath. "Because her birthday is next week and my friends are coming over to help me make a surprise gift," he lied.

"Susan's birthday is next week? Really?" said Glen.

"Really," confirmed Ortega. "She's turning 185-billion years old and I want to do something special for her, so can you come over and keep her out of my hair for an hour? Please?"

Glen chuckled almost as deeply as Ortega had chuckled. The sound made Ortega feel strangely comforted, and he had a sudden urge to reach out and touch Glen.

But, of course, that wasn't possible.

"Sure thing, little buddy," said Glen. "See you then."

Saturday morning, Peter's mom dropped the kids off at the lab. Dr. Susan had just said good-bye to her and was about to pull the main doors of the lab closed when Glen strode off the open elevator carrying two coffees and a bag of doughnuts.

"Glen," said Dr. Susan, blinking in surprise. "What are you doing here?"

"I was in the neighborhood."

Ortega and Peter exchanged knowing glances. Eugene started to giggle, but Janice shut him up with a sharp elbow to the ribs.

"Oh," said Dr. Susan, looking thoroughly nonplussed. "But ... but — how did you get up here without signing in at the security desk and getting buzzed through?"

"Mohammed from the physiology lab let me in the side door in exchange for a jelly doughnut," he whispered with a conspiratorial grin.

"Dr. Whitmore will have a fit if he finds out," frowned Dr. Susan. "He's a real nut when it comes to security, you know."

"I know, but it was a matter of life and death!" explained Glen earnestly. "If I hadn't gotten inside quickly, there's a very good chance that the rampaging Ortegasaurus that lives behind the doughnut shop would have torn off my legs and stuffed them down my throat!"

Ortega was so embarrassed by the fact that Glen had mentioned the Ortegasaurus in front of his friends that he clapped one hand over his eyes and made a flapping gesture with the other one in the hope that Glen would take the hint and remove himself from Ortega's sight.

Dr. Susan laughed. Glen smiled down at her.

"Come on," he coaxed. "Why don't we forget about Dr. Security Nut and go drink our coffee while it's still hot? I'll even help you transcribe this week's tapes, if you like."

Dr. Susan seemed taken aback. "Well, the project funders *will* be looking for their quarterly update soon, and I won't be able to finish it until I have all the data analyzed," she murmured, looking up at Glen with an odd expression on her face. "Are you sure this is how you want to spend your Saturday morning?"

"Oh, absolutely," he smiled.

The minute Glen had squired Dr. Susan safely to her office, Eugene asked Ortega what Glen and Dr. Susan had been talking about.

"At the end of every day, Dr. Susan interviews me about what I did. Sometimes she uses a video camera, but mostly she just uses a tape recorder. Afterward, everything I said — plus everything else anyone has observed and recorded about me — gets entered into the computer, and a whole bunch of programs are run to analyze the information," explained Ortega.

"This happens every *day*?" asked Eugene.

"For as long as I can remember," said Ortega.

"And do they ever tell you what the analysis says about you?" asked Eugene curiously.

The question startled Ortega. "No," he blurted. "I mean, not directly, although I pick up a lot at scientific conferences."

"You go to scientific conferences?" said Peter.

Annoyed by the hint of enthusiasm in the voice of his friend, who couldn't *possibly* imagine what those conferences were like for him, Ortega cut the conversation short by galloping over and disabling the lab's central video camera. He knew the only reason Dr. Susan hadn't insisted on observing this visit with his friends was because she was recording everything for later analysis.

"At least that's what she *thinks*," he muttered savagely, tugging the little yellow wire at the back of the camera just enough to cut power.

He turned in time to see Peter pulling his own video camera out of his knapsack. A few minutes later, Janice and Eugene returned from the bathroom, where they'd been making themselves up to look like the sole survivors of a terrorist plot involving lethal viruses and zombie killers. With dark circles under their haunted eyes and fake gashes all over their faces and hands, they were such a startling sight that Ortega let out a bark of surprise.

"That's it!" cried Peter, whirling around to face him. "That's the sound I want to hear at the end of the scene when you reach out and drag Eugene into the supply closet."

"No problem," said Ortega, with a businesslike clap of his hands. "What sound do you want me to make when I start to eat him?"

Eugene tried to protest that this wasn't funny, but Janice interrupted, saying, "He doesn't care what sound you make, just as long as you chew with your mouth closed, right, Pete?"

Peter grinned and nodded. "Now, places, everybody," he ordered, shooing them into position. "Lights ... camera ... action!"

Glen kept Dr. Susan busy for so long that the friends had finished filming, cleaned up and were lounging behind Ortega's beanbag chair giggling and whispering together by the time anybody bothered to check on them. The scene had unfolded perfectly, with lots of unexpected, creepy little extras. Like the way Janice's footfalls had echoed when she'd run through the darkened lab in search of a place to hide, or the way Eugene's eyes had bugged out for real when Ortega's long, hairy arm had shot out of the supply closet and closed around his throat. Peter was elated — he said it was even more spine-tingling than he'd hoped it would be, and that he couldn't wait to shoot the river scene the next day.

"Me neither," said Ortega jubilantly. "It's going to be great!"

"It's cold," complained Ortega, snatching his toe back from the muddy water.

"It's not *that* cold," said Peter. "And anyway, you'll only be in it for a few minutes. Just long enough to crouch down behind the boat and then burst out of the water roaring with hunger for human flesh."

"But I'm not hungry," protested Ortega. "And I can't swim."

"You don't have to swim," said Peter, casting an anxious glance over his shoulder in the direction of his mom's trailer. "It's a very shallow river."

"How do you know?" asked Ortega.

"Because one time my mom and I took a boat ride to the city to have dinner at Pizza Pizzazz and got stuck on sandbars half a dozen times during the trip," explained Peter impatiently. "Now will you please get out there so we can film this scene? My mom isn't going to be on the phone with my dad forever, you know, and if she comes out and sees us using the boat without permission, supervision *or* life jackets, I am dead meat."

Reluctantly, Ortega waded into the water, trying not to freak out as his feet sank deep into the sucking muck at the bottom of the muddy river. Ten feet from shore, Janice was rocking the boat and laughing like a hyena while Eugene clutched the sides and bleated for her to stop. Then Peter shouted "Action!" and they both scrambled into position. Ten seconds later, Ortega leaped out of the water as best he could, roaring and snapping his fearsome canines. Janice pretended to do kung-fu moves on him until he slid back into the water. Then, ignoring the small outboard motor, she and

Eugene paddled madly for shore. When they got there, they jumped out of the boat, scrambled up the riverbank and took off into the woods at a dead run in desperate search of the rare weed that could be stewed into an antidote for zombie venom. The scene ended with a dripping Ortega giving an unearthly scream before dropping from a high branch to face the ultra-tough, time-traveling zombie killer (Janice) below.

Later, back in the tree fort, Peter played back the "raw footage" for the others to see. It was grainy, and a little shaky, but that only seemed to add to the effect, especially at the end when Ortega dropped out of the tree, because all you saw was a giant shrieking blur and then the screen went blank.

"You are *really* talented," sighed Ortega. "I'll bet your mom and dad have been on the phone so long because they can't stop talking about how talented you are."

"I doubt it," said Peter. "My parents don't talk — they argue."

"About what?" asked Ortega.

"Me, mostly," said Peter matter-of-factly. "My mom gets mad at my dad for buying me expensive gifts — like the video camera, or the boat — instead of paying child support, and she gets *really* mad when he makes promises he doesn't keep. She can't seem to understand that he's doing his best, you know? He's not irresponsible *or* a quitter. Things come up, that's all. Plans change. It's the way life is sometimes."

Ortega nodded wisely, as though he knew all about life and its mysterious ways.

Suddenly, Eugene sat up and looked over at Ortega with a puzzled expression. "Hey, Ortega," he said. "Do you have parents?"

Janice gave Eugene an incredulous look. "Of course he has parents," she said. "What do you think — the laboratory found him at the bottom of a cereal box?"

"I don't know where they found him," retorted Eugene, sticking his thumb to his nose and wiggling his fat fingers at her. "That's why I'm asking."

Janice gave a derisive snort and tried to look bored, but she couldn't resist sneaking a peek at Ortega. Peter, too, gave him a curious sideways glance. Ortega felt the hair along his crest begin to rise, the way it did at Dr. Whitmore's stupid scientific conferences when all those eggheads crowded around trying to get him to do something remarkable. Then he remembered that when he'd asked Peter about his parents, Peter had answered without hesitation. No one knew better than Ortega how unfair it was to only ever ask the questions — sometimes, you had to answer them, too.

So instead of folding his arms across his chest and refusing to do anything but scowl (which is what he usually did to the eggheads), Ortega turned to Eugene and said, "They found me in, um, a zoo. My mother wasn't taking very good care of me, so they took me away from her and gave me to Dr. Whitmore. And that's all I know."

The long moment of silence that followed was eventually broken by Eugene, who gave him a bleak look and said, "That's not very much to know, Ortega."

"No," he replied slowly. "I guess it isn't."

———————

By the time Ortega got back to the lab that evening he was looking forward to building himself a cozy little nest in the corner behind his beanbag chair and settling in for a good long snooze. Hanging out with his friends had been fun, but they didn't seem to enjoy napping nearly as much as he did. They were so full of energy, all the time — even Eugene, who wasn't in very good shape at all. In truth, Ortega had found it rather exhausting trying to keep up with them.

Unfortunately, just as he finished shaping his dirty clothes into a nice, comfy pile with an Ortega-sized hole in the middle of it, Dr. Susan walked into the room and asked him if he had any idea who had tampered with the lab's central video camera.

He immediately collapsed into the hole and pretended he was in a coma.

"Dr. Whitmore had planned to use yesterday's recording at an upcoming scientific meeting to illustrate your level of social integration," said Dr. Susan. "Imagine how upset he was when he discovered that the only thing he had a recording of was you climbing up onto a chair and reaching for the back of the camera."

Ortega moaned slightly, the way he figured a coma patient might if he wanted someone to go away and stop pestering him.

"Get up!" ordered Dr. Susan, leaning over to give him a tickle.

Ortega yelped and tried to skootch away from her, but she had him trapped behind the beanbag chair, so after a few moments of helpless wriggling he gave up and opened his eyes.

"You wrecked my nest," he complained, gesturing to the flattened pile of dirty laundry.

Instead of answering, Dr. Susan took a notepad and a pen out of the pocket of her lab coat. Ortega knew that meant she was about to start asking him some important research questions, but before she could even open her mouth, he sat up and said, "Who are my parents?"

Dr. Susan was so startled by his question that she nearly dropped her pen. "What?" she asked.

"Who are my parents?" he repeated. "Where are they? All you've ever told me is that my mother lived in a zoo. That doesn't mean anything — it's like me telling you your mother lived in a city. What was my mother's name? Did she even have a name? Is she still alive? Do you know who my father was? Do I have any brothers or sisters?" For some reason,

Ortega could feel himself getting angry. "WHAT DID YOU THINK?" he shouted suddenly, snatching up a handful of heavy-duty building blocks and hurling them across the room with such force that they left tiny dents in the wall. "DID YOU THINK IT DIDN'T MATTER BECAUSE I WAS JUST A STUPID GORILLA?"

Dr. Susan was so shocked by his outburst that for a moment she could only stare at him with a stricken expression on her face. Then, abruptly, she collapsed onto the beanbag chair. "Oh, Ortega," she said. "Of *course* I didn't think anything like that. It's just, well, after you learned to talk you seemed so different from … from …"

"From those stupid gorillas in the zoo who walk around naked and eat without using utensils and grunt like a bunch of *animals*?" he asked scornfully.

Dr. Susan hung her head. "I'm sorry … I guess I just started to think of Grandma and me as your family and —"

"Did either of you adopt me?" interrupted Ortega.

"No, but —"

"THEN YOU'RE NOT MY REAL FAMILY!" he bellowed.

Dr. Susan flinched but didn't turn away from the gust of hot gorilla breath in her face. Instead, she lifted her head and looked into Ortega's eyes for so long that he started to worry he might blink first.

"Fair enough," she said at last.

Something in her voice made Ortega want to reach out and touch her, but he resisted the temptation.

"I'll find out what I can about your birth family, okay?" she continued quietly.

For a moment, Ortega just sat there scowling at the fresh dents in his walls and plugging his nose so he wouldn't be comforted by the smell of Dr. Susan's shampoo. Then: "Whatever," he grunted moodily as he flopped back into his ruined nest.

Dr. Susan gazed at him with enormous tenderness. "You look tired," she murmured, tentatively reaching down to smooth the hair on his heavy brow. "Would ... would you like me to sing you a lullaby?"

"I don't care," he yawned. "But get Mr. Doodles for me before you start, okay?"

Dr. Susan fetched the ratty old stuffed bear, tucked him gently into Ortega's arms and began to sing.

At the sound of her lilting voice, Ortega yawned again, reached for her hand and nudged it against the hair on his brow. She immediately began smoothing it once more, and Ortega gave a low grunt of contentment and drifted off to sleep dreaming of a nameless, faceless mother who looked just like him.

Chapter Seven

Ortega awoke Monday morning with a bad case of the sniffles, so Dr. Susan kept him home from school. Gorillas were very susceptible to catching pneumonia — in the wild, older, weaker mountain gorillas often succumbed to the disease during the rainy season — so Dr. Susan and Dr. Whitmore never took any chances. The slightest sniffle, the smallest fever and the mildest cough were treated with complete bed rest and, if his symptoms didn't disappear in a day or two, a visit to Dr. Mike.

"He's a real doctor," Ortega reminded Dr. Whitmore, when he came in to check on Ortega mid-morning. "You know — one who actually helps people."

"He doesn't help *people*, Ortega," corrected Dr. Whitmore absently as he leaned over to take Ortega's pulse. "He's a veterinarian."

"He's a genius," declared Ortega, sneezing runny yellow boogers all over the front of Dr. Whitmore's lab coat.

With a cry of disgust, Dr. Whitmore fled the room to clean up. Ortega wrapped his long arms around himself and rolled around on the bed, kicking his feet in the air and chuckling deeply until Dr. Susan came into the room carrying a tray, at which point he let his arms flop listlessly to his sides.

"Hello," he croaked weakly. "Did you bring me another bowl of tapioca?"

"Yes," she smiled, "and also two peanut-butter-and-jelly sandwiches, a big bunch of grapes and a yogurt smoothie."

Ortega grinned as his nose — which had been temporarily cleared out by his previous well-timed sneeze — began to run again.

"Are you feeling any better?" asked Dr. Susan, holding a tissue to his nostrils.

Ortega sighed melodramatically, then pushed her hand away and began shoveling sandwiches into his mouth.

Dr. Susan sat cross-legged at the edge of the bed humming quietly to herself and examining her frizzy hair for split ends until Ortega was almost finished his snack, at which point she gave him a sideways glance and said, "Are you *sure* you have no idea how you might have caught the sniffles, Ortega?"

Ortega thought back to the scene in the river — and to the cold, muddy water that had seemed to suck more and more of the heat out of his body with each passing minute.

"No idea," he said with a violent shiver as he reached for his smoothie. "No idea at all."

Ortega's sniffles weren't completely gone the next day, but he demanded to be allowed to go to school anyway. He knew Miss Rutherford was going to require him to make up any work he'd missed, and this took a good deal of the joy out of lying in bed watching TV and being waited on hand and foot by Dr. Susan. Besides, Peter's movie was almost finished, and Ortega didn't want to be the cause of any delays.

Dr. Susan was okay with Ortega going back to school as long as he promised to dress warmly and stay dry, but Dr. Whitmore was dead set against it. He didn't want Ortega exposed to all sorts of bacteria and viruses that his weakened immune system might not be able to handle.

"I thought you said bacteria and viruses couldn't jump between species," said Ortega, trying not to sniffle as he pulled on his knapsack. "I thought you said that was one of the exciting things about the technology I represent."

"I said *some* bacteria and viruses couldn't jump between species, Ortega," said Dr. Whitmore with a condescending little smile. "But some can, and that's why I'm concerned about you."

Ortega blinked in surprise. Then, in a voice that sounded much younger than his eleven years, he said, "Are ... are you really concerned about me, Dr. Whitmore?"

"Of course!" replied Dr. Whitmore, as though surprised by the question. "Without you, Ortega, there is no Project Ortega. I would be out of a job, as would Susan and all of our support staff. Not only that, but the company would suffer the loss of important funding and one of its most valuable assets."

"Oh, yeah?" muttered Ortega, knuckle-stomping off in search of Dr. Susan. "What asset is that?"

"You."

———◦◦◦———

In the end, Dr. Whitmore kept Ortega home from school for another two days. By the morning of the third day, Ortega was so eager to see his friends that he was bouncing off the walls — literally.

"You're not going to get to school any faster this way," smiled Dr. Susan, jingling the car keys at him.

"THAT'S YOUR OPINION!" whooped Ortega as he barreled around the room, tumbling and smashing into things.

The drive to school seemed interminable to Ortega, but it was well worth it, because when he finally walked into his classroom, Peter, Janice and Eugene looked just as happy to see him as he was to see them. It was a heady feeling for him — to be liked, by friends his own age, for his own sake and nothing more. As though he were just a person like any other; as though he were an equal.

The deep sense of contentment this brought him lasted all the way until lunchtime, when Peter announced his intention to shoot the final scene of the movie that weekend.

"Good idea," said Janice, joining the conversation for the first time since lunch began. "Because I'm pretty sure the anniversary of that drifter's murder is coming up, and even I don't think it would be a good idea to get caught wandering around in that factory when his ghost rises."

To emphasize her point, she nodded knowingly and drew her finger across her bare throat.

Eugene's eyes bulged. "Maybe it's not a good idea for us to be wandering around in there at all!" he exclaimed. "I mean, we don't know for sure the ghost only rises on the anniversary. Maybe he gets up early — you know, to get a head start on scaring people to death!"

Janice threw back her head and laughed so wildly that Ortega cringed. "Don't be ridiculous, Eugene," she said. "Ghosts don't get up early. We'll be perfectly safe as long as we go in soon and avoid the attack dogs."

"What attack dogs?" cried Eugene, clutching his chest.

"The ones pictured on the No Trespassing signs someone nailed up around the property last week. It's probably just a scare tactic to keep vandals away — like that health department notice on the front door that says the place is infested with rats — but we won't know for sure until we get inside. In fact, we won't know *anything* for sure until we get inside, so we'll just have to be prepared for everything," said Janice with obvious relish. "Isn't that right, Peter?"

Peter — who looked even more alarmed than Ortega felt — nodded reluctantly as he watched Janice do a few kung-fu moves to illustrate her own personal preparedness. Janice nodded back and then, without warning, rounded on Ortega.

"I've even figured out what we're going to do about *you*," she said, flourishing her index finger like a cutlass.

"Do about me?" he echoed, not liking the sound of that one bit.

"That's right. See, as soon as we started talking about where and when we were going to shoot the final scene, I realized we had a big problem. We had to figure out a way to get you to the factory at night without anyone finding out. It seemed impossible at first. I mean, even if we could bypass all the security features at your lab — the cameras, the locks, the mad scientists who are always hanging around — we'd still have to sneak you past the guard downstairs. And even if we could do *that*, we'd have to somehow make it from the city all the way out here — *without you being recognized.* We'd have to do it all *and* shoot the scene *and* get back to the lab before anyone realized you were missing."

"Sounds pretty impossible to me," said Eugene hopefully, taking an enormous bite of coconut-frosted sponge cake.

"But then I was sitting in class, see," continued Janice, "and I overheard Myra and her bubbleheaded friends talking about how everyone is going to see the new Derek Blackheart movie that's opening tonight at the town theater."

"So?" said Peter.

"*So,*" said Janice, smiling a triumphant pirate smile. "We tell our parents — or, uh, whoever," she said, glancing at Ortega, "that we want to go to the show, too. Then, after we all get dropped off, we ditch the theater and head to the factory. It's only five or six blocks away, so it shouldn't take us long to get there, and since no one will be expecting the movie to let out for a couple of hours, we'll have plenty of time to shoot the scene and get back to the theater. Isn't that the most perfect plan *ever*?"

"Perfect," said Eugene unhappily, "all except for the part about us getting chased by ghosts, attacked by dogs and eaten by rats."

Janice brushed aside his concerns with an impatient wave of her hand. "It's very unlikely that all of those things will happen, Eugene."

"But how unlikely is it that *some* of them will happen?" he asked, anxiously licking a bit of frosting off the empty sponge-cake wrapper.

"How should I know? That's what makes it so exciting!" said Janice. When she noticed that her words of comfort had failed to wipe the look of terror off Eugene's face, she added, "Listen, if it makes you feel any better, I'll stay right by your side the entire time and protect you no matter what happens, okay?" Lifting up both arms, she flexed her biceps to show Eugene the raw power that would stand between him and certain death.

Ortega — who was so worried that he could hardly see straight — looked over at Peter, who appeared ready to vomit. It was clear that neither of them wanted to go ahead with this insane plan, but it was equally clear that neither wanted to be the first to admit it in front of this dark-haired girl with the flashing blue eyes.

Janice sighed contentedly and reached for her sandwich.

Friday night, Ortega spotted Peter, Eugene and Janice the minute Dr. Susan brought the Chevette Scooter to a skidding halt at the curb in front of the movie theater. They were waiting in the shadows, slightly apart from the noisy lineup of young people eager to be terrorized by a movie that had somehow avoided a Parental Guidance rating. Eugene appeared to be clumsily attempting to model the kung-fu moves Janice was demonstrating, while Peter stood by looking smaller and skinnier than ever.

"Looks busy," said Dr. Susan as she rifled through her purse for ticket money.

Instead of answering, Ortega took a deep breath, buried his face in Mr. Doodles's back and screamed so shrilly that Dr. Susan jumped and let out a little scream of her own.

"What on earth is wrong!" she cried, turning in her seat to face him.

"Nothing," he replied calmly. "Why do you ask?"

"Because the last time I heard you scream like that was when you found the rubber snake Rupert had hidden in the cookie jar," she grumbled, handing him his ticket money.

"What's your point?"

"My point is that you only scream like that when you're scared."

"Not true. I also scream like that when I'm excited about going to the movies with friends who think of me as an equal — unlike some people," he retorted, giving the seat beside him an aggressive slap. "You don't know everything about me, you know. Just because you get to see the results of your stupid analysis and I don't doesn't mean that you know me better than I know myself!"

"I never said it did," protested Dr. Susan, throwing up her hands as though to ward off his sudden anger. "Would you like to see the results of our analysis sometime?"

"Not really," he muttered, rolling his eyes. "Can I go now?"

"Absolutely," she said. "Can I have a kiss?"

"Absolutely not."

Dr. Susan chuckled. "Have fun tonight," she said, reaching back to touch his cheek. "Call if you need me."

"I will," he replied, as he kicked open the car door and stepped out into the heavy heat of the night. "And I won't."

"It's about time," said Janice the minute Ortega knuckle-walked up. People were looking at him, of course — people were always looking at him — but the crowd was mostly kids, and since they all went to the same school as Ortega, it wasn't the first time they'd seen him.

The novelty was wearing off.

"Okay, here's the plan," continued Janice. "In a couple of minutes, we'll get into line. Act casual, like nothing's going on. Then, just before we get to the ticket booth — after pretty much everyone else has already gone in — I'll act like I just remembered something important and —"

"Hey," interrupted a voice.

Swiveling on one callused knuckle, Ortega saw a middle-aged man in a cheap theater uniform standing before them.

"I hope you're not thinking of bringing him into the theater," said the man, giving his greasy head a jerk in Ortega's direction.

"Why not?" demanded Janice, who seemed to have forgotten that going into the theater wasn't even part of the plan.

"Well ... because!" spluttered the man, gesturing with his hands. "He's an animal."

"You're an animal," snapped Janice.

"I am *not*," huffed the man indignantly. "I'm a person."

"He's a person," insisted Peter, pointing at Ortega.

"No, he ain't!" cried the man, who seemed to be getting very frustrated. "Just ... just look at him!"

Janice, Eugene and Peter looked at Ortega. He looked away, only to see Duncan and his idiot friends standing nearby, laughing at him.

"I don't know what you see when you look at him, mister," said Eugene in a genuinely perplexed voice. "All I see is a guy who likes brown sugar and cherry suckers."

The man hesitated for the merest instant before jamming his hands into his sweaty armpits. "All the same, he ain't coming into my theater," he said gruffly. "So unless you're looking for trouble, you all had best be on your way."

"Just keep walking," said Janice, tugging her pirate kerchief farther down on her head.

"But people are watching," said Eugene, with a worried glance over his shoulder. "I thought the plan called for us to slip away unnoticed."

"That was Plan A," explained Janice, breaking into a light run. "We've moved on to Plan B. Plan B calls for us to think on our feet."

This didn't sound like much of a plan to Ortega, but he didn't bother to mention this as he loped silently after Janice and the boys. He knew that he should be feeling grateful to his friends for having stood up for him in front of the theater man, but instead he felt annoyed by the fact that they were so sure they knew what he was when he wasn't even sure himself what he was.

"Why do I have to be a person *or* an animal, anyway?" he huffed as he loped along behind the others. "Why can't I be both?"

"What was that?" panted Peter, over his shoulder.

"Nothing," grunted Ortega.

The friends kept to deserted side streets and back alleys, ducking behind dumpsters to avoid detection when car headlights threatened to expose them. Ortega's eyes swept the shadows in search of danger; his leathery nose curled at the unfamiliar smells that hung heavy in the hot, muggy night air. From time to time he looked back, certain he'd heard footsteps or voices. Even though he never saw a thing, instinct told him to gallop faster.

Janice didn't slow down until they were halfway across the field behind the school. Except for the ragged sound of Eugene gasping for breath, the night was as quiet as death.

The sky was dark and getting darker as storm clouds from the east rolled in, blotting out the stars one by one. On the hill in the distance, the haunted factory loomed. Even from where he stood, Ortega thought he could feel the menace of the place — as though an unspeakably evil presence had taken hold of the very building itself.

He shuddered with dread.

"Get out your camera, Peter," ordered Janice in a hushed voice.

Swallowing hard, Peter slipped off his knapsack and fumbled inside for his video camera. With shaking hands, he flicked a small switch at the top of the camera. Instantly, the faces of his friends were bathed in sickly yellow light.

Eugene squinted and held his hand up to shield his eyes. Janice didn't even blink.

"Keep filming no matter what happens, okay?" she whispered, with a quick glance over her shoulder.

Peter nodded mutely. At that moment, a flash of sheet lightning lit up the sky to the east. Ortega braced himself for the crack of thunder that would follow, but it never came.

"The storm is still too far away," breathed Janice, as though reading his mind. "Okay, you guys. Let's go. Follow me and stay close. We'll enter the property by the cover of the trees, then make for the broken window at the side of the building. Be careful climbing in — you don't want to get cut, because the smell of blood attracts all kinds of things. We get in, we shoot the scene, we get out. If we get split up, we'll meet at the flagpole in front of the school."

"Why would we get split up?" cried Eugene, his voice sounding pitifully small in the vastness of the night.

But Janice was already moving again, so he just hurried to catch up with her. Peter stayed a little way back so he could film them as they jogged silently through the trampled yellow grass. Every once in a while, Eugene looked back. Ortega, who was knuckle-walking along beside Peter, supposed that the expression of naked terror on Eugene's face was probably just what Peter was looking for, but it did nothing to calm Ortega's own nerves, which were screaming with alarm.

As they approached the silent thicket of trees outside the factory, he found himself whipping his head this way and that.

Something was not right here.

He could feel it in his *bones*.

Suddenly, there was an unearthly shriek about ten feet in front of him. Turning his gaze forward, he saw something leap from behind the nearest tree. His heart gave a lurch of terror as another bolt of lightning lit up the sky, illuminating the creature that would have looked like a boy except ... except ...

Except for the fact that it had no head!

Eugene and Janice screamed in unison, then bolted in opposite directions, only to find another moaning, lurching, headless creature, and another, leaping out from behind other trees, forcing them back. His instinct to protect raging, Ortega charged silently forward, his fearsome canines bared, his eyes fixed on the back of the nearest creature.

But just before he leaped at it with all of his considerable strength, lightning flashed again and he saw that one of the creatures he was about to attack had suddenly sprouted a head! In a panicked flash, Ortega realized that these so-called headless creatures were nothing more than boys who'd tucked their heads into their T-shirts. And not just any boys, either — it was Duncan and his idiot friends! They must have followed them from the theater!

As he veered sharply in order to avoid contact, Ortega's foot caught on a root and he went crashing into a nearby tree. The headless boys surrounding Janice and Eugene jumped when Ortega bellowed in pain, and Eugene used the momentary distraction to lower his head and run as hard as he could into the belly of the biggest one. The boy exhaled in a mighty *whoosh* and dropped like a sack of potatoes. Eugene was on him in a second, pummeling with all his might and spitting oaths of unbridled fury. Such was his rage that none of the other still-headless boys dared to intervene, and it wasn't until the one pinned beneath Eugene started howling for mercy that Eugene finally eased off. For a moment, he just sat there on his victim's chest, panting with exertion. Then all at once, he began to cry — big, blubbery tears of relief and exhaustion. The boy beneath him heaved him off, got to his feet and — without popping his head through his collar to reveal his identity — slunk off into the night with his companions.

When they were gone, Ortega started toward Eugene, his heart hammering as he tried to think of what to say to comfort his sniffling friend. Before he'd taken three steps, however, Janice shoved past him and ran up to Eugene.

"You were awesome!" she cried, giving his arm a lusty punch. "When those headless idiots jumped out at us, I lost it, I really did! I mean, I thought I was ready for anything, but who the hell is ever ready for something like *that*? I was so stunned I couldn't do a single kung-fu move. Not a single one! It didn't matter, though, did it? Because you were right there watching my back the whole time," she enthused as she gave him another slug in the arm. "Just like a real live zombie killer!"

Eugene smiled and wiggled his eyebrows at Ortega.

Ortega smiled back. Then he thought of something and stopped smiling. Looking up at the empty factory that seemed to stare back with icy malice, he gave a shiver and, with great trepidation, asked, "So ... uh ... what now?"

"Now we go back to the theater," announced Peter as he stepped forward and closed the view screen on the video camera. "I caught everything on tape," he explained. "The stormy night — the headless dudes — Ortega's charge — Eugene putting the beat on that one that sounded a lot like

Duncan — Janice running to Eugene's side. It was all so real and scary that there's no point sticking with the original script." He grinned and waved his arms expansively. "I've already got everything I need to put together the best film ever. That sorry old factory can kiss my —"

Suddenly, a deafening crack of thunder shook the air around them. The clouds swallowed up the moon with amazing speed, and the sky opened up and poured rain down upon them.

With a cry, Peter shoved his camera into his waterproof knapsack and ran after the others, who were already pelting across the field and away from that terrible place. They ran until they were breathless, then slowed to a walk. Ortega licked the rivulets of warm rainwater that streamed down his leathery face, and purposely knuckle-walked through the dirty puddles that had begun to gush down the streets around him. When Peter and Eugene noticed him blissfully splashing along, the two of them started stomping behind him, singing silly songs at the top of their lungs, kicking up great geysers of water with their soaking sneakers and laughing at their own recklessness. For a while, Janice tried to look uninterested in their display of carefree abandon, but before long she, too, was dancing in the rain and whooping like a maniac.

It was a wonderful release after the tension of the evening, and the friends were in high spirits as they rounded the corner right next to the theater.

Which is probably why it came as such a shock when they saw the crowd of shouting people who — as far as Ortega was concerned — looked every bit as scary as anything they'd faced yet.

Hastily, the friends ducked back into the shadows.

"They're shouting about us," whispered Eugene worriedly.

"I doubt it," said Janice, looking unconvinced.

"They are. I know it," insisted Eugene. "People must have heard how we argued with that man about Ortega, and then how we just ran away without telling anyone where we were going. So much for thinking on our feet! Oh, this is great. Just great," moaned Eugene softly, wringing his chubby hands. "I knew all along this was a bad idea. Running around in the dark without supervision *or* permission? My mom and dad are going to kill me!"

"Pull yourself together!" ordered Janice harshly. "This is no big deal, okay? Even if they are here about us — so what? We'll just mostly tell the truth. Namely, that we wouldn't abandon Ortega after the theater manager refused to let him in, so we spent the evening hanging out in the field behind the school instead."

"But that's not how we spent the evening!" cried Eugene.

Janice rolled her eyes. "I know. That's why I said we'd *mostly* tell the truth. Weren't you listening?" she asked, giving his ear a little tweak. "No one with half a brain is going to get mad at us for sticking up for someone. Adults love that kind of thing. If anything, they're going to get mad at that theater dolt for putting us poor, innocent children in the position of having to choose between our dear friend Ortega and a tub of popcorn. I promise you — by the time we're finished telling them the mostly truth, we're going to be heroes!"

Before Ortega could point out that *they* would be heroes and he would still be the big, hairy lump that got turned away from the theater for being an animal, someone in the crowd outside the theater spotted them and the shouting got louder. At first, Ortega supposed this meant Eugene had been right — that the crowd was there because of them — but then a shrill voice rose above the rest, shouting, "There it is! There's the gorilla! Out roaming the streets of our town unsupervised, doing God knows what to our poor children!"

Angry voices joined with the shrill voice; people began to spill out from under the theater marquee, oblivious to the rain that still poured down. Some shook fists at him; others just stared with faces twisted in expressions of varying ugliness. Mrs. Harding stood at the front of the mob clutching Myra's wrist in what seemed to be an iron grip, her mouth curled into a thin-lipped smile.

Shocked at unexpectedly finding himself the focus of so much hostility, Ortega shrank back from the noisy confusion, his stomach churning in distress. The hair on the back of his neck began to bristle; his throat felt so tight that he had to pant through his open mouth just so he wouldn't feel as if he was suffocating. Peter edged closer and tried to say something to him, but Ortega ignored him. There was nothing Peter could say that would matter right now, nothing. The crowd wasn't here about Peter, and Peter had no idea what it felt like to be screamed at by so many strangers who hated him for no reason at all, and who could kill him in a heartbeat without ever having to worry about being called murderers.

Suddenly, at the back of the crowd, Ortega spotted the silhouette of a woman with hair like a witch. She was desperately trying to shove her way through the crowd, and Ortega's heart turned to ice when he caught a glimpse of what she clutched under one arm.

It was a gun.

At that moment, something inside Ortega snapped. Pushing himself upright, he threw back his head and bellowed into the stormy night. It was such an otherworldly sound that people in the crowd screamed in panic and tripped over one another in their haste to get back. Even his friends skittered away from him, each wearing the shocked expression of a child who had been carelessly playing with matches and accidentally set the house on fire. The hurt this caused him hardly registered. The witch with the gun was almost upon him.

He had to get away.

Unfortunately, the precious seconds he'd spent roaring out his rage and terror had cost him dearly, because just as he dropped to his knuckles and turned to flee, the witch burst from the crowd and launched herself at him.

Only it wasn't a witch at all.

And she wasn't clutching a gun.

It was Dr. Susan, whose hair had gone berserk on account of the humidity, and tucked under her arm was an umbrella, which she hadn't bothered to pop up because she'd been so frantic to get to Ortega's side.

At the sight of the only mother he'd ever known, Ortega let out such a heartrending cry of anguished relief that some of the people in the mob suddenly looked uncertain, and Peter, Janice and Eugene hurried back to his side.

But Ortega wanted nothing from anyone but Dr. Susan.

"Oh, honey," she breathed as she cupped his massive head in her hands and placed a gentle, lingering kiss on his forehead. "Are you okay?"

Trying not to sniffle or sneeze or do anything that would make her stop holding his head, Ortega nodded.

"Do you think it's time to go home?" she asked softly.

Gulping past the lump in his throat, he nodded again.

Popping up the umbrella, Dr. Susan carefully held it over his head in order to shield him from the rain that had slowed to a misty drizzle. Then she turned and began to lead Ortega through the now-silent crowd toward the car. As they walked past Myra and her mother, Mrs. Harding opened her mouth to say something, but shut it again fast when she saw the look on Dr. Susan's face.

"She's the one who tried to kill me," whispered Ortega.

"She can try it again over my dead body," said Dr. Susan through clenched teeth.

Ortega grinned a little. "I like it when you act tough," he murmured as he gently rubbed her small, pale hand against his leathery cheek. "It almost makes up for the fact that you're wearing a poncho."

"Almost?" inquired Dr. Susan, giving his hand a squeeze.

"Well, it's a very ugly poncho," said Ortega.

"That's your opinion," whispered Dr. Susan.

Both of them smiled.

—

By the time Dr. Susan got Ortega safely settled into the car, Peter's mother had arrived to take him and the others home, and, much to Mrs. Harding's apparent dismay, the milling mob had begun to disperse in clumps of two or three, like dandelion fluff in the wind. Feeling suddenly famished, Ortega ransacked the car for something to eat, then sat back and watched as Myra's mother angrily stalked off in the direction of her big, ugly sport-utility vehicle without so much as a backward glance at Myra, who was scrambling to keep up with her. Myra's hair was plastered to her head, and her wet clothes clung to her scrawny frame. She looked as small and pathetic as a drowned kitten, and for one brief moment Ortega almost felt sorry for her. Then she looked up, saw him watching her and stuck her tongue out at him.

Ortega — who was feeling much improved after having devoured the three packages of peppermint breath mints he'd found lying at the bottom of Dr. Susan's purse — was about to kick open the car door, gallop over and lick Myra across the face in order to show her what tongues were *supposed* to be used for, when Dr. Susan's face loomed on the other side of the foggy window.

"Don't even think about it," she warned, her voice sounding muffled through the glass.

"Don't boss me around," said Ortega without moving his lips.

"What was that?" asked Dr. Susan as she opened the car door and started to slide into the driver's seat.

"NOTHING!" hollered Ortega.

Pausing mid-slide, Dr. Susan arched an eyebrow at him. "Nice try, but I don't startle that easy, pal."

Then she plopped right down on top of the jumbled contents of her emptied purse, gave a yelp of surprise and jumped so high that she hit her head on the ceiling of the car.

Ortega covered his mouth with both hands and snickered.

"I'm glad to see you've recovered so nicely from your harrowing ordeal," grumbled Dr. Susan as she shoveled the junk from her seat back into her purse. "Now buckle up. It's time to go home."

Chapter Eight

That night, Ortega slept like a log. The next morning when he awoke, he felt battered, bruised and so worn out that when he limped into the kitchen and discovered that no one had laid out breakfast for him, he didn't even have the energy to dump cottage cheese into the heating vents.

Retrieving a bag of gingersnaps from the cupboard, a jar of peanut butter from the counter and a neatly folded brown paper lunch bag from the fridge, Ortega knuckle-walked slowly back to his room and climbed into bed.

He'd eaten all the gingersnaps, demolished the contents of the lunch bag and was just struggling to reach the last bit of peanut butter in the jar with his long, juicy tongue when Dr. Whitmore strode into his room.

"Ortega!" he cried. "What do you think you're doing?"

"I think I'm eating," replied Ortega in a bored voice as he flung the plastic peanut-butter jar to one side. "What do you think I'm doing?"

"I think you are once again purposely flouting laboratory rules," said Dr. Whitmore sternly. "You know very well you're not supposed to eat in ... Uh! Is that my lunch?" he cried, pointing at the shredded remnants of brown bag Ortega was clutching between his toes.

"I don't know," admitted Ortega. "Did you have peanut butter and jelly?"

"No, I had cucumber on rye bread."

"Oh. Then yes, it is your lunch. Or rather, it was," grinned Ortega, belching richly.

Dr. Whitmore stared at him without saying anything for so long that Ortega began to feel uneasy. Gently, he released the shreds of bag from between his toes and began to smooth them out, as though this might somehow make up for having purposely pigged out on Dr. Whitmore's sandwich.

Suddenly, Dr. Whitmore spoke.

"You know, Ortega," he said softly, "when I rescued you from the zoo you weighed less than four pounds."

Ortega looked up quickly, his heart beating fast at the thought that he might learn something new about where he'd come from.

"Colleagues told me I was a fool to work with a gorilla," continued Dr. Whitmore. "They cited studies that showed gorillas to be stubborn, uncooperative and far less intelligent than chimpanzees."

"Then you met me and realized what a bunch of morons your egghead friends were," guessed Ortega, hoping he didn't sound as hurt and disappointed as he felt.

"No," said Dr. Whitmore thoughtfully. "Then I did some research and discovered that there were no suitable chimpanzees available for purchase. The funding for the project was already in place, so I had no choice but to make do with you."

"And that made it all right to steal me away from my mother."

"Your mother had already rejected you, Ortega," said Dr. Whitmore. "She was refusing to nurse or groom you. She was making no effort to protect you from the aggression of her mate's rival silverback. You would have died without the intervention of the zookeepers and me."

Ortega crossed his long arms over his massive chest. "You're a liar," he said flatly.

Across the room, Siggy reared up, clutching the bars of his cage and peering around with bright eyes.

"My point in telling you all this," continued Dr. Whitmore gently, "is that I knew going into Project Ortega that I might someday run into difficulty maintaining dominance and control over you, so I made provisions."

"What does that mean?" snorted Ortega.

"It means that there is a plan in place to shut down Project Ortega if it ever appears as though, due to your obstinate behavior, we are no longer making meaningful scientific advances."

"What happens if you do that?"

Dr. Whitmore sighed. "Susan and I go on to other things, I suppose. Your part-time handlers will be out of work and —"

"No," interrupted Ortega, more loudly than he'd intended. "I mean what happens to *me*?"

Dr. Whitmore gave him a hard look but ignored the question. "Susan has received a two-day suspension for what happened at the theater last night."

"What?" Ortega jumped up in alarm. "But what happened had nothing to do with her! It was that theater man — he wouldn't let me in to see the movie, so my friends and I, we ... uh ... went and hung around the field behind the school and ... uh ..."

"Susan did not ask for my permission to release you into the custody of those children —"

"She didn't release me into the custody of anybody," protested Ortega, flapping his arms in agitation. "She dropped me off to spend time with my friends! She was trying to make me happy!"

"She did not follow any of the protocols designed to ensure your safety and security in uncontrolled social situations."

"But she came back and rescued me!"

"She forgot what you are, Ortega, and what she is relative to you," said Dr. Whitmore in a hard voice. "You are a gorilla, and the valuable subject of a cutting-edge scientific study. She is a researcher who has an obligation to remain detached so that she can make decisions that are in the best interests of Project Ortega."

"In case you're wondering, she didn't walk me directly into the theater *because* she thought it would be best for the project," explained Ortega hastily. "See, she was wearing this very ugly poncho, and she knew if she got out of the car in front of all those kids from school that I'd probably kill myself, or die of humiliation, and then where would the project be?"

"I'm getting tired of having these conversations with you, Ortega," said Dr. Whitmore. "Disconnected video cameras ... lack of cooperation in the language studio ... being secretive, rude and inconsiderate. I won't put up with it much longer. Winning a Nobel Prize isn't worth half the grief you put me through some days. Consider yourself warned."

And with that, Dr. Whitmore turned on one cheap heel and strode out of the room.

The rest of the weekend passed quietly. Saturday afternoon, one of the more annoying part-time handlers came by to administer a new series of intelligence tests, which Ortega dutifully completed after eating just two copies of the test, snapping only three pencils in half and making a mere dozen screeching demands for chocolate ice cream in exchange for his cooperation. He didn't believe for a minute Dr. Smarty Pants's stupid threats, but he figured it couldn't hurt to be on his best behavior until Dr. Susan got back. The guy was obviously losing it.

"As if Dr. Susan and Grandma would ever let anything happen to me," he whispered to Mr. Doodles on Sunday night before bed.

The tired, tattered old stuffed bear looked up at Ortega from his seat on the beanbag chair, sympathy, understanding and loyalty positively shining from his one remaining button eye.

Suddenly, Ortega's heart swelled with such love that he thought he might burst. Hooting loudly, he snatched Mr. Doodles up by one leg, crushed him to his chest in a fierce hug and galloped around the room, bellowing and crashing into things until exhaustion overwhelmed him. At that point — after tenderly replacing a lump of stuffing that had escaped from the tear in his teddy's backside — Ortega wearily knuckle-walked over to the pile of dirty clothes behind the beanbag chair, made himself a little nest and bedded down with the beloved Mr. Doodles tucked safe in his powerful arms.

———

Monday morning, Dr. Susan made breakfast and drove Ortega to school as usual. Although she seemed genuinely concerned for him and how his weekend had been, whenever she thought he wasn't looking, she kept smiling to herself. The strange, secretive feel of these stupid little smiles had really gotten on Ortega's nerves by the time they arrived at school.

"You could at least pretend that you missed me," he griped as he climbed out of the car.

"I've already told you I missed you," said Dr. Susan in an exasperated voice. "I've said it at least a dozen times."

Ortega started to roll his eyes, then stopped when he noticed something hanging around her neck. "What is *that*?" he asked, pointing through the open driver's side window at what looked like a giant tooth.

"This?" Dr. Susan twirled the thing around her neck and smiled. "It's a present, from Glen. A model of the tooth of a carnivorous dinosaur he found on his dig last summer. He turned it into a charm and put it on a gold chain. Isn't that just the neatest, most original thing you've ever heard of? Anyway, we … I mean, well, I saw him over the weekend and he gave it to me then. For some strange reason, he thought it was my birthday."

"Oh yeah?" said Ortega. "What a weirdo."

Dr. Susan smiled again. "Actually, he's pretty —"

"I've got to get going," interrupted Ortega, who'd just caught sight of Peter, Eugene and Janice heading into school. Absently, he reached up and gave his forehead a fretful rub.

Dr. Susan's smile was instantly transformed into a frown. "Are you okay?" she asked, searching his eyes with her own. "You're not still feeling the effects of the stress you experienced on Friday night, are you? You need to tell me if you are, Ortega, because these things can be very serious. I've told you before — in the wild, gorillas have been known to leave trails of bloody diarrhea a mile long when fleeing from pursuit."

"That is completely disgusting," he complained. "Are you trying to make me barf up my breakfast or something?"

"I'm trying to make sure you're okay."

"Well, I'm sure Miss Rutherford will let you know the minute I start leaving trails of bloody diarrhea all over the classroom," he grumped.

"There's no reason to be sarcastic," said Dr. Susan, reaching up to touch her tooth necklace. "I just want to make sure you're fine."

Ortega snorted and was beginning to walk away when he stopped suddenly and turned back to face Dr. Susan.

"Did you know that I weighed less than four pounds when you and Dr. Whitmore stole me away from my mother?" he asked.

Dr. Susan blinked at him for a moment before replying. "That's not true. You weighed four pounds and two ounces, and I should know because I was there when they put you on the scales. You didn't like it one bit," she said, smiling at the memory. "You squirmed and fussed and then peed all over the zookeeper. Who, I might add, looked a lot like Dr. Whitmore."

Ortega didn't smile. "Was *that* when you stole me away from my mother?" he persisted.

Dr. Susan flinched as though he'd just bitten her. "It wasn't like that," she said. "Your mother — she loved you, I'm sure she did — but she was very young, and she'd been born in a zoo herself. She'd never been part of a wild gorilla family, never watched other gorilla mothers taking care of their babies, never had a chance to practice being a mother to the offspring of her female relatives. She didn't know what to do with you, Ortega, and there was no way to teach her in time to save you."

"Where is she now? You said you were going to find her for me."

"I've been trying," said Dr. Susan. "Unfortunately, the zookeeper at the zoo where you were born has been on an extended vacation, and no one else has been willing to talk to me. As soon as the zookeeper returns, I hope to be able to give you the information you're looking for."

"Good," muttered Ortega. "Because my real mother is more like me than you'll ever be."

At the look of hurt in Dr. Susan's eyes, Ortega immediately regretted the comment — which he wasn't even sure he believed — but before either of them could say anything, he turned and loped silently off toward the school.

After the way he'd left things on Friday night — ditching Peter, Eugene and Janice for the safety of Dr. Susan's car — Ortega was a little worried about how his friends would act toward him when they saw him again.

As it turned out, they were worried about the same thing.

"We felt bad about ditching you when you ... you know ... stood up and, uh, roared," mumbled Peter at lunchtime, as his ears slowly turned pink. "We didn't mean to leave you all by yourself to face that crazy mob. It's just that ... well, you kind of ..."

"Scared the living crap out of us," said Eugene with a shiver that made him jiggle so hard he could barely peel the foil top off the tapioca pudding he'd traded Ortega for two jelly doughnuts.

"*Totally*," agreed Janice, looking up from her book. "I mean, one minute you're regular Ortega and the next minute — pow! — you're I'm-going-to-rip-out-your-liver-and-eat-it-raw Ortega."

"I wasn't going to hurt anybody," said Ortega defensively, taking a nibble of his doughnut. "I was ... I felt threatened. They were all yelling at me." He paused before adding, "I thought they were going to kill me."

"I know," said Peter. "That's why we were so sorry that we didn't stick by you."

The knowledge that his friends wished they'd had the courage to face *death* with him made Ortega feel so giddy that he wanted to overturn something big and breakable for the sheer pleasure of hearing it smash. Instead, he said, "Would it make you feel any better if I promised to use you all as a human shield next time I'm under attack?"

"Yes!" said Peter fervently.

"I guess," shrugged Janice.

"Absolutely not!" squeaked Eugene, pulling his face out of his pudding cup so fast that he got tapioca all over his nose.

Peter, Janice and Ortega laughed as Eugene wiped pudding off his nose. Then Janice returned to her book and Ortega asked Peter if he'd finished putting together the movie.

"Almost," he said eagerly. "I spent most of the weekend editing. It took me a lot longer than I originally thought it would because so much of the final scene was unscripted, but in the end, it came together nicely. Now all I have to do is make a few minor adjustments to the soundtrack and put in the credits, and then I can post it online for my dad to see."

"And for Derek Blackheart to see," reminded Eugene.

Smiling, Peter nodded and took a big bite of his sandwich.

———

That afternoon when Dr. Susan picked Ortega up from school, instead of taking him straight back to the lab, she drove him across town to Dr. Mike's office. Dr. Mike had been Ortega's veterinarian for as long as he could remember. Not only had he taken countless X-rays, scans and blood samples, but he'd also assisted in all four of the surgeries required to maintain and upgrade the artificial voice box that had been implanted in Ortega's throat when he was a baby. Recovering from those surgeries had been difficult and painful, but Dr. Mike had always been the best — caring for Ortega, joking with him, writing out prescriptions for chocolate ice cream. The first time he'd done that, Dr. Whitmore had told him not to be ridiculous. Dr. Mike had responded by wordlessly taking back the prescription, adding "fudge sauce, nuts and plenty of whipped cream" to it, and solemnly handing it back to a flabbergasted Dr. Whitmore.

Ortega had been slavishly devoted to Dr. Mike ever since.

"I still don't see why we're here," complained Ortega as he paced around the examination room. "Like I told you this morning, I feel perfectly fine. I only had a bit of stress-related bloody diarrhea at school today when I realized that you hadn't put any cherry suckers in my lunch. *Again.* Oh, and P.S. — I've been meaning to tell you that I'm not a four-pound-two-ounce baby anymore and that I'm no longer comfortable with you sitting around gawking at me in my underwear while Dr. Mike examines me and finds out that the only thing wrong with me is that you overreact to every little thing."

"There's a difference between overreacting and taking responsible precautions," observed Dr. Susan, glancing up from her *Reader's Digest* magazine. "And P.S. to you — I don't gawk."

"So you say," sniffed Ortega. "But even if it is true — don't I deserve a little privacy after all I've been through in my short life?"

Dr. Susan rolled her eyes, but since she'd already proven that she was willing to take risks to give him the small freedoms that were suddenly so important to him, he wasn't a bit surprised when she grumbled, "If I leave the room, do you promise to wait nicely and to cooperate with Dr. Mike when he gets here?"

Ortega clasped his hands beneath his chin. "I will be like a big, hairy angel who floated down to earth to bless Dr. Mike for not being a complete jerk like Dr. Smarty Pants," he promised.

"Wow," said Dr. Susan as she headed for the examination room door. "I can't tell you how your words have reassured me."

The minute Dr. Susan was gone, Ortega opened all the drawers in the desk, riffled through every bit of paper in sight, chewed a handful of wooden tongue depressors to shreds and sniffed every cat-food sample he could get his hands on. Then he scampered over and opened the examination room door, wondering if there was any way he could sneak into the back room and let all the barking dogs out of their kennels without getting caught.

Suddenly, the door of the exam room down the hall burst open. Hastily, Ortega slammed his own door shut. As he did, he heard the sound of a little girl running down the hall, sobbing. It was such a pitiful sound that he thought his heart might break. Seconds later he heard the sharp clip-clop of high-heeled shoes following after the little girl, and then the soft, heavy sound of men's shoes heading toward his own door. Hastily, he skittered backward.

Seconds later, Dr. Mike opened the door.

"Ortega!" he cried, smiling as though finding Ortega in his examination room was a lovely but unexpected surprise. "How's my favorite patient?"

"Fine," replied Ortega. "Why was that little girl crying?"

Dr. Mike sighed. "Her cat is sick, and unfortunately her mother has decided to have it euthanized."

"What does that mean?" asked Ortega.

"She wants to have the cat put down," explained Dr. Mike. When Ortega looked at him blankly, he elaborated. "You know — put to sleep."

Ortega was horrified. "She wants to have the cat *killed*?" he cried. "But why?"

"Like I said, the cat is sick," said Dr. Mike as he crossed the room to his desk. "The medicine that could cure it is relatively inexpensive, but the cat is old and there's no guarantee he won't get sick again. So the mother says she doesn't want to pay for ... Ortega, where are you going?"

But Ortega didn't bother to respond — he was already out the door and halfway down the hall. By the time Dr. Mike caught up with him, he'd burst into the sick cat's examination room, released the unfortunate creature from its cage and was tenderly cradling it in one arm.

Dr. Susan — who'd heard the commotion and guessed who was at the bottom of it — showed up half a second later.

"Ortega!" she cried. "What are you doing? Put that cat down this —"

"It needs medicine and you need to pay for it," he interrupted. Hurriedly, he explained the hideous fate that awaited the poor cat. Somewhere in the distance, the little girl cried on and on.

Dr. Susan sighed. "Ortega, it's not that simple," she said gently.

"It's exactly that simple!" he screeched, stomping his foot. "Either you pay for the medicine so that the cat can get better or the cat dies. What could be simpler than that?"

"Ortega," Dr. Susan tried again. "This has nothing to do with us ..."

"SO WHAT!" he hollered. "WOULDN'T YOU WANT SOMEONE TO RESCUE ME IF I WERE ABOUT TO BE KILLED FOR NO GOOD REASON AT ALL?"

The silence that followed his shout was deafening. Then Dr. Susan said, "Yes, I would."

Turning to Dr. Mike, she nodded firmly. Dr. Mike hesitated, then reached up and retrieved a small bottle of pills from the top shelf of the cupboard.

Satisfied that he'd accomplished his mission, Ortega tried to hand the tired old cat to Dr. Mike, but Dr. Mike shook his head.

"You saved his life, pal," he said. "You take him out and give him back to the one who loves him."

With shining eyes and a swelling heart, Ortega looked from Dr. Mike to Dr. Susan. Then, holding the cat protectively against his big, hairy belly, he one-arm knuckle-walked past the two adults, who followed him out of the exam room and down the hall toward the waiting room. The little girl's sobs got louder and louder as Ortega approached, and Ortega's smile got broader and broader as he imagined the joy that would light up her face when she got over the shock of seeing a gorilla in dress pants barreling toward her and realized that her cat was saved.

Unable to contain his eagerness, Ortega half galloped the last few steps down the hall and into the waiting room. There, he came upon a sight so shocking that his smile vanished instantly and he nearly dropped the cat onto its poor old head.

Myra Harding.

She was the sobbing little girl. Myra — the one who'd tried to stomp Siggy to death, the one who'd almost certainly helped her mother egg on the bloodthirsty mob at the movie theater.

She was staring at him now, looking almost as startled as he felt. Her red-rimmed eyes darted in confusion from his face down to the cat in his arms and back up again. Then she saw Dr. Mike standing behind Ortega with a smile on his face, and hope lit up her tearstained face like a sudden shaft of sunlight in a world full of shadows.

The cat in Ortega's arms mewled pitifully, reminding Ortega why he was there. Averting his eyes, he took a hesitant step toward Myra, held out the cat and muttered, "I told Dr. Mike I'd buy the medicine your cat needs so that he doesn't have to be killed."

Wordlessly, Myra took her cat and buried her nose deep in its fur. When she was done, she looked up at Ortega and opened her mouth as though she was about to say something. At that moment, however, her mother clip-clopped briskly back into the waiting room. When she saw Ortega and Dr. Susan, her eyes narrowed into mean little slits, but they flew open again when she noticed the cat in her daughter's arms.

"What ... what is the meaning of this!" she cried. "What is *he* doing here?" she demanded, wrinkling her nose at Ortega. "And why isn't that cat in his cage, where he belongs?"

Dr. Mike stepped forward. "You said you were concerned about the cost of Peepers's kidney medication, Mrs. Harding, and that you would have liked to save him if it weren't for the expense," he said. "Well, as luck would have it, Ortega and Susan have decided to donate the money required to buy the medication. So Peepers can be saved after all!"

Instead of looking grateful, or even pleased, Mrs. Harding looked livid. "Who do you think you are, allowing that … that *monster* to interfere in my family's personal business?" she hissed. "What kind of a so-called professional are you that you would make a decision like this without consulting me first?"

Dr. Mike recoiled as though he'd just been slapped. "But I thought —"

"You thought, you thought!" she interrupted. "Ha! Well, there's nothing to be done about it now, I suppose," she said sourly, snatching the pills out of Dr. Mike's hand and giving her daughter a little shove toward the exit. "Come along, Myra, and when you wake up one of these mornings and find Peepers dead at the foot of your bed, remember that that is what happens when you stick your nose into other people's business."

And without so much as a glance at the monster that had so heroically saved the family cat from an untimely death, they were gone.

Chapter Nine

That night, Ortega had a terrible dream.

In it, he was trying to rescue Myra's cat, Peepers, from a tree so tall that the top of it disappeared into the clouds. Higher and higher he climbed after Peepers, who was mewling plaintively and leaping ever upward from branch to branch. Suddenly, Ortega's head broke through the clouds that shrouded the top of the tree. He pleaded with Peepers to come to him, but the cat was now leaping nimbly toward the sunny edge of the cloud. Ortega was terrified by the idea of letting go of the tree and stepping out onto nothingness, but he knew that if he didn't go after Peepers, the cat would fall off the edge of the cloud and plunge to his death. So Ortega took a big step and ... BANG! He felt a bullet whiz past his head. Rearing up in alarm he spun around to see a monstrous Mrs. Harding clutching a gun under one arm. She was at least twenty feet tall, with rotting teeth, hair that hung in filthy, matted clumps, and a coat made of murdered lab animals, stitched together whole. Throwing back her head, she let out a hideous cackle, aimed the gun straight at his heart and fired ...

Ortega awoke with a start. For a long moment, he was too scared to do anything but lie rigid in his bed clutching his blankets. After that, he bellowed for Dr. Susan a few times. When she didn't appear, he climbed out of bed and went looking for her.

As soon as he stepped into the hall, he heard the sound of her laughter coming from her office. Sucking his lips in annoyance, Ortega immediately decided to punish her for failing to hear his previous calls for assistance, and also for being happy while he was still quaking inside. Tiptoeing up to her office, he was about to roar at the top of his lungs when he heard the murmur of a man's voice coming from inside. Curious, Ortega peeked around the corner and was startled to see Glen, the paleontologist with the weird taste in birthday gifts.

He was sitting with his back to Ortega. And sitting on his lap — *wrapped in his arms!* — was Dr. Susan.

Ortega was so dumbstruck that for a minute all he could do was stand there with his mouth hanging open. Then, without quite knowing why, he shrank away from the intimate scene, turned and loped to his bedroom as quietly as possible in order to try to fall asleep.

Alone.

———

Early the next morning, Dr. Susan sleepily walked into the kitchenette, flicked on the lights and nearly jumped out of her skin when she saw Ortega sitting at the kitchen table, as still as a hairy statue.

"What are you doing up this early?" she cried.

Without a word — and without taking his eyes off her — Ortega slipped out of his chair and slowly knuckle-walked over to where she was standing. Pushing himself upright, he stared at her for so long that she started to seem uncomfortable.

"Listen, Ortega ..."

Without warning, he flung his long arms around her and squeezed hard enough to take her breath away. "I just want to say that I'm sorry I said those mean things about my real mother being more like me than you are, and also that I don't care if you ever find out about my gorilla family," he lied fervently. "They're just a bunch of animals who don't know the difference between verbs and nouns, anyway. The important thing is that I've got you, and nothing — not even a stupid paleontologist — can come between us, and no matter what happens we'll always be together." To emphasize his warm feelings, he rained juicy kisses all over her face, leaving a trail of saliva that she was unable to wipe off on account of the fact that he still had her arms pinned to her sides. "Okay, that's all I wanted to say," he murmured, releasing her so abruptly that she almost fell over. "You can start making my breakfast now while I go get dressed."

"Ortega ..." began Dr. Susan.

But he was already gone.

Myra didn't say anything nice to Ortega at school that day, but she didn't say anything mean to him, either. Nor did she make faces at him, whisper to her stupid friends about him or arrange to have her mother cut off his head and mount it on the wall in her living room.

It was a start.

Duncan was also ignoring him. After the pounding Duncan had taken from Eugene on Friday night, Ortega had been sure he and his friends would suffer some kind of horrible retribution involving spitballs and public humiliation, but so far Duncan seemed to be keeping his distance. Peter thought it was because he didn't want anybody else in the class to find out that Eugene had put the boots to him, Janice thought it was because he was afraid Eugene would put the boots to him *again* and Eugene thought it was because an alien with a much nicer personality had taken over his brain. Ortega didn't know what to think and didn't spend much time worrying about it. Things were working out, and that was all that mattered.

As he sat in class trying to work a tangle out of the hair on his forearm, Ortega recalled how, when Dr. Susan and Dr. Whitmore had first told him they were going to make him go to school, he'd been so upset that he'd given in to the burning need to snap Dr. Whitmore's new cell phone in half. In all his years, he'd never faced anything nearly as scary as a room full of strange eleven-year-olds, and he'd been sure that it would end in disaster.

But, against all odds, he seemed to be making it. He'd outlasted the protesters, conquered his enemies and made friends who'd more or less agreed to lay down their lives for him. He was still a dunce when it came to schoolwork, but he wasn't the only one in the class who struggled, and anyway, no one expected him to become a brain surgeon someday.

"What do they expect you to become?" asked Eugene on Thursday while they sat in the tree fort waiting for Peter to shout up that the sandwiches had arrived.

"What do you mean?" asked Ortega, squinting at a picture of Peter and his dad.

"Well, what are you going to be when you grow up?"

"I'm going to be a gorilla," he replied absently, as he tried to imagine what a picture of him and *his* dad would look like.

On the other side of the tree fort, Janice looked up from her book.

Eugene let out a great guffaw. "I know *that*," he chortled. "What I mean is, what are you going to do? You know — with your life?"

Ortega looked at him blankly. No one had ever asked him that question before — probably for the same reason he'd never thought about the answer: because talking gorillas didn't have the right to make those kinds of choices. In fact, they didn't have any rights at all. There was no place for Ortega in the world of animals, and no place for him in the world of human beings beyond that which Dr. Whitmore had created. Someday, Janice, Eugene and Peter would get to make all their own decisions about their own lives, but that day would never come for Ortega.

The thought made his belly twist in anger and his heart ache with sadness. "I'm thinking about becoming a brain surgeon, if I can get my marks up," he grunted, turning away.

Eugene guffawed again.

Suddenly, they heard a door slam, followed by a long, thin squeal. Flying to the tree-house balcony, Janice, Eugene and Ortega watched in alarm as Peter bolted across the scraggly yard, plunged into the wooded area and scrambled up the tree-house ladder. The minute he got to the top, Janice grabbed him by the front of the shirt.

"What is it?" she cried, shaking him back and forth. "What's wrong?"

"Wrong?" panted Peter. "*Wrong?*" He gave a laugh that sounded more like a bark. "Nothing is wrong. Everything is right. No — better than right. Everything is perfect!"

Janice looked slightly disappointed.

"Did your mom put honey *and* jam on the sandwiches this time?" asked Eugene hopefully.

"She could have put rubber chickens and dog turds on them for all I care!" whooped Peter. "I just got off the phone with my dad. He said he showed Derek Blackheart my movie and Derek was so impressed by it that he wants to meet us as soon as possible!"

Eugene and Janice both started jabbering at once. Ortega hooted, spun in circles and drummed madly on the floor of the tree house with the palms of both hands until something occurred to him.

"Are ... are you sure he wants to meet *all* of us?" he asked tentatively, wondering if someone as cool as the world's most famous horror film director would even consider hanging out with someone as ... as *hairy* as the world's most famous talking gorilla.

"Yes, I'm sure," nodded Peter.

"Even me?"

"*Especially* you," said Peter. "My dad wants to personally introduce you to Derek. He thinks that with the right representation, you could go far in Hollywood."

Ortega's mouth dropped open. "Really?" he cried, agog at the thought. "He said that? Oh, *wow*! What else did he say about me?"

"Just that he'd never seen anything like you before and that he couldn't wait to meet you," said Peter shortly before turning back to Eugene and Janice. "Anyway, I've already asked my mom and, like usual, she wasn't happy about my dad springing something big like this on her at the last minute. But she said I could go as long as he comes and picks me up. The movie he's working on is being shot two hundred miles from here, so it's going to mean a three-hour drive for him — there *and* back — but when I told him, he just laughed, like it was nothing." Peter grinned up at a big, glossy picture of his dad, looking handsome and dashing in a cherry-red sports car. "He's going to pick us up after school tomorrow, but he needs to know tonight how many of us are going so he can borrow a bigger vehicle if he has to. So give me a call as soon as you get home and let me know if you've got permission go, okay?"

"Okay!" cried Eugene and Ortega in unison.

Janice just smiled.

———— ∘◦∘ ————

That afternoon, when the last bell rang, it took every last drop of Ortega's rather limited supply of self-control for him not to burst out of his seat and gallop through the crowded halls bellowing with excitement and shoving people aside in an effort to get to Dr. Susan's car as quickly as possible. He wanted to meet Derek Blackheart so badly that he could taste it, but he had a feeling that leaving a trail of broken bodies behind him wouldn't do much to convince Dr. Susan that she should fight to get him permission to go.

When he finally did emerge from the school — after having patiently waded through a pack of tiny kindergarten students who wouldn't stop touching him and asking him silly questions — he was dismayed to discover that Dr. Susan wasn't waiting for him. Before he could start scowling in earnest, however, he spotted a sight that made his heart sing.

Grandma!

She was sitting at the curb in her jazzy silver hybrid vehicle, waving at him. With a bark of delight that made several students nearby start in alarm, he bounded down the walk and flung open the car door.

"HI, GRANDMA, IT'S ME. WHAT ARE YOU DOING HERE?" he shouted excitedly.

Instead of telling him to use his indoor voice — which is what Dr. Susan would have done — Grandma explained that Dr. Susan's afternoon meeting had run late, so she'd called Grandma and asked her to pick him up from school. "Hop in," she smiled. "I brought along some banana-chocolate-chip muffins for us to snack on while we drive."

Ortega heaved a deeply contented sigh as he climbed in. The whole car smelled like fresh baking, and it was perfectly spotless except for the large vomit stain Ortega had made three years ago after eating one too many blueberry turn-overs at the county fair.

"You are, like, the best grandma that ever lived," he mumbled through a giant mouthful of muffin. "When I'm a big Hollywood star someday, I'm going to buy you a diamond-encrusted apron and a solid gold spatula."

Grandma seemed very pleased to hear that she was going to be showered with such practical riches and spent the entire drive back to the lab listening to Ortega talk with his mouth full. Once or twice, she tried to get a word in edgewise — for example, when Ortega mentioned that he was probably going to have to drop out of Grade 5 in order to pursue his movie career — but he just kept talking.

"It's not that I don't appreciate everything Dr. Susan has done for me," he explained as they walked off the elevator hand in hand. "But I have to find a place for myself in this world, you know? And the opportunity to meet Derek Blackheart — and maybe even star in one of his movies — well, that doesn't come along every day ..."

Ortega's voice trailed off when he saw Dr. Whitmore standing at the open glass door of the lab, smiling broadly.

"Good news, Ortega!" he cried, clapping his hands together. "The keynote speaker at the Tenth Annual Conference of Language Development Specialists has just been hospitalized with kidney stones!"

"That is good news!" cried Ortega sarcastically. "With any luck, he'll be dead by morning!"

Dr. Whitmore laughed as though this was the funniest joke he'd ever heard. "No, no," he said, wagging his finger in Ortega's face, "the good news is that I've been asked to take his place. So, hurry inside and start packing. We leave first thing in the morning."

For an endless moment, Ortega just stared at Dr. Whitmore, trying to figure out if this was a joke, or a lie, or some sick experiment designed to see how Ortega would react to the emotional strain of not being allowed to meet someone famous. When at last he decided that it was none of those things, but something infinitely worse — the truth — he folded his arms across his hairy chest and said, "Sorry. I've got other plans."

Dr. Whitmore laughed again.

"I'm serious," said Ortega. "I would really love to go to your stupid conference with you, but it's not going to happen."

Dr. Whitmore stopped laughing. "This is not a stupid conference, Ortega," he said sternly. "It's a very important one. Many of the Project Ortega funders are going to be there, not to mention representatives from some of the most prestigious scientific journals in the world. I am honored to be attending in the capacity of keynote speaker, and you should be, too."

In response, Ortega lifted up one leg and farted. "I'm not going," he said.

"Yes, you are," snapped Dr. Whitmore.

"Excuse me but —" began Grandma.

"This is none of your business, Mrs. Gannon," interrupted Dr. Whitmore.

Ortega gasped. "DON'T YOU DARE TALK TO MY GRANDMA LIKE THAT!" he hollered, clobbering Dr. Whitmore with his knapsack.

With a yelp, Dr. Whitmore skittered backward into the lab. Ortega chased after him with Grandma hot on his heels, urging him to stop.

"She's not your grandmother, Ortega," bleated Dr. Whitmore as he tried to fend off Ortega's knapsack attack. "She's the mother of your primary handler. While I've always been pleased by your ability to form emotional attachments — we couldn't have accomplished nearly so much without it — it is very important that you and everyone else involved with the project not lose perspective and start pretending that — OOF!"

Dr. Whitmore exhaled hard as Ortega caught him in the belly with the knapsack.

"That's it, I'm calling security!" he wheezed, fumbling for the intercom as Ortega continued to rain down blows upon him. "And if you don't cooperate with them, I'm going to give them permission to tranquilize and restrain you!"

Hurriedly, Grandma stepped forward to try to do something to get the situation under control before security arrived. Unfortunately, Ortega didn't realize that she was so close behind him, and the next time he swung his knapsack back to clobber Dr. Whitmore again, he accidentally hit her with it.

With a gasp, he spun to face her.

"Don't worry, honey," she said quickly. "It was an accident. I'm fine."

Ortega was too horrified to reply. Dumping the knapsack (on Dr. Whitmore's head), he dropped to both knuckles, galloped to his bedroom and slammed the door.

Ortega huddled on his bed with his head buried under his comforter for what seemed like a very long time, feeling sick about what he'd done to Grandma — feeling sick about *everything*. It was all so unfair that he would have cried if he could have. Instead, he lay curled in the darkness, silent and alone.

He should have felt comforted when the door finally opened and he heard Dr. Susan walk into the room, but he didn't. He felt angry — angry that she hadn't prevented him from hurting Grandma, angry that she hadn't warned him about the conference, angry that she wasn't going to be able to arrange things so he could meet Derek Blackheart with his friends. Angry because he knew why she was there — to soothe him, and to talk him into cooperating with Dr. Smarty Pants. To act as if she wanted him to do it for his own good, when the truth was that she only ever wanted him to do anything for *her* own good — and for the good of Project Ortega.

Sitting up slowly, he eased himself onto his haunches and glowered at her.

"Hi," she murmured, acting as though she didn't notice his threatening manner. "I heard you got some bad news this afternoon."

Ortega grunted but said nothing.

"Grandma called me on my cell phone to let me know what happened," she continued softly. "I got here as soon as I could. She asked me to let you know that she tried to come in to see you after you ran to your room, but Dr. Whitmore wouldn't let her. She said to tell you that she's not a bit hurt and that although she knows that as a responsible adult she's not supposed to say that Dr. Whitmore got what he had coming to him, Dr. Whitmore got what he had coming to him."

Ortega didn't smile.

Dr. Susan took a deep breath. "I'm sorry I wasn't here to break the news about the conference," she said, taking a step toward him. "I didn't even know about it until I talked to Grandma. I know you're disappointed —"

"You don't know ANYTHING!" he bellowed, grabbing poor Mr. Doodles by one leg and flinging him at her so hard that a wad of stuffing popped out of him. "So why don't you just get out of here and go kiss your stupid boyfriend who gives you stupid gifts when it isn't even your birthday!"

"Ortega …" began Dr. Susan, taking another step forward.

"Go away!" he shouted, rearing up and bristling at her. "Get out of here! I don't need you — I hate you! And do you know what else? I'm never going to speak to you again!"

With that, he beat on his chest with all his might, then whirled around on his bed and plopped down hard with his back to her. And there he sat, sucking his lips so hard that they ached, until at last she stepped out of the room and closed the door behind her.

———

The next morning, Dr. Whitmore woke him early.

"I was watching from the other side of the two-way mirror when you confronted Susan last night," he said, looking even more prissy than usual in a cheap button-down shirt and an ugly new bow tie. "And I want you to know that if you decide you'd rather not work with her anymore, I will see to it that she is removed from the project team. All I ask in return is that you cooperate at the conference this weekend."

"And if I don't?" grunted Ortega, nestling deeper into the nest of dirty clothes he'd constructed for himself the night before.

Dr. Whitmore stared down at him. "Get up and get dressed," he said flatly. "We leave in twenty minutes."

Ortega dawdled getting dressed in order to give Dr. Susan time to come and try to set things right with him. When she came, he was going to pretend that she didn't exist, of course, but that was beside the point. The point was that he was still very upset about not getting to meet Derek Blackheart, and very anxious about having to attend a noisy, busy conference with no one to protect him but stupid old Dr. Whitmore, who was about as useful in that department as a Kick Me sign. The point was that Ortega needed to see Dr. Susan and hear her and smell her and possibly even taste her (if he could get away with it) in order to calm his nerves.

But she didn't show up — not when he was getting dressed, not when he was eating breakfast, not when he was dumping out the fifth-floor window a stack of carefully prepared conference handouts that repeatedly referred to him as "the sub-human specimen."

In fact, by the time Dr. Smarty Pants had laid the plastic sheet down over the expensive leather seats in the back of his fancy new car and buckled Ortega in, he had come to the conclusion that because of the way he had treated her the previous evening, Dr. Susan wasn't going to show up — not now, and maybe not ever again.

Closing his eyes against the unthinkable possibility, he leaned his forehead against the window and made a sad noise low in his throat.

"Please don't vocalize like that at the conference, Ortega," said Dr. Whitmore as he slid into the driver's seat. "It will almost certainly be used by my detractors as proof that you haven't truly adopted spoken language as a primary method of communication."

Ortega was about to give Dr. Whitmore the middle finger (as more proof that he hadn't truly adopted spoken language as a primary method of communication) when he saw Dr. Susan come charging out of the lab building with Mr. Doodles tucked under one arm. Her face was red with exertion, her scrawny legs were flying beneath her long, flouncy skirt and her hair was a frizzy mess.

Ortega thought he'd never seen her look so beautiful.

"You're not forgiven," he announced the minute she flung open his door.

"I know," she said as she tucked Mr. Doodles into his arms and then leaned down to give him a long hug and a big kiss. "Have a safe trip."

Seeing Dr. Susan so buoyed Ortega's spirits that it wasn't until he and Dr. Whitmore stood on the windy tarmac waiting to board the small, chartered plane that would take them to the conference that he suddenly remembered he was supposed to have called Peter the night before to let him know that he hadn't been able to get permission to meet Derek Blackheart.

"I need to borrow your cell phone," he said, tugging so hard on the hem of Dr. Whitmore's sports coat that he nearly pulled him over.

Dr. Whitmore yanked his coat out of Ortega's hand. "Absolutely not," he huffed.

"Come on!" complained Ortega. "I need to let my friends know that I can't have fun with them this weekend because I'm going to be stuck with you at the geek convention instead."

Dr. Whitmore pursed his lips in annoyance. "Perhaps if you hadn't run off while I was going through the security check we might have had time for phone calls," he said, glancing down at the giant armpit stains he'd developed while chasing Ortega through the airport terminal. "As it is, we do not. Remember this moment the next time you decide to cause trouble for me."

"Believe me," muttered Ortega, as the door of the small plane slowly swung open, "I will."

The plane ride to the convention was long and boring, except for the twenty minutes they spent bouncing through turbulence, which so terrified Ortega that his fear odor filled the entire cabin and he couldn't stop whimpering, which resulted in another fussy speech from Dr. Whitmore about using spoken language.

When they finally landed, airport officials refused to let Ortega off the plane without being collared, leashed and escorted by armed guards. If Dr. Susan had been there, she would have argued and pleaded with them until they backed off, but Dr. Whitmore was in such a rush to get to his precious conference that he acquiesced immediately. Ortega proceeded to spend almost ten minutes barreling around the cabin hooting about all the things that would fly out of Dr. Whitmore's rear end before he'd set one foot outside with a collar on.

Then Dr. Whitmore ordered the armed guards to board the plane.

At the sight of their guns, and their unsmiling faces, Ortega froze. "Please, Dr. Whitmore," he begged. "*Please.* I'm sorry for saying that your own mother would fly out of your rear end. All I want you to do is to *talk* to the airport officials. Explain to them that I'll be good — tell them that I'm not an animal, not the way they think. Tell them ... tell them that I'm just a guy who likes cherry suckers."

Dr. Whitmore pursed his lips. "I don't even know what that's supposed to mean, Ortega," he said primly. "What's more, I cannot tell the airport officials you'll be good because I don't know that for a fact. Now, stop making a big deal out of nothing. Put this collar on and —"

"*Stop making a big deal out of nothing?*" he screeched, unable to stop himself.

The armed guards jumped.

"Put the collar on, Ortega!" barked Dr. Whitmore.

Ortega's knees gave way beneath him, but even as he slid to the floor of the plane, he shook his head in defiance. *No.*

Dr. Whitmore leaned forward. "I'd advise you not to do anything to provoke those men, Ortega," he hissed. "They look nervous enough as it is."

Ortega started to disagree, but his voice deserted him when he saw the agitated expressions on the guards' faces, and the guns in their clutching hands. Dr. Whitmore used that moment of distraction to deftly slip the heavy leather dog collar around Ortega's neck and snap on the hated leash. Giving one sharp tug to bring Ortega stumbling to his feet, he then turned and started briskly off the plane. Every time Ortega tried to hang back or duck behind him, Dr. Whitmore gave the leash another tug, and at the bottom of the stairs he allowed one of the airport officials to take a short video of Ortega self-consciously complaining of a stomachache. Then Dr. Whitmore led Ortega across the tarmac and through the airport to the conference van that was waiting to take them to the hotel. People gawked and chattered and crowded and pointed and took picture after picture after picture, things that would have upset Ortega at the best of times but which utterly humiliated him now. All he could think about was one of his classmates — or worse, a friend who saw him as an equal! — logging on to Video-Junkie and seeing a clip of Ortega being paraded around on a *leash.*

It was such a mortifying prospect that he would have screamed if he hadn't been so afraid of getting shot.

"I hope you're happy," he muttered at Dr. Whitmore as he clambered awkwardly into the waiting van and scooted down out of the sight of the guards. "Because of you, I may never be able to go to school again."

"You'll go if I say you will," said Dr. Whitmore, absently adjusting his bow tie.

That's what you think, screeched Ortega, in his mind.

Out loud, he said nothing.

For the rest of the weekend, Ortega was on his worst possible behavior. While Dr. Whitmore was checking them in, Ortega snuck a pair of Dr. Whitmore's threadbare gray underwear out of the suitcase and galloped around the lobby wearing them on his head and merrily waving to the other conference delegates who were also checking in.

He attended the packed opening session of the conference, but only so that he could fart and point at Dr. Whitmore every time there was a pause in the discussion. In some later sessions he sat like a lump, examining his belly button and refusing to answer even a single question. In others, he agreed to answer questions, but only if people answered his questions first — questions such as, "How much do you weigh?" and "When was the last time you had bloody diarrhea?" and "Why do *you* think Dr. Whitmore has never had a girlfriend?" Once, he had a screeching temper tantrum when Dr. Whitmore refused to interrupt his speech in order to run to the vending machine and get him a chocolate bar; another time, he pretended to slip into a coma, collapsing to the floor and moaning so persistently that Dr. Whitmore was forced to cancel the session early. When Dr. Whitmore tried to introduce him to important scientists and funders, Ortega galloped away, or licked them, or lay down on the floor and counted his toes. At meals, he ate with his feet and chewed with his mouth open and threw hissy fits when Dr. Whitmore refused to let him drink syrup right out of the bottle. Short of marching him around at gunpoint again, Dr. Whitmore did everything to try to get Ortega to behave — he threatened, he begged, he bribed, he cajoled. Nothing worked.

By the time the conference ended, Dr. Whitmore had dark circles under both bloodshot eyes, a giant cold sore on his upper lip and a pinched expression that bespoke a thoroughly nasty temper. So nasty, in fact, that Ortega emerged from the fog of recklessness that had enveloped him since being dragged around in public by a leash and decided it might be a good idea to back off a little during the flight home. Dr. Whitmore had acted like a stupid jerk, but there were worse things he could do.

Much worse.

Unfortunately, Dr. Whitmore completely ignored Ortega's attempts to be less hostile and even accused Ortega of licking his in-flight meal while he was using the bathroom. This accusation made Ortega so indignant that he slapped his seat and hooted loudly before turning his back on Dr. Whitmore and refusing to speak to him again for the duration of the trip. He *had* licked Dr. Whitmore's in-flight meal — even the mashed turnips, which looked like a pile of watery yellow puke — but Dr. Whitmore had no proof he'd done it, and that was the thing that really irked Ortega. It so irked him, in fact, that he wasn't sure he was going to be able to resist slobbering on his finger and poking it into Dr. Whitmore's ear at some point during the drive home.

Luckily, Dr. Susan was waiting for him at the airport, so he was spared that test of his resolve. Instead, he got to go to Pizza Pizzazz for dinner and watch the boats cruise up and down the murky river while he told Dr. Susan about his weekend. It wasn't until he'd eaten his fill of pizza and they'd wandered down for a walk by the river that he quietly told the worst of it — how Dr. Whitmore had dragged him from the plane by a leash, and how he'd let men point guns at

Ortega's head. After he said this, it took Ortega a minute to realize that Dr. Susan was no longer walking beside him. When he looked back, he was shocked to see that she had her hands over her mouth, as though she'd just witnessed a gruesome accident. Then all at once she crumpled to her knees and began sobbing hard. Thoroughly alarmed, he galloped back to her side.

"What is it?" he cried frantically, giving her shoulder a shake. "What's wrong?"

Instead of answering, Dr. Susan just cried and cried until Ortega didn't know what else to do but to sit close by her side and make low, comforting noises until the worst of it had passed.

After she stopped crying, Dr. Susan apologized for everything. When Ortega asked if she could be a little more specific, she laughed softly and talked about what a mess she'd made of things, and how Dr. Whitmore was right when he said she was the worst kind of scientist — brilliant and full of potential but unable to keep her emotions out of her work. She talked about how long she'd felt trapped into doing things she knew were wrong and even unethical because she was worried that if she ever got fired there would be no one around to protect Ortega.

"The thing is, for all of that I just can't bring myself to regret what we did to you, Ortega," she said softly, touching the back of her hand to his cheek. "Because if we hadn't done it, you wouldn't be you, and I just can't imagine a world without you."

Ortega didn't even bother trying to make sense of the jumble of emotions her startling words had stirred up inside him. Instead, he sighed deeply, lay back on the grassy bank beside Dr. Susan and quietly listened to the sound of the frogs and the crickets until the chill of the evening crept over him and it was time to go home.

———

That night, as he was climbing into bed, Ortega found on his pillow a snooty handwritten note from Dr. Whitmore promising him that the next day they'd have a long discussion concerning his behavior at the conference.

That's your opinion, he thought.

And with a harsh bark of laughter, he stuffed the note into his mouth, swallowed it in one gulp and bellowed for Dr. Susan to come sing him a lullaby.

Chapter Ten

The next morning at breakfast, Dr. Susan told Ortega she had to go away for a few days.

"What!" he exclaimed, letting his messy yogurt spoon drop to the floor with a clatter. "Why?"

Dr. Susan fetched a clean spoon and wiped up the mess on the floor before sliding into the seat beside him. "I've got some vacation time coming to me, so I thought I'd use it to —"

"But you can't go! I need you here," he complained, flinging his long arms into the air. "For one thing, I'm still feeling totally traumatized by my experience at the conference!"

"So is Dr. Whitmore," said Dr. Susan, sounding grimly pleased at the thought.

"Well, that's the other thing, isn't it?" continued Ortega. "Dr. Whitmore is losing it. Farting in public, accusing people of things he has no proof they did. One day you say you're worried about protecting me, the next you're leaving me in the clutches of a madman. Frankly, I wouldn't be a bit surprised if you came home and found me *euthanized*," he said dramatically before shoving a big bunch of grapes into his mouth, stems and all. "Besides, who's going to drive me to school if you're not here?"

"Glen said he'd help out."

"I don't want him to help out," said Ortega in a crabby voice. "He's a weirdo."

"He is not."

"He is, too," insisted Ortega, reaching for a slice of honey-dew melon. "Do you know that he goes around licking other people's meals for no reason at all?"

"Really?" said Dr. Susan, popping a freshly washed rasp-berry into her mouth. "Well, that certainly sounds like the kind of thing a weirdo would do."

Ortega scowled.

Dr. Susan smiled and patted his hand. "It's only for a few days, and when I get back I'll have a surprise for you. Besides, this will give you a chance to get to know Glen better." She paused before continuing. "I like him, Ortega, and I'd like you to give him a chance. Will you do that? For me?"

Ortega glowered at his breakfast for a moment before suddenly snapping his piece of melon in half with a deadly flick of his wrists.

"I'll try," he said in a garbled voice as he crammed both halves of the melon wedge into his mouth. "But I'm not making any promises."

"The promise to try is good enough for me."

———

Glen drove Ortega to school that very day. When he showed up at the lab, Ortega puffed out his chest and swaggered back and forth snapping pencils and flinging the pieces in Glen's general direction. He kept waiting for Dr. Susan to rush in and scold him, or for Glen to try to stop him, but neither of those things happened. Glen just stood there yawning, rubbing his eyes and ducking flying pencil pieces until eventually, Ortega ran out of pencils and, feeling foolish, knuckle-walked moodily to the bathroom to take a pee.

When he was done, Dr. Susan made him pick up the pencil pieces, then handed him his lunch.

"See you in a few days," she said when she leaned over to give him a kiss on the cheek. "Remember your promise."

Ortega was about to remind her that technically he hadn't promised her anything, when she straightened up and gave Glen a kiss on the *lips*!

Grunting in annoyance, Ortega rattled his lunch bag at Glen and used his free hand to shoo him away from Dr. Susan. Glen didn't resist. Instead, he gave Dr. Susan a sleepy smile, picked up Ortega's knapsack and headed for the door, whistling in a way that, inexplicably, made Ortega want to follow.

"Go easy on him, Ortega," murmured Dr. Susan as she reached out to untwist the collar of his shirt. "He's one of the good guys."

Glen's car wasn't a car at all. It was an ancient van with tinted teardrop windows and shag carpet up the walls in the back. The paint was rusted in half a dozen places, and the back fender was crumpled beyond repair.

"Ortegasaurus got to it," he said matter-of-factly when he saw Ortega looking at the fender.

Ortega sniffed and looked away.

"Mangled it with his bare hands," continued Glen as they climbed into the van. "Remember I told you about the one that lives behind my favorite doughnut shop? Well, last Tuesday I was in a real rush to get my morning coffee, and I guess I parked too close to his nest."

"He sleeps in a nest?" Ortega couldn't help asking.

"Well, sure, what did you think?" shrugged Glen. "I told you he was smart and talented, remember?"

Ortega nodded. Glen leaned over to put the keys in the ignition.

"Wait," blurted Ortega. "You haven't finished the story."

"I haven't?" said Glen, sitting back in surprise. "Oh, I guess you're right. Well, anyway, I was on my way out of the shop with an extra large coffee in one hand and a bag of fresh doughnuts in the other when all of a sudden I heard a bloodcurdling scream. Turning around, I saw the Ortega-saurus coming straight for me. His handsome face was contorted in rage, his elegant hands were balled up into fists and he was charging with a speed and grace remarkable for a creature of such raw power."

Ortega's mouth dropped open slightly. "What did you do?" he breathed.

Glen frowned. "Well, my first instinct was to run, obviously," he explained. "But I really didn't want to spill my coffee, and plus I thought — maybe this guy'll back off if I explain that I wasn't trying to threaten him or take over his territory."

"You just parked near the nest because it was a good parking space," observed Ortega.

"It was a *great* parking space — the best parking space ever," agreed Glen.

Ortega nodded. "So what happened?"

"Well, I stood my ground and when the Ortegasaurus was so close that I could smell his lovely peppermint breath, I explained everything."

"And what did he do?" asked Ortega in a hushed voice.

"He roared in my face so loud I dropped the coffee on my sneakers," sighed Glen unhappily. "Then he chased me to my van and was so furious when I managed to slip inside before he got a chance to disembowel me that he took it out on my poor fender." For a moment, he looked glum. Then his face brightened, and twisting in his seat, he pulled a bulging bag of doughnuts from behind him. "Look, Ortega!" he cried. "I still have the doughnuts from that fateful day. Would you like one?"

Eyeing Glen suspiciously, Ortega reached into the bag.

"Are you trying to butter me up or something?" he asked through a mouthful of apple fritter still warm from the oven.

"Absolutely," said Glen. "Is it working?"

Ortega swallowed, grunted and reached for another doughnut. "I'll let you know when the bag is empty."

The bag was empty by the time Ortega got to school twenty-five minutes later, but he grabbed his knapsack and jumped out of the van without telling Glen if his bribe had worked or even bothering to say good-bye to him. He'd spent the weekend trying not to think about the fun his friends were having with Derek Blackheart, but there was no way he was going to be able to avoid hearing about it now. In truth, he was so jealous that he wanted to rip off his locker door and hurl it down the hallway. It wasn't just that they'd gotten to hang out with a famous person all weekend — it was that they'd gotten to do it *together*. Before becoming friends with Peter, Eugene and Janice, Ortega had been so far removed from the rest of the world that he hadn't even realized he was being left out of things.

Now he did.

Still, he thought as he lumbered into the classroom before class began, *these are the only people in the world who have ever told me they'd die for me. The least I can do is pretend to be happy for them.*

"So, how was it?" he asked, plopping down into his seat.

"How was what?" asked Peter, without looking up from the doodle he was making at the top of his science homework.

"The weekend," said Ortega, trying to smile. "Hanging out with Derek Blackheart and your dad."

Peter looked up with an inscrutable expression. "It didn't happen," he said.

"What do you mean?" asked Ortega in surprise.

"I mean it didn't happen," said Peter. "The scene they were shooting on Friday ran late and my dad couldn't get away."

Eugene and Janice exchanged a look that Ortega didn't understand. He started to ask what was going on, but Peter cut him off.

"My dad was busy, *okay?*" he said loudly. "Someone in his position can't just come and go as he pleases. If Derek tells him he's got to stay and keep working, he's got to stay and keep working. At least *he* called to let me know plans had changed," he muttered, returning to his doodle with a scowl.

Ortega stared down at the top of his friend's head. "I couldn't call," he said after a long moment. "Dr. Whitmore wouldn't let me. I told him I wanted to go with you, but he made me go to his stupid scientific conference instead."

"Whatever," muttered Peter. "It doesn't matter."

Ortega could tell that it did matter — a *lot* — but he had no idea why Peter seemed angry with *him*. "Okay, well, anyway, I'm sorry if I did anything to mess things up," he mumbled awkwardly.

Peter gave Ortega an incredulous look. "How could *you* have done anything to mess things up?" he asked. "Our plans falling through had nothing to do with *you*. I mean, what do you think — my dad would cancel a weekend with *me* just because *you* couldn't be there?" He shook his head in disgust. "God, you are so full of yourself sometimes."

Ortega was so shocked that he didn't know what to say. It didn't really matter, though, because at that moment, Miss Rutherford strode briskly into the classroom, clapped her hands together sharply and announced that it was time for the lesson to begin.

Later that morning, when Peter left to go to the bathroom, Janice and Eugene hastily explained that Peter's dad hadn't canceled until he'd found out that Ortega wasn't going to be able to make it. Janice said she figured the whole weekend had only ever been about showing Ortega off to Derek

Blackheart; Eugene nodded solemnly and added that this wasn't the first time Peter's dad had done something like this. Ortega was outraged. It had never occurred to him that somebody's own dad could be such a complete *jerk*. Why, the guy was almost as bad as Dr. Whitmore — worse, maybe, because Dr. Whitmore never pretended to like Ortega. Peter's father pretended to *love* him! Clenching and unclenching his fists, Ortega angrily asked Janice and Eugene why they'd let Peter get so excited about the weekend if they'd known all along his dad might back out.

"Because we thought he might not," said Eugene lamely.

Janice shrugged and looked away.

The rest of the day, Peter didn't say much to Ortega. Ortega tried not to take it personally, but it was hard. After all, it wasn't his fault that Peter's dad was a jerk. At least Peter *had* a dad. Oh, and P.S. — Ortega's own weekend hadn't exactly been a barrel of laughs, either, not that anyone had bothered to ask him about it. If anyone was full of himself it was Peter, acting as if the whole world revolved around him.

As if he was the only one who had problems or something!

Grumbling to himself about the fact that Peter really wasn't the friend he'd pretended to be, Ortega climbed into Glen's van at the end of the day and flung his knapsack into the back.

"Do you have any more doughnuts?" he asked without preamble.

"No," said Glen.

Ortega sucked his lips in annoyance, as though Glen had purposely run out of doughnuts in order to make Ortega even more miserable than he already was.

"Would it help if I offered to drop you back at the lab and then run out and get us a couple of submarine sandwiches for dinner?" asked Glen, putting the van into gear.

Ortega, who loved sub sandwiches so much that he started to salivate at the mere mention of them, shrugged moodily and asked, "Can I get extra lettuce on mine?"

"You can get whatever you like," said Glen, raking his fingers through his messy hair. "Now, do you think we could just drive quietly for a while? I've had a rough day, and to be honest with you, I really don't feel like talking about it."

"I know exactly how you feel," sighed Ortega, settling back in his seat.

"I thought you might," said Glen.

Ortega felt a lot better by the time he got back to the lab. Dr. Susan was right — Glen *was* one of the good guys.

"It doesn't mean I think it's okay that he's dating Dr. Susan," he advised the Lancaster-Stone family as he watched them buzz excitedly around the piece of overripe banana he'd just dropped into their jar. "I mean, that's just gross, plus —"

"What's gross?" asked a voice behind him.

Ortega whirled around, instinctively rearing up and throwing his long arms in front of his pets in a protective gesture that would have seemed poignant to anyone but the person who stood before him.

Dr. Whitmore.

"What do you think you're doing sneaking up on me like that?" complained Ortega, dropping back onto his knuckles in order to resume feeding his pets.

"My job," said Dr. Whitmore. "Perhaps if I'd done a little more 'sneaking up,' as you call it, things might have turned out differently."

Ortega shrugged and handed Siggy a sunflower seed.

"Because of your antics at the conference last weekend, two of our major funders have backed out of Project Ortega," continued Dr. Whitmore in a strangely calm voice. "They accused me of falsifying data because I was unable to reproduce my published results at the conference. In other words, after observing you in action, they didn't believe you'd achieved as much I'd reported you'd achieved."

Pleased that Dr. Smarty Pants was getting a taste of his own medicine — namely, that he was getting an idea of what it felt like to be made to look like a fool in front of people who mattered to him — Ortega permitted himself a small smile.

Dr. Whitmore took a step closer.

"I don't know what you're smiling about," he said softly. "This means the end of Project Ortega."

Ortega's smile froze on his face as a tiny seed of anxiety took root in the pit of his stomach. "What do you mean?" he asked.

"We no longer have enough money to pay for even the most basic project expenses," explained Dr. Whitmore with a shrug. "It. Is. Over."

The anxiety in Ortega's stomach bloomed so fast that he could feel it pressing against his rib cage, making it hard to breathe. "But what do you *mean*," he persisted, unable to believe what he was hearing.

"The lab is going to be shut down," said Dr. Whitmore, his eyes never leaving Ortega's face. "The staff will be laid off, and the assets will be sold or redistributed to other projects."

"What about me?" blurted Ortega, who was suddenly too upset to be bothered by how pitiful and weak he sounded. "What's going to happen to me?"

"You ... well, I'm sorry to say that the company has decided to sell you," said Dr. Whitmore, not sounding sorry at all.

"SELL ME?" cried Ortega in horror. "Sell me to *who*?"

"I'm not sure," said Dr. Whitmore vaguely. "Another lab, perhaps, or a zoo, or ..."

As Dr. Whitmore's voice trailed off, Ortega started shaking his head back and forth, faster and faster, as though this might somehow change the terrible things that Dr. Whitmore was saying. "No," he said. "No, no, no. You're wrong. I know you're wrong. Dr. Susan won't let this happen — she'll protect me!"

"Susan is an employee, Ortega," said Dr. Whitmore. "There is nothing she can do."

"Yes. Yes, there is. She can take me. She can buy me!" he said. He took a stumbling step toward Dr. Whitmore. "Please, Dr. Whitmore. Please!" he begged, clasping his hands beneath his chin. "Please let her buy me!"

Dr. Whitmore took a hasty step back and reached for the doorknob without taking his eyes off Ortega. "She wouldn't be able to afford you, Ortega. As I've told you before, you are a very valuable animal. Besides, Susan has her whole life ahead of her," he pointed out. "A life that will most likely include a husband and children. Do you really think there would be a place for you in that life?"

Ortega was too devastated to reply.

Dr. Whitmore opened the door. Just before he walked through it, he paused and looked back.

"I warned you that this was a possibility, Ortega," he said shortly. "I guess we'll both spend the rest of our lives being sorry that you didn't believe me."

———

The minute Dr. Whitmore left the room Ortega staggered over and collapsed on his bed. He had never felt so ... so *destroyed* in his entire life. With all his heart, he wanted to believe that Dr. Whitmore was lying, that he had only said those awful things to get back at Ortega for what had happened at the conference. But he knew it wasn't possible. Nobody — not even Dr. Whitmore — could be that cruel.

Ortega had made a terrible, terrible error in judgment, and he was about to pay for it in the worst way possible.

The thought filled him with such cold dread that he began to shiver. Everything and everyone he loved best in the world were about to be ripped from him. He was going to be thrust into the treacherous unknown, handed over to people who didn't care for him at all, who didn't care if he lived or died except for what it would cost them. What if he was sold to a lab that shaved down his head and inserted needles into his brain to see the effect of different kinds of chemicals? Or one that injected him with drugs to see how long it would take him to die or develop cancer? It didn't seem possible that he could be doomed to a place like that, but Ortega knew better than anybody what could happen in animal laboratories, and that the people who owned him could — and would — do whatever they liked with him.

Unless ...

Ortega sat bolt upright in bed, his heart hammering hard at the idea he'd just gotten. It was a very slim chance, but it was a chance, and that made it better than nothing.

Snatching up Mr. Doodles, he pressed the raggedy teddy to his nose and began to inhale deeply in order to calm himself. Before he'd inhaled more than twice, however, the bedroom door burst open.

Ortega screamed.

"Don't worry — I got extra lettuce!" cried Glen.

Ortega nodded and tried to smile. "Can we go eat outside?" he asked, clutching Mr. Doodles so tightly he wasn't sure he'd ever be able to let him go. "I ... I just had another blow-up with Dr. Smarty Pants, and I really need some fresh air."

Glen smiled. "Sure, little buddy. Let's go."

Ortega meekly followed Glen out of the lab and into the waiting elevator. He was still holding Mr. Doodles, still sniffing him when he thought Glen wasn't looking. He was nervous, but he'd been nervous before. He'd also been alone before, and succeeded in the face of overwhelming odds.

He could do this.

Ortega followed Glen past the security desk and out into the late-afternoon sun. Ortega noticed that Dr. Whitmore's favorite tulips were making a comeback after the stomping they'd received on Ortega's first day of school. He would have liked to take a moment to destroy them beyond recognition, but there was no time.

It was now or never.

Shoving Mr. Doodles down the front of his shirt, Ortega bolted. Soundlessly he loped around the side of the building and shot off across the back lawn. He didn't bother to look over his shoulder to see if Glen was chasing him because he couldn't run any faster anyway. He was running as fast as he could — as though his life depended on it.

When he got to the back parking lot, Ortega vaulted over the low fence and headed straight for the gate. The parking lot attendant ran out of his booth when he saw Ortega but made no move to stop him. Ortega shot past him and headed off down the street, ignoring the shouts of startled pedestrians and the pain in his knuckles as they slammed down on the pavement again and again.

He took a left turn at the first set of lights. In the distance, he could hear the faint sound of a siren. He'd known they'd be coming after him — he just hadn't realized it would happen so fast.

It didn't matter. He didn't have far to go. Another few blocks and he'd be there and it would be all over, one way or another.

Putting his head down, he shot across a street without bothering to check for traffic. He heard the squeal of brakes and the crunch of metal on metal. His breath coming in ragged gasps, Ortega gritted his teeth against the cramps that had begun to shoot through his gut as he barreled up the front steps of Grandma's house.

"GRANDMA!" he bellowed, hammering on the closed door with both fists. "IT'S ME, GRANDMA. OPEN UP — QUICK!"

The only response from inside the house was silence. Outside, the sound of the sirens was growing louder.

"PLEASE, GRANDMA — THEY'RE COMING FOR ME!" Ortega sobbed. "I NEED YOUR HELP! PLEASE!"

Suddenly, he heard a loud thwacking noise right above him, and an updraft made his hair stand on end. Squinting into the sky, he saw a news helicopter hovering so close that it looked as if it was going to land on top of him.

With a shriek, he leaped off Grandma's porch and galloped toward the street. Before he was halfway there, however, two police cars came to a screeching halt at the curb in front of him, blocking his flee path. A big van came roaring up behind them; from the back of the van jumped masked men carrying rifles. A crowd had started to gather on the other side of the street; Grandma's nosy neighbor was staring at him from the other side of the hedge. One of the police officers pulled out a megaphone and starting shouting things at Ortega, but he couldn't hear a thing over the sound of the helicopter overhead.

"LEAVE ME ALONE!" he screamed, clapping his hands over his ears.

But they wouldn't. They were coming nearer; they were trying to surround him.

"GO AWAY!" he roared, charging forward and running back, desperately searching for an escape route. He ripped handfuls of leaves and twigs off Grandma's decorative hedge and hurled them at his attackers; he snapped his teeth and whacked at the ground with his big hands. Finally, he reared up on two legs and beat upon his chest, bellowing with all his might.

It was an extraordinary display of bravery by the young gorilla who was on the verge of losing everything, which is probably why all of nature stood still when the shots rang out.

Ortega staggered backward one step, then two.

Then he fell to his knees.

And everything went dark.

Chapter Eleven

When Ortega came to, he was lying on the wire-mesh floor of a large cage. His head was throbbing, the images in front of his eyes kept swimming in and out of focus and his mouth was so dry that his tongue was swollen.

After a moment of lying still, Ortega gingerly rolled into a sitting position. Stabbing pain shot through his right shoulder when he did so; looking down, he saw a tiny crust of blood around a small puncture in his shirt. He tried to move his right arm. It was stiff and sore.

Blinking hard, he looked around for Mr. Doodles, but he was nowhere to be seen. Ortega's teddy had vanished.

The room in which the cage sat was large and harshly lit. Empty cages of varying sizes were stacked against one wall; a stainless-steel sink and cleaning supplies could be seen along the other. Directly across from Ortega, there was a door.

"Hello," he croaked. "Is anybody there?"

No one answered.

＊

Some time later, a man in a blue jumpsuit walked into the room. The crest above his shirt pocket said Animal Control.

"I'm not an animal," whispered Ortega. "Not the way you mean it."

The man shrugged nervously. Ortega bowed his head.

"I need something to drink," he rasped.

The man walked over to the sink and filled a large plastic container with water. Walking back over to the cage, he slipped it through a little door in the back.

Ortega gulped it down noisily, so fast that water ran out of his mouth and down his chin. When he was done, he saw that the man was watching him intently. Wordlessly, Ortega wiped his mouth with the back of his hairy hand and pushed the container back through the little door.

"I'm hurt," he said in a subdued voice. "And I have to go to the bathroom. And you should call Dr. Whitmore at the company laboratory. He'll be looking for me."

The man hesitated. "You're not really hurt — it was only a tranquilizer dart," he said, his eyes straying to the speck of blood on Ortega's shirt. "And I'm sorry, but I can't let you out to use the bathroom. That Dr. Whitmore fellow saw your capture on the news and called us even before you were brought in. He said he'd sue if anything happened to you while you were in our custody."

"Dr. Whitmore knows I'm here?" said Ortega, his heart giving a wild thump. "But then ... why hasn't he come to pick me up?"

The man shrugged again.

After a long silence, Ortega averted his eyes and quietly repeated his request to use the bathroom.

Red-faced, the man gestured to the newspaper-lined tray beneath the wire mesh on which Ortega was sitting, but didn't say a word.

Ortega's mouth dropped open. "You expect me to go on the floor?" he asked in an anguished voice. "Like a dog in a *kennel?*"

"I'm sorry," the man repeated, looking everywhere but inside the cage. "I really am."

Instead of answering, Ortega stared at the empty cages along the far wall, wondering if the prisoners who had occupied them had felt as trapped and scared and humiliated as he did.

Somehow he doubted it.

"I'll send in your, uh, doctor the moment he arrives," promised the man.

But Ortega didn't answer. He was no longer listening.

Ortega held it for as long as he could, but eventually the cramps that had begun back at Grandma's house got the better of him. Crouching low in the far corner of the cage with his eyes on the door, Ortega relieved himself. He was not surprised to see flecks of blood in the diarrhea. When he was done, he tiredly crawled to the opposite end of the cage and leaned his forehead against the cold bars.

What happened next would have intrigued Dr. Whitmore and his colleagues had they been there to witness it. It was an unprecedented event, an unexplainable event, an event that blurred the line that separated Ortega from the human species almost as dramatically as did his ability to speak.

For as he sat there contemplating the utter hopelessness of his future, one very small, very bright tear trickled slowly down the young gorilla's still face.

Ortega was crying.

Eventually, Dr. Whitmore showed up to get him. He didn't notice the tearstain on Ortega's dusty cheek, but he did notice the stained newspaper in the bottom of the cage. Frowning, he made a note on the little pad of paper he had tucked into the breast pocket of his cheesy-looking sports jacket.

"How are you feeling, Ortega?" he asked gently, his pen still poised above the pad.

Ortega didn't have the energy to do anything more than grunt.

"Use your words," said Dr. Whitmore, less gently. "I know this has been a difficult experience, and I am not without sympathy, but I must point out that no one forced you to run away. That was your decision. Decisions have consequences. There is nothing to be gained by falling apart at this point — in fact, there is much to lose."

Ortega emitted a bark of laughter that sounded more like a sob. How could there be much to lose? He'd already lost everything.

Dr. Whitmore's face clouded over. "Do you think this has been easy for me?" he hissed. "I have spent the last three hours answering to the media, my boss and the corporate board of directors, not to mention trying to avoid Susan's mother and all the other crackpots out there who can't seem to grasp what you are. I am not trying to suggest that your life is expendable, Ortega, or that I am unconcerned with your welfare. Far from it — I have always taken great pains to see that you are well cared for. But the fact is that I am *trying* to undertake groundbreaking scientific research with implications far beyond anything you could possibly imagine, and I am plagued at every turn by roadblocks — lack of cooperation, lack of understanding, lack of vision. I am constantly explaining myself to those who don't appreciate what I am doing, and it is becoming frustrating almost beyond endurance!"

One very tiny piece of this long-winded speech pierced Ortega's consciousness.

"Grandma called?" he asked, turning his face ever so slightly toward Dr. Whitmore.

"I wish that was all she'd done," he said sourly. "Unfortunately, she showed up outside the lab building and made such a scene that I would have called the police if I hadn't been so intent on avoiding additional publicity. She made it sound as though it was my fault she wasn't home when you got there, and she threatened to hit me with her purse when she found out I hadn't yet come down to release you. Worst of all, without having a single fact to back up her accusations, she blamed me entirely for the fact that you'd run away in the first place. As if you'd never done something like that under your own steam!"

For the first time in what seemed like a hundred years, Ortega smiled.

Dr. Whitmore stared at him hard before jerking his head at the man in the blue jumpsuit, who silently walked over and unlocked and opened the cage door. For a moment, Ortega just sat there, looking at the opening. Then, with a great sigh, he hoisted up his bulky body and slowly knuckle-walked across the cage and down the ramp to the concrete floor of the animal-control warehouse.

"Good luck," said the man, lightly brushing his fingers against Ortega's uninjured shoulder as he lumbered by.

"Thank you," said Ortega, pausing to stare down at the man's hand. "And ... thank you for the water. It helped."

The man nodded, then turned away.

The minute Ortega stepped out into the night, he felt better. Not completely better, of course, but better in the way he did when he awoke from a nightmare — still shaky, still frightened, but at least able to breathe again. Closing his eyes, he turned his face into the breeze that felt so cool against his hot skin.

He wasn't in a good place, but he was in a far better place than he'd been moments before.

The drive back to the lab was uneventful. Dr. Whitmore kept trying to get Ortega to say something, but he refused. At first, he did so because he felt too drained to speak, but after a while, it had more to do with the satisfaction he got out of seeing Dr. Whitmore twitch every time he grunted. There was a certain freedom in knowing that there was nothing more he could do to Ortega, no matter how badly Ortega behaved.

He had already done his worst.

With this in mind, Ortega made a point of knuckling through the flower bed at the front of the lab building in order to maim as many tulips as possible, and followed this up by tracking wet mud through the foyer and into the elevator. Dr. Whitmore didn't say anything, but made another long note in his obnoxious little notepad before popping it back into the pocket of his sports jacket.

Ortega smiled as he imagined how Dr. Whitmore would react if he were to grab that stupid pad, rip out every last page and gobble up the ones that looked especially important.

"Feeling a little better, are we?" said Dr. Whitmore with a small smile of his own.

Ortega grunted.

Dr. Whitmore's smile vanished. "Go to your room. I'll bring you something to eat shortly."

"I thought I wasn't supposed to eat in my room," said Ortega.

"In light of what happened today, certain rules have changed," replied Dr. Whitmore primly. "Until further notice you will be confined to your room unless accompanied by an escort of my choosing."

"What? But that's not fair!" cried Ortega, slapping his hands against the floor in protest. "I should at least be free to walk around here without being treated like a criminal!"

"Oh, really?" said Dr. Whitmore, folding his arms across his chest. "You mean so you can remove the letter *E* from every keyboard in the lab? So you can pour chunky noodle soup into my briefcase? So you can change the message on my answering machine to say that I'm in the bathroom having a poop?"

In spite of his distress — which was extreme — Ortega couldn't help snickering at this last one.

Instead of looking upset, Dr. Whitmore looked almost relieved.

"This is the way it's going to be for now, Ortega," he said briskly. "When you have demonstrated that you deserve additional freedoms, I'll consider giving them to you. Now, go to your room and think about what you need to do in order to ensure that you do not completely lose your head the next time you find yourself in a stressful situation."

Instead of doing what he was told, Ortega stared at Dr. Whitmore until the scientist blinked and looked away.

"Why are you doing this to me?" asked Ortega quietly. "I don't understand. What difference does any of this make to you? Project Ortega is over, remember? Pretty soon, I'm not going to be your problem anymore. Can't you just leave me alone until then?"

Dr. Whitmore hesitated.

"For reasons I cannot explain, that is not possible," he said in a way that suggested he was choosing his words carefully. "But I can say this: cooperate with me now, Ortega, and you may be surprised by how things work out in the end."

Because he was exhausted and had nowhere else to go, Ortega went to his room. As soon as the door closed behind him, he heard the *click* of Dr. Whitmore locking the door from the outside.

"Jerk," he muttered, blowing a raspberry at the locked door.

The door said nothing.

Ortega looked around the room. His beanbag chair was missing, as were his books, his framed pictures of Grandma and Dr. Susan and most of his toys. The room looked barren, the way it used to when he was small and thought nothing of unleashing wholesale destruction on everything in sight if he didn't get his own way.

Wandering over to the desk where his pets still sat, Ortega wondered about Dr. Whitmore's last comment. It had almost sounded as if there was hope — like maybe, if he was very, very, *very* good, his whole world wouldn't fall apart after all. Like if he cooperated, in the end he wouldn't have to lose *absolutely* everything. Maybe he'd still get sold, but he'd be able to continue attending school and seeing his friends. Maybe he'd have to go live at another lab, but Dr. Susan and Grandma could still come and visit him whenever they wanted. Some things would change, but the things that really mattered would stay the same. Closing his eyes, Ortega briefly allowed himself to cling to this hope, and to experience the sweet rush that surged through his body at the thought of it.

Then he opened his eyes and let hope slip away, like dust in the wind.

He knew better than to think that Dr. Whitmore was actually trying to comfort him. More likely, he was looking for a way to dominate him until the very end — to force Ortega to cooperate by dangling the one carrot he knew Ortega couldn't possibly resist reaching for.

It was almost certainly a trick.

But what if it wasn't?

Ortega didn't know what to think.

Before he could ponder the question further, he heard a commotion out in the lab. Scampering over to the two-way mirror, he cupped his hands around his eyes and could just barely make out the source of the commotion.

It was Peter! He was standing on the other side of the bulletproof glass at the front of the lab, and he was shouting at Dr. Whitmore!

Ortega jerked his face away from the mirror. His heart was hammering so hard that it actually hurt. Why was Peter here? Why was he yelling at Dr. Whitmore?

Hastily squashing his face back up against the mirror, Ortega was shocked to see Dr. Whitmore angrily letting Peter and his mother into the lab. The three of them spoke rapidly for a moment. When Dr. Whitmore began to shake his head vehemently, Peter slung his knapsack off his shoulder, snatched out a handful of photographs and shoved them at Dr. Whitmore, who flipped through them quickly, his eyes bulging in horror. Slamming his pasty fist on the nearest counter, he glared at Peter, then abruptly stormed toward Ortega's bedroom with his keys in his hand.

Ortega barely had time to turn around before the door opened, Peter slipped inside and Dr. Whitmore slammed the door behind him.

"I knew it!" gasped Peter, pointing to the tiny bloodstain on Ortega's shirt. "You're hurt!"

"It's nothing," lied Ortega, who did not want to talk about it. "What are you doing here?"

"Janice and Eugene and I have been having *fits* ever since we saw you get shot on TV!" explained Peter breathlessly. "We kept calling and calling, but that stupid jerk out there wouldn't tell us anything except that you were fine. Fine! Ha! Eventually, Janice figured you must have been killed and that the company was going for a full cover-up. She said if that was the case, the three of us could all expect to meet with unfortunate accidents at some point in the very near future. You can imagine how much Eugene appreciated the warning."

Ortega chuckled deeply, warmed by the thought of his other two friends. "But I don't understand. Why did Dr. Whitmore let you in to see me?" he asked. "He wouldn't even let my grandma in!"

Now it was Peter's turn to chuckle. "Remember the footage I took of you pretending to attack and eat Janice and Eugene? Well, I showed him a couple of stills from it and told him that if he didn't let me see you, I'd upload the whole clip to

VideoJunkie and call all the newspapers. I guess he figured having the whole world watch you try to rip Eugene's legs off might not go over so well with his bosses."

"Or with his buyers," added Ortega with a pang.

"What?" said Peter.

"Nothing," replied Ortega tersely before abruptly turning and knuckle-walking over to where Siggy was busily chewing a toilet-paper roll.

After a moment, he felt Peter sidle up next to him. He waited tensely for the boy to start asking questions or to tell him that friends didn't say "nothing" to each other in situations like this, or even to get angry at Ortega for clamming up on him after all he'd gone through to get there.

But Peter did none of those things. Instead, he picked up a sunflower seed and, with a slightly shaking hand, gently poked it through the cage at Siggy.

"I acted like such an idiot at that conference last weekend that a bunch of money got taken away from the lab," confessed Ortega after a long moment. "My project — Project Ortega — is being shut down. Dr. Whitmore says the company is … going to sell me."

Peter looked at him blankly. "What do you mean "sell you?"

"You know — like, put a price tag on my forehead," said Ortega, gesturing impatiently. "Give a free toaster to whoever buys me."

"Yeah, right," said Peter, rolling his eyes.

"It's true," said Ortega.

"I don't believe it," said Peter, folding his arms across his chest. "You're just kidding around." When Ortega didn't say anything, Peter said, "You're joking, right?" When Ortega *still* didn't say anything, Peter's face fell and his gray eyes grew large. In that moment, he looked every bit as young as he had the first time Ortega had ever seen him. "You're not joking?" he said in a tiny, incredulous voice.

Ortega shook his head.

"But ... but they *can't*," said Peter, shaking his head in the same bewildered fashion that Ortega had shaken his when he'd first heard the news.

"They can," said Ortega.

"But *how?*" asked Peter, his voice rising. "I don't understand. You can talk and do the eight-times table and everything!"

"But I'm not a person."

"Don't be stupid," snapped Peter. "Of course you're a person!"

Ortega locked eyes with his friend. "But not a *human* person," he said.

Just then, the door opened.

"Time's up," said Dr. Whitmore tightly, glaring at Peter as though he'd like to be able to sell *him* — in the form of ground sausage. Ortega watched in fascination as a dozen explosive expressions flitted across Peter's small face — anger, grief, panic, hatred, defiance. Then his thin body sagged a bit, and with a resigned sigh he threw his arms around Ortega.

"I'm sorry I was such a jerk at school today," he mumbled, hugging Ortega so hard that his injured shoulder began to throb.

Ortega squeezed his eyes shut and said, "I'm willing to let bygones be bygones if you are."

"I am, I totally am!" replied Peter, half-laughing, half-sniffling. "What's a bygone?"

Ortega tried hard to smile. "Say hi to Janice and Eugene for me," he said, swallowing past the lump in his throat.

"I will," said Peter, squeezing harder still.

"You've been a good friend," Ortega whispered. He paused before adding, "I want you to know that I'll always think of you as an equal." At this, Peter started to cry in earnest. "Me too!" he gulped as he stepped away from his friend and began furiously wiping away the tears with the back of his hand. "Good-bye, Ortega. Good luck!"

Ortega spent most of the next day in his closet, which was the only place he could get a little privacy now that Dr. Whitmore had taken away his beanbag chair. He ate his meals in there, played with his mouse in there, missed his friends, Dr. Susan and Grandma in there, worried about what was going to happen to him in there. At one point, he even made a halfhearted attempt to share his fears with Smelly Boy, the sock puppet Grandma had made for him years ago using one of Dr. Susan's old sweat socks, but it was such a painful reminder that dear, faithful Mr. Doodles was lost forever that he set Smelly Boy aside almost at once.

Instead of being frustrated by Ortega's unwillingness to get spied on, Dr. Whitmore seemed to be getting a strange sense of satisfaction from the fact that Ortega exhibited no signs of claustrophobia. Under normal circumstances, Ortega would have taken this as his cue to run out of the closet screaming that the walls were closing in on him. Present circumstances were anything but normal, however, and having Dr. Whitmore mostly leave him alone suited him just fine.

That evening, after serving Ortega a supper that consisted of three peanut-butter sandwiches and a big pile of limp vegetables that didn't appear to have been washed properly, Dr. Whitmore announced that he — and he alone! — would be spending the night in the lab.

"I canceled a trip to the science gallery with my nephew, Rupert, in order to be here for you tonight, Ortega," he said in a long-suffering voice as he handed Ortega a walkie-talkie. "I'm going down to the cafeteria to get some dinner right now, but I can be back up here in a minute if you need me. Just press the button and talk."

Slowly, Ortega lifted the walkie-talkie to his lips, pressed the red button and screeched, "I WON'T NEED YOU."

Dr. Whitmore jumped halfway out of his skin. "Really, Ortega!" he huffed. "Is that any way to —"

"OVER AND OUT."

Ten minutes later, Ortega heard scuffling noises in the main lab. Sucking his lips in annoyance, he was just about to screech into the walkie-talkie for Dr. Whitmore to shut up when he heard something that made his hair stand straight on end.

"Ortega?" whispered a voice just outside his bedroom door.

Tumbling out of the closet, Ortega galloped to his bedroom door with such speed that he nearly slammed into it face-first. "Janice?" he whispered back. "Is that you?"

"Of course it's me. Who else —"

"Hi, Ortega," sang Eugene from somewhere down at Ortega's feet.

Ortega immediately lay down on the ground. Through the crack at the bottom of the door, he could see a bit of a jolly smile, a patch of pudgy cheek and one crinkly eye.

"How are you doing?" asked Eugene, as though this was the most natural place in the world to have a conversation.

"Terrific," said Ortega. "What are you doing here?"

"Helping you escape so that they can't sell you," explained Eugene.

A sliver of Janice's face appeared at the crack. "This is for real, Ortega. We're busting you out. Is there anyone else here we should know about besides the dingdong in the bowtie?"

"No ..."

"Okay, good."

Abruptly, Janice's face disappeared. There was the soft patter of feet running down a hall, a jingling of keys and then, to Ortega's absolute and utter amazement, his bedroom door swung open and his three friends stood before him dressed in the same dark clothes they'd worn during the night shoot at the haunted factory.

"Ready to go?" asked Janice, looking around with her hands on her hips.

"I ... um ... go where?" asked Ortega.

The three children exchanged uneasy glances.

"Some place that isn't this place," Peter finally said.

"Some place where they won't sell you," added Eugene.

"We'll explain on the way," finished Janice.

"But how —"

"No time," she interrupted. Reaching for his arm with an expression that clearly said she'd drag him to safety if she had to, Janice paused when she noticed the walkie-talkie he was still clutching in his leathery hand. "Is that what I think it is?"

"If you think it's a walkie-talkie, then yes, it is," said Ortega. "Dr. Whitmore told me to use it to call him if I need him."

Janice flashed her pirate smile. Ortega was dazzled.

"This is working out even better than I could have hoped," she whooped softly. Grabbing the walkie-talkie out of Ortega's hand, she thrust it at Peter. "You know what to do."

Three minutes later, Ortega was standing in a shadowed doorway just around the corner from the elevator when he heard the sound of himself screaming at the top of his lungs. Startled, he looked at Janice for an explanation, but she just put her finger to her lips. Thirty seconds later, Dr. Whitmore staggered out of the stairwell. There were large, yellow sweat stains in the armpits of his dress shirt, his thin, greasy hair was disheveled, and he was gasping for breath. From the walkie-talkie clipped to his fake leather belt came the sound of Ortega screaming on and on.

By standing on his tiptoes, Ortega was able to watch as Dr. Whitmore fumbled with his security pass and then dashed across the main lab toward his closed bedroom door. Then he couldn't see anything. Feeling so agitated that he thought he might start screaming for real, Ortega bugged his eyes out at Janice in the hope that she would tell him what the heck was going on, but she just gave her head an impatient shake and pressed him farther into the shadows.

Next thing Ortega knew, Peter was flying out of the lab with a scared smile on his face.

"Did it work?" asked Janice.

Peter nodded.

"Are you sure?" persisted Janice. "He can't get out?"

Peter nodded again.

"Will someone please explain what just happened?" wailed Ortega softly.

"Later," said Janice tersely. "Follow me."

One after another they ducked into the stairwell and started rapidly and silently down the stairs. Disaster almost struck on the second-floor landing when they heard the sound of people approaching the stairwell, but Ortega took a fast flying leap from the top of the stairs, landed soundlessly and braced himself against the door, pinning it shut. There were a few tense moments while a loud man with a southern accent and a bad temper repeatedly threw himself at the door in an effort to force it open, but at last someone called out that the elevator had arrived and everyone on the other side of the door drifted off to take the easy way down.

The team moved on.

When they reached the basement, Janice stuck her head out the door, checked in all directions, then led them quickly through a creepy-looking tunnel whose glistening cement walls were lined with hissing pipes and bulging wads of pink insulation. Ortega was just about to tell Janice that if this was where they were taking him, he'd rather be sold (not true), when the tunnel opened up into a set of crumbling stairs going up. Still leading the way, Janice took the stairs two at a time. When she got to the top, she waited impatiently for the others to catch up. Eugene arrived gasping for breath, but before he could inhale even once, Janice had spun him around by one shoulder, dug into the back of his knapsack and pulled out what looked like a big handful of black rubber. She handed some to Peter and some to Eugene.

Ortega frowned and was about to ask the obvious question when, in unison, the three kids pulled gorilla masks down over their faces.

Ortega's mouth dropped open. "What on *earth* are you doing?" he cried.

"It's dark and we don't have far to go," said Janice in a slightly muffled voice. "But just in case someone catches a glimpse of us, I thought it would be better if we all looked like gorillas. You know, so that maybe people wouldn't know which one of us to chase if we have to split up."

The notion that anyone would ever mistake this slim girl with eyes like blue fire for a big, hairy gorilla was so ridiculous that Ortega almost started laughing. Before he could, however, she turned and swiped what looked like a security pass through the locking mechanism next to the door. There was a tiny click, then she shoved open the door and slipped silently into the night.

"You're nuts, you know," Ortega called after her in a whisper.

As he loped alongside his friends under the cover of the foliage that surrounded the corporate buildings, Ortega's mind raced. Had he actually just been broken out of the lab, or was this some bizarre dream? Looking around, he could easily imagine the latter. The rubber gorilla masks were so lifelike that his skin tingled whenever he caught a glimpse of one out of the corner of his eyes. It was as if his family — his real family, the one he'd been stolen from — had arrived to save the day.

Ortega turned to tell Peter what an amazing feeling it was, when suddenly the ground dropped away beneath his feet. With a gasp, he started to fall. Bumping and sliding through grass and mud, whipped in the face by branches, unable to see a thing, Ortega was just about to bellow in terror when the moon broke through the clouds and he slid to an ungraceful halt at Janice's feet.

"Get up and put this on," she said, handing him a life jacket. "We have a long ride ahead of us."

Chapter Twelve

"*Now* will you tell me how you did all this?" asked Ortega, clutching the side of Peter's boat, which was puttering along near the shore just fast enough to make Ortega feel like throwing up.

"It wasn't easy," said Janice with relish.

Peter — who was sitting in back steering the outboard motor — nodded.

"But when Peter came back from seeing you yesterday and said you were going to be *sold*," said Eugene, who couldn't seem to get over the fact that someone would actually do something like that to a guy who liked to eat brown sugar and cherry suckers. "Well, it really wasn't a question of 'if' we could get you out, it was a question of 'how' and 'when'."

"That's two questions," said Janice, who was scouting the shoreline as though expecting to be attacked by ninjas at any moment.

Eugene stuck his tongue out at her. Ortega smiled.

Then the boat lurched and he screamed.

"Quiet!" hissed Janice, flapping her hand at him.

"It's nothing," said Peter. "We just hit a sandbar." He paused before adding, "Somebody needs to get out and give us a push."

There was nothing Ortega wanted less than to leap into the cold, murky water that was probably filled with slimy things just waiting to drag innocent gorillas to their watery graves. However, he was so much bigger and stronger than the rest of them that it would have been ridiculous to suggest that someone else do it. Besides, his friends had gone to so much trouble to save him — this was the least he could do.

And so, cautiously — but without complaining — he lowered himself out of the boat and into the icy water. It wasn't at all deep, but the bottom sucked at his feet as though it were a living thing. Biting down on his lip to keep from crying out, Ortega waded to the back of the boat, put his uninjured shoulder against it and gave a mighty heave. The boat sprang forward with alarming swiftness; Ortega ran after it, splashing like a deranged water buffalo. By the time Eugene had grabbed the back of his pants and hauled him into the boat, Janice was ready to kill him.

"You would make, like, the worst secret agent *ever*," she said severely.

"Not to worry," replied Ortega airily as he tried without success to squeeze water out of his shirt. "I'm planning on becoming a brain surgeon, remember?"

At this, Eugene began to chortle so hard that he started snorting. Peter — who didn't quite get the joke — shook his head and smiled.

They got stuck six more times over the next two hours. Each time, Ortega insisted on pushing, and each time he climbed back into the boat feeling colder and more exhausted than the time before.

In between, Janice, Peter and Eugene told him everything.

It had all started the night before when Peter had come to visit Ortega. Standing there in Ortega's bedroom, he'd made the split-second decision that something had to be done to save his friend. Not wanting to raise Dr. Whitmore's suspicions, however, he'd cleverly acted all weak and blubbery, as though he'd accepted the fact that Ortega's fate was sealed. Then, on his way out of the lab, while his mother was giving Dr. Whitmore one last piece of her mind, he'd palmed Dr. Susan's security pass, which was just lying on the counter next to a can of pencils.

"Palmed means stole," explained Peter, sounding inordinately pleased with himself.

Ortega nodded and gestured for him to carry on.

When he got home, he called Janice and Eugene and they worked out the details. They'd sneak out, take Peter's boat to the city and moor it as close to the lab building as they could. To avoid the security guard at the front desk, they'd hide in the bushes at the back of the building, wait until somebody came out the back door that Glen had used on the morning they shot the lab scene, then slide a stick in the door to keep it from closing. When the coast was clear, they'd slip inside and head up to the lab.

"Other than disconnecting the video cameras, we weren't exactly sure what we'd do next," admitted Janice. "There was no way to know how many people would be inside and what additional security precautions they were taking with you."

"All we knew for sure was that we had to be prepared for anything," said Peter with a smile in his voice.

Eugene did a kung-fu kick that nearly tipped the boat over.

Janice ignored them both. "Almost as soon as we got there, we saw the nerdy professor walk onto the elevator," she explained. "We scoped the place out for another couple of minutes, and when we figured that the coast was as clear as it was ever going to be, we used the security pass to sneak inside. After all the cameras were disabled, Peter found the key to your room.

"That first night we became friends, you showed me where Dr. Jerky Pants hid the extra key to his office and how to get into his secret drawer, remember, Ortega?" piped Peter. "I even licked his keyboard, for old time's sake."

"You shouldn't have done that," said Janice disapprovingly. "We were on a very tight schedule and it was a waste of precious time."

"It was totally worth it," said Peter.

Ortega hooted in agreement.

"After that, the only thing left to do was to slow down Dr. Whitmore in order to give ourselves time to escape," interjected Eugene, pulling a handful of caramels out of his pocket and handing three to Ortega.

Janice nodded. "Peter had brought along a portable tape recorder with a looped tape of a bunch of the screams you'd made while filming his movie," she said. "We had an idea that we might be able to use it to lure that jerk doctor into some kind of trap. The problem was figuring out how to do it without one of us getting caught."

"When we saw the walkie-talkie it was almost too perfect to believe," continued Peter. "I just walked into your closet, taped the red button down in the Talk position and hit Play on the tape recorder. Then I hid in the hallway until I saw Dr. Fussy Pants go flying into the bedroom, at which point I ran over, slammed the door and locked him inside." Peter's grin faltered just a little bit there, and his voice grew timid. "He ... he was *really* mad — you should have seen him, hollering, throwing things, hammering on the two-way mirror. I-I actually thought he might have a heart attack."

"Impossible," said Ortega, sneezing so hard he blew his caramel over the side of the boat. "He's got no heart."

Chortling, Eugene leaned over and gave Ortega a hearty high five, causing the boat to wobble dangerously. Ortega held his breath until it steadied, then sighed with a contentment he would not have thought possible a few hours earlier.

All of a sudden, he saw a blinking light on the shoreline.

"Look out!" he whispered fearfully. "I think there's someone out there!"

"Thank goodness," murmured Peter as he steered the boat into a slow turn toward the light. "I was beginning to worry we'd missed it."

Ortega shivered violently, his feeling of contentment gone. They were here.

Wherever "here" was.

He watched in alarm as a small, shadowy figure skidded awkwardly down the riverbank and stood at the edge of the water. When they got close enough, Janice — who was seated at the front of the boat — stood up and threw one end of a rope to the figure. The figure caught it and slowly began hauling them to shore. There was a soft scraping sound as the bottom of the boat slid along small stones and then the boat shuddered to a halt.

"Everybody out," ordered Janice, shrugging off her life jacket and jumping into the water with her shoes on as though she were a platoon commander with bigger things to worry about than wet feet.

Ortega — whose feet had just finished drying following his last leap into the water — unbuckled his own life jacket, clambered to the front of the boat and climbed out only after carefully testing with his toes to make sure he was on solid ground.

Then he turned around and came face to face with Myra Harding.

"What's she doing here?" he cried, dropping to his knuckles so he could flee the instant her crazy mother came flapping out of the bushes with a butcher knife clamped between her teeth.

"Helping us," said Janice.

"Helping us?" gasped Ortega. "Helping us how? Helping us *why?*"

Janice shrugged before turning to chastise Eugene, who had just starting chuckling noisily in response to something Peter said.

Ortega stared at Myra. In the faint starlight, her face looked as pinched as ever, and she appeared to be scowling. Ortega couldn't imagine for the life of him what she could possibly have to gain from helping someone like him, and he was just about to warn Janice that it was probably some kind of trick when Myra cleared her throat.

"I, um, saw what happened on the news," she said. There was a pause, and then: "My mother laughed when they shot you."

Ortega didn't know what he was supposed to say to this, so he said nothing.

"I didn't," continued Myra. "Laugh, I mean. I ..." She paused again, as though struggling to collect her thoughts. "Peepers died," she said abruptly.

"I'm sorry," blurted Ortega.

Myra nodded. "Because of you, I found him dead at the foot of my bed, just like my mother said I would."

"I'm sorry!" he blurted again, this time so loudly that Janice interrupted her lecture to Eugene to reach back and give Ortega a jab in the ribs.

Myra stared out across the water. "I'm not," she said in an odd voice, after a moment's silence. "I mean, I'm sad he's gone, of course, but ... the foot of my bed was his favorite place in the world. It's where he would have wanted it to happen."

This sounded like a good thing to Ortega, but he couldn't be sure.

"Everybody ready?" asked Janice, hoisting a duffel bag onto her shoulder before pausing to pull her pirate kerchief lower on her forehead.

Myra nodded and picked up the flashlight she'd set down on a nearby rock. Peter and Eugene fell in behind Ortega.

"All right, then," said Janice crisply. "Let's go."

Wordlessly, Myra turned and began scrambling up the grassy slope.

"Wait!" said Ortega, more loudly than he intended.

Pausing mid-scramble, Myra looked back at him. "What?" she asked in an impatient whisper.

Folding his long arms self-consciously across his broad chest, Ortega averted his eyes and muttered, "Where are you taking me?"

Myra's thin eyebrows peaked in surprise. She looked at Janice and the two boys. "You didn't tell him?" she said.

"Tell me what?" asked Ortega, his dark, deep-set eyes darting from one face to the next.

Janice frowned. Eugene made an unhappy mewling noise.

Peter took a deep breath. "We're taking you to the one place no one would ever think of looking for you, Ortega," he explained. "We're taking you to ... to the haunted factory."

Myra's huff of annoyance mingled with Ortega's bark of alarm to send a very interesting-sounding echo shooting across the still water.

"My mother's factory is not *haunted*," complained Myra.

Ortega's muscles bunched beneath him as he prepared to take flight into the night.

"Please don't," blurted Peter, grabbing Ortega's wet sleeve. "I ... I know it's bad. But we couldn't think of anywhere else to take you!"

"We didn't tell you earlier because we didn't want to freak you out," added Janice.

"Myra says it's not half bad once you get inside!" said Eugene in a cheerful, high-pitched voice that fooled exactly nobody.

Ortega yanked his sleeve out of Peter's hand and, digging his knuckles hard into the soft ground at his feet, tried desperately to think of somewhere else to go. Somewhere that was safe and warm and full of comforting smells, where no one would ever find him and where he wouldn't end up a half-eaten, mangled, strangled corpse stuffed into a vat of tanning chemicals.

But no matter how hard he tried, he couldn't think of such a place, because he was just a high-priced, overgrown lab rat on the run from a scientist who would stop at nothing to get him back, and that meant that there was nowhere safe for him to go — not now, and probably not ever again.

The thought made him ache all over.

"Please, Ortega," begged Peter, leaning close. "You only have to stay there until we can figure out what to do next."

And what happens if you can't figure out what to do next! Ortega screeched, in his mind.

Out loud, he said nothing.

Soundlessly, Myra led the four friends up over the crest of the grassy riverbank and on toward the dark and silent factory. The clouds had drifted over the moon again, and there wasn't a breath of wind in the air. Even so, the stillness of the place seemed unnatural — as though something evil was holding its breath. Listening … and waiting.

When they got closer to the building than Ortega had ever been before — so close that he could see what looked to be dragging finger marks down the inside of the grimy windows — Myra came to an abrupt halt.

"Here's the key to the padlock on the front door," she whispered as she thrust an old silver key at Janice. "The offices are in the basement — like I said, they'll be dark, but probably more comfortable than the factory floor."

"Safer, too, right?" asked Janice, sounding a lot less crisp than she had down by the river.

Myra shrugged nervously. "Now, remember that you promised never to tell anyone that I helped you," she said, "not even if you were being tortured."

"I remember," said Janice.

Peter and Eugene nodded.

"Good," said Myra with obvious relief, as she began to back away, "because I'm leaving now and I don't ever want to talk about this again."

Ortega blinked in surprise. Eugene's mouth dropped open.

"You mean you're not coming inside with us?" he blurted.

Myra pinched her lips together and shook her head as she slowly continued to back away into the shadows.

"But I don't understand!" Eugene cried as loudly as he dared. "Why aren't you coming in with us? What are you afraid of?"

But Myra had already been swallowed up by the darkness, and the only answer to Eugene's question was the deafening silence of the night.

———

For a long moment, the four friends just stood staring after Myra.

"I know why she left!" gasped Eugene suddenly. "Because this is the anniversary of the night her mom boiled that guy alive in a vat of — OOF!"

"Oh, Eugene," said Janice in a voice filled with concern. "What's wrong?"

"I think you ruptured my spleen," he wheezed, clutching his belly where Janice had just landed a kung-fu kick.

Ortega smiled weakly.

"Come on," murmured Peter, giving Ortega a nudge in the injured shoulder, which had begun to ache again. "Let's do this thing."

———

Gingerly, they tiptoed up to the front door of the factory. Swallowing hard, Janice slid the key into the padlock and turned. It opened suddenly with a dull clunk. Slipping the lock into her pocket, Janice unwound the heavy, rusted chain as quietly as she could. Nevertheless, it rattled against the metal door like machine-gun fire in the night. Ortega cringed and bit his lip to keep from screaming aloud.

When at last the chain lay on the ground at their feet, Janice reached into her duffel bag, pulled out some flashlights and wordlessly handed them out.

"Ready?" she whispered.

They nodded and bunched closer together.

Slowly, she pushed open the door and they all stepped inside.

The factory had the distinct look of a place that had been abandoned abruptly, possibly in somewhat of a panic. Under the low ceiling, in the thin, yellow light of the flashlight beams, the friends saw scarred workbenches scattered with coffee mugs, cutting tools and dried-up strips of leather. Here and there, mannequins wearing half-finished leather coats stared unblinking into the dusty light, their fake hair askew, their mouths red slashes in their impossibly perfect faces. Under a bench near the back, Ortega noticed a pair of ancient boots and what looked like a pile of dirty old clothes; in the darkness beyond that stood row upon row of open tanks that appeared to be crusted over with the toxic remains of long-evaporated chemicals.

Ortega shivered and tried not to think about what other remains those tanks might contain.

"Close the door quietly," ordered Janice in a hushed voice.

Eugene nodded just as the door slipped from his sweaty fingers and slammed shut behind him. The crashing noise of metal on metal reverberated throughout the entire factory. Eugene shrieked in terror, Ortega clapped his hands over his ears and Peter stiffened as he heard the sound of many small things scurrying in the darkness.

Janice glared at Eugene. "Come on," she whispered, her breath coming in ragged gasps. "Myra said the stairs are at the back corner of the shop."

Without another word, she began to pad soundlessly around the workbenches and past the mannequins, into the farthest, darkest recesses of the workshop. Heart hammering wildly, Ortega knuckled after her as carefully as he could but still managed to kick over two mannequins and send Eugene shrieking again as they toppled stiffly toward him with their dead eyes and outstretched plastic arms. Once, in the dying echoes of Eugene's shrieks, Ortega thought he heard something else — a whispered moan, perhaps, or a muffled footfall — but he couldn't be sure and he was too petrified to even *think* about stopping to investigate.

When the four friends reached the back wall of the factory, they groped their way along it until they found the staircase. Here, Janice paused for so long that Ortega wondered if she was having second thoughts. Before he could ask, however, she began to edge her way down, pressing her back to the wall as she went, as though this might offer her some kind of protection. Against what, Ortega refused to think.

The stairs descended into a darkness so profound that the beams of the flashlights soon appeared pathetically feeble. Sightless, soundless heaviness pressed against Ortega from all sides, making it hard for him to breathe. Suddenly, Janice stopped, so abruptly that Ortega nearly ran into her. They had made it to the bottom of the stairs and were standing at the end of what appeared to be a narrow corridor lined with closed doors. Janice inched her way forward and tried the doors. The first two were locked, but the third was not. After wiping the back of her hand across forehead and exhaling once, loudly, Janice turned the knob and slowly eased the door open. Ortega and the others held their breath, but nothing bolted, lunged *or* scurried out the open door. In fact, nothing moved at all. With a slightly shaking hand, Janice held her flashlight high above her head and peered inside. After a long moment, she stepped aside and gestured for Ortega to come forward.

"What do you think?" she whispered, leaning so close that Ortega could smell the green-apple shampoo she'd used to wash her hair that morning. "Could you stay here by yourself for a while?"

Wordlessly, he looked past her into the office. It was a small room, thinly carpeted, with a picture of a boat hanging crookedly on the wall behind the desk. There was a filing cabinet, a garbage can and a bookcase but, strangely, no chair. Thin stacks of paper sat at odd angles on the desk, like the work of someone trying to look busy.

If not for the fact that the office was located in the basement of a derelict, rat-infested haunted factory, it would have been merely depressing.

Closing his eyes, Ortega breathed deeply of the green-apple-shampoo smell and tried not to cry. Up until now, none of this had seemed quite real — the daring escape from the lab, the lurching boat ride in the night, the sudden appearance of Myra Harding, even the harrowing passage into the heart of the dreaded factory. At times, it had almost felt as though they were shooting a scene in a movie.

But they weren't shooting a scene in a movie, of course. They were trying to save Ortega from being sold away from everything he'd ever known. Without warning, he had a sudden memory of smiling, frizzy-haired Dr. Susan singing "Feelin' Groovy" at passing Jersey cows. With a pang, he wondered where she was, and whether she'd be sad when she finally returned home and learned that he was gone.

Opening his eyes, he looked at his friends.

"Staying here isn't going to change anything, you know," he said in a low voice. "There's nowhere on earth I can go that Dr. Whitmore won't find me. In the end, he's going to be able to do whatever he wants with me."

"Maybe, but that doesn't mean we have to make it easy for him," said Peter savagely. "That doesn't mean we shouldn't *try*."

Ortega didn't say anything. Suddenly, he was very tired.

"We brought everything you're going to need," said Janice, abruptly shouldering past him into the shabby little office. Dumping the duffel bag onto the desk, she unzipped it and started pulling out supplies. "I brought a sleeping bag and a foam mattress, a camping lantern with extra batteries, some bottled water, a couple of books, some toilet paper and ... uh ... this thing," she muttered, sounding embarrassed as she tenderly set a small, threadbare stuffed dog next to the lantern.

"And I brought food," said Eugene eagerly, presenting Ortega with a large bag of brown sugar and too many cherry suckers to count.

Janice looked up from the floor behind the desk where she was now hastily arranging the sleeping bag. "Eugene, that is not *food*," she said severely.

"It sure the heck is," said Ortega as he tentatively knuckle-walked into the room and reached for a sucker.

Eugene beamed. Janice rolled her eyes. A few minutes later, after she'd finished setting the garbage can behind the bookcase so that Ortega would have a safe, private place to go to the toilet in the absence of running water, she checked her glow-in-the-dark watch, looked over at Peter and jerked her head toward the door.

Peter nodded once and turned to Ortega. "Listen, we've got to go now if we're going to make it back across town to the theater before the double-feature lets out. My mom thinks we're inside watching it, and there'll be serious trouble if we're not there when she comes to pick us up," he explained hurriedly as Janice zipped up the empty duffel bag and slung it over her shoulder in preparation to leave. "You'll be okay here until we can figure out what to do next?"

Still not believing that a few days was going to make any difference, but not sure what else to do, Ortega nodded.

Peter stepped forward and gave him a hug. "You know what?" he whispered. "Gorillas can be pretty brave sometimes."

Ortega clutched Peter as though he might never let him go. "So can boys," he whispered.

The two of them stepped back, smiling. Then Ortega's smile faded and his lower lip began to quiver. "Hurry back," he said in a tremulous voice.

"Count on it."

Chapter Thirteen

For a long time after Peter, Eugene and Janice had left, Ortega stood staring through the half-open door. First, he watched the dark silhouettes of his friends get swallowed up by the greater darkness. Then he watched the bobbing beams of their flashlights as they entered the stairwell and disappeared from sight. After that he closed his eyes and strained to hear the sound of their footsteps padding up the stairs and across the cold and dirty factory floor. He smiled briefly when he heard a noisy clatter and the sound of Eugene shrieking. A few moments later, he heard the scrape of metal on metal, the rattle of a chain and then silence.

He was alone.

As softly as he possibly could, Ortega closed the door. For a moment, he didn't move at all. Gradually, however, he began to realize how cold he was, and how tired. The dart wound in his shoulder had begun to ache again, sending a dull throb down his arm. Slowly, Ortega backed away from the door, limping slightly as he favored his injured shoulder. When he reached the sleeping bag, he eased himself down onto his side. He tried to tuck the sleeping bag around his body, but it wouldn't stay in place, so after a while he had to content himself with nestling in as best he could. It smelled faintly like the green-apple shampoo that Janice used, but instead of comforting Ortega, it made him homesick. He closed his eyes several times, but opened them again almost immediately to check that the camping lantern was still on. Then he noticed that he was still clutching the cherry sucker he'd picked up earlier. Tearing the wrapper off with his teeth, he popped it into his mouth and began to suck. Slowly, slowly his eyelids drooped until at last they closed for good. A short while after this, the cherry sucker silently fell out of his mouth and lay on the sleeping bag in a small but growing puddle of cherry-flavored drool.

In the dream, Ortega was trapped at the bottom of a hole so deep the light that poured into the opening at the top was nothing more than a distant speck. Over and over he tried to climb his way out, but every time he neared the top the walls grew slick and he plummeted to the bottom again. In a panic, he clawed at the darkness around him in the hope of discovering a hidden opening, but the only thing he uncovered was Dr. Whitmore's head, huge and grotesque, sitting in the middle of a fruit platter, droning on and on about how Ortega had brought this on himself. In despair, Ortega bellowed and beat his fists against his chest, but though this resulted in Dr. Susan's face suddenly appearing at the top of the hole, she merely looked puzzled, as if she didn't understand what the problem was.

And then she was gone.

Ortega awoke with a start. He had no idea how much time had passed. The light from the camping lantern seemed weaker, and so did he. The wound on his shoulder was hot to the touch and his forehead was wet with sweat. He drank a little water, then peeled the half-eaten sucker off Janice's sleeping bag and popped it in his mouth. Propping his back against the wall, he listened anxiously for the sound of lurching footsteps or murderous moans, but the only sound he heard was silence. With a cough, he reached for the ratty stuffed dog Janice had left for him. It, too, smelled like green apples. But if he closed his eyes, hugged it tight and tried very hard, he could almost imagine it was good old Mr. Doodles.

Twelve cherry suckers and two naps later, Ortega ripped open the bag of brown sugar. He ate ravenously and afterward lay down with a rather upset stomach. Somehow, eating brown sugar wasn't half as much fun when a person wasn't sneaking it out of his own kitchenette and then galloping down the hall shrieking with laughter as his favorite handler chased after him, scolding and shaking her frizzy hair at him. An image of Dr. Susan bloomed before his eyes. Ortega grunted and reached for it, but even as he did, it began to morph. Frizzy hair shortened and darkened, brow thickened, shoulders broadened, arms lengthened. He was looking at himself, but not himself — a mother who looked just like him. She hooted softly, then knuckle-walked slowly to his side and, after a moment's hesitation, reached out and gave him a chin tickle. Ortega squeezed his eyes shut and inhaled deeply, breathing in the musky scent his body could never forget — the scent of the animal who'd given him life, the scent of the one who'd first clutched his tiny, frail body to her chest. Uncertain what to do with the squalling, squirmy thing in her arms, she'd done her best for as long as she could — Ortega was suddenly sure of it. Hooting plaintively, he reached for her, but when he opened his eyes again, she was gone.

The world of people, the world of animals. Miss Rutherford was right — he belonged in both places, and neither.

Ortega cried out once, from the depths of his soul.

And then he wept.

Time passed. At one point, Ortega thought he heard the distant sound of the chain at the factory door rattling. Heart hammering, he sat up so fast he got dizzy. Breathing hard, he listened with all his might, but he didn't hear anything else, and after a long time he eased himself back down onto the sleeping bag, telling himself it had only been the wind, but that Janice, Peter and Eugene would surely be back soon.

"Ortega?"

He moaned and winced as someone shook him gently by the sore shoulder.

"Ortega, are you okay?"

The voice sounded concerned. Dragging himself from the depths of troubled sleep, Ortega fuzzily pondered this until all at once, his eyes flew open.

"You came back!" he croaked, staring up into the worried faces of his friends.

"Of course we came back," said Janice. "What did you think?"

Ortega struggled to sit up. Coughing wetly into the back of his hairy hand, he asked how long he'd been down there.

"Almost two days," said Peter. "I'm sorry we couldn't get back any earlier. It's been crazy, Ortega. Really crazy."

Eugene nodded solemnly and reached for a cherry sucker.

"Your disappearance is all over the news," continued Peter. "There's, like, hourly coverage on the news stations and all the newspapers have run front-page stories. Some people are freaking out and refusing to let their children out of sight until you've been 'recaptured'; others have started petitions demanding an inquiry into how you've been treated and what precautions were in place to protect you. Girls are laying flowers and stuffed toys and bananas in the tulip patch at the front of the lab building."

"Weird," said Ortega faintly.

Peter nodded.

"Also, the police are involved," added Janice, in a voice lacking in its usual bravado. "They interviewed all of us — Peter, Eugene and me. Took us out of class one by one, questioned us for ages. Wanted to know what we were doing the night you disappeared."

"I stuck to the story," said Eugene, sounding extremely defensive.

"I don't think it matters," murmured Janice. "I'm pretty sure they know — or at least suspect — that we were involved. Everyone does. Duncan and his goons have been sticking to us like glue. Probably hoping to find you and collect the reward money."

"There's reward money?" asked Ortega weakly, feeling pleased in spite of the fact that the ache in his shoulder seemed to have spread to the rest of his body.

Peter nodded. "Dr. Susan even came to see me," he said.

Ortega's heart leaped. "She did?"

Peter nodded again. "She was really upset, Ortega. She … she looked like she'd been crying hard for a long time. Her nose was red and shiny and there were these big splotchy patches all over her face."

Affection for Dr. Susan swelled in Ortega's chest. "It's not a very good look for her, is it?" he asked.

"Not really," admitted Peter with a small shudder. "Anyway, she begged me to tell her where you were. *Begged* me. It was awful, Ortega. She said she tried to get a flight home the minute Glen called to tell her about you getting shot, but there were problems with the airline, and by the time she got back you were gone. She said to tell you that Dr. Stinky Pants lied about the funding being cut — she said you don't have to be scared about being sold because the company has no plans to do that, and besides, she'd die before she'd ever let it happen."

Ortega coughed again but didn't say anything.

"She also gave me this," said Peter. Slipping his knapsack off his shoulder, he reached inside and pulled out ... Mr. Doodles! He was missing both eyes now, and it looked as though his head had been repeatedly run over by a truck with very dirty tires, but it was undoubtedly, joyfully, him.

Flinging the stuffed dog to one side, Ortega reached out and crushed his beloved teddy against his chest, wondering why his heart felt as if it was breaking.

"So," said Peter tentatively, after a moment. "Do you think she was telling the truth?"

"Yes," said Ortega, hugging Mr. Doodles tight.

"So ... do you want to go home?" said Janice, who was carefully cradling the abandoned stuffed dog.

Ortega nodded weakly.

Eugene looked enormously relieved.

"Okay," said Peter, as Janice began to quickly load up the duffel bag. "Then let's get you out of this place, work out a story we can all stick to —"

At this Janice bugged her eyes out at Eugene, who stuck out his cherry-red tongue at her.

"— and figure out a way to get you home."

Getting Ortega out of the basement proved harder than anyone realized it would be. Because he'd spent most of the last two days lying around, even Ortega himself hadn't realized how sick he was. He couldn't put any weight at all on his injured shoulder, and he had to stop every few paces to catch his breath. By the time they were halfway to the front door of the factory (which didn't actually seem frightening at all in the light of day), Ortega was so exhausted that he insisted on resting before going any farther.

Although they tried hard not to show it, Janice, Eugene and Peter were frantic with worry. Janice fanned Ortega's sweaty forehead while Eugene hand-fed him lumps of brown sugar and Peter paced back and forth trying to decide what to do.

"Eugene, give me your phone," he said abruptly, after deliberating for only a very short while.

Wordlessly, Eugene handed it over.

"What are you going to do?" murmured Janice.

"I'm going to call Dr. Susan," said Peter tightly. "I'm going to let her know that Ortega is here and that he's very sick. Then I'm going to stay with him until she gets here and I'm going to make sure she helps him." He jerked his head at Janice and Eugene. "You two are going to get out of here. I won't tell her you were involved. You'll be safe."

Janice and Eugene blinked at Peter for a moment, then turned back to Ortega and wordlessly resumed their ministrations.

Peter lifted the phone and began to dial, but before the call could go through, he heard a noise in the distance.

Sirens.

Snapping the phone shut, he ran to the nearest window.

"Police cars! Trucks! They're coming this way!" he cried. Turning, he bolted back to where Ortega sat, arriving just in time to see Janice rip Mr. Doodles out of Ortega's arms.

"It was a trap!" she said fiercely, shaking poor Mr. Doodles so hard he started to leak stuffing. "They must have bugged this thing — how else could they have found us?" Gripping Ortega by one arm, she attempted to haul him to his feet. "You know what this means, don't you?" she snarled. "That your Dr. Susan probably lied! About every-thing! We've got to get you out of here!"

Ortega lumbered to his feet with difficulty.

Eugene, who had jogged over to the window during Janice's tirade, called, "They're almost here!"

Peter ran his small fingers through his thick hair, a wild look in his stormy gray eyes. "It can't end like this, it can't!" he muttered to himself. Then he looked down at the cell phone he was clutching in his hand and gasped. "Ortega, stay right where you are. I've got an idea."

———————

Two minutes later, the four friends heard cars come to a skidding halt on the overgrown gravel road in front of the factory. Loud shouts and the sound of slamming car doors could be heard outside, and then suddenly the front doors flew open and officers in combat gear poured inside.

"There he is!" someone cried.

The officers spread out in a ring around Ortega, who stood hunched in the center of the factory floor — Janice by his side, Eugene covering his back and Peter in front, standing as tall as he possibly could. "Step away from the gorilla," called one of the officers, in a deep, authoritative voice.

Janice, Eugene and Peter didn't even blink.

Before the officer could repeat his command, there was a flurry of activity at the door as Dr. Whitmore shoved his way inside.

"Aha! I knew it!" he cried, spraying a heavyset man in a dark blue suit with saliva. "I told you they were involved, Detective, and there they are!" he said, jabbing his finger into the man's face. "Well? Why aren't you arresting them?"

"We need to secure the scene," said the man impassively. "We need to separate the children from the gorilla —"

"His name is Ortega!" hollered Janice.

The detective nodded in her direction before continuing. "We need to separate the children from Ortega before deciding if further steps need to be taken with them."

"What do you mean 'if' further steps need to be taken?" asked Dr. Whitmore furiously. "Of course further steps need to be taken — those children need to be arrested for the crime they committed!"

Eugene squeaked in fear and poked his head around Ortega. "We didn't commit any crime!" he protested. "Ortega wanted to come with us, right, Ortega?"

Ortega nodded — too sick to think about fleeing and unwilling to abandon his friends in any case.

"You see!" said Eugene hopefully. "We didn't kidnap him!"

Dr. Whitmore snorted derisively. "I don't want them charged with *kidnapping* — I want them charged with theft. That gorilla is —"

"HIS NAME IS ORTEGA!" screamed Janice, snatching the nearly empty bag of brown sugar out of Eugene's hand and flinging it at Dr. Whitmore.

The scientist ignored her. "That gorilla is a very valuable animal. I want them charged with theft and —"

"No," said Ortega. He spoke quietly, but with a conviction that silenced everyone, even Dr. Whitmore. "Leave my friends alone and I'll go quietly. You can do whatever you want to me."

Peter, Janice and Eugene immediately started shouting in protest, but Ortega gently shoved them aside, picked up Mr. Doodles and, limping badly, knuckle-walked slowly over to where Dr. Whitmore stood.

"That was a wise decision, Ortega," he said sternly, giving his bow tie a fussy tug.

Ortega didn't bother answering him. There was nothing left to say.

"How did you find me?" asked Ortega a short while later as he sat on the plastic sheet in the back of Dr. Whitmore's car, his hot forehead pressed up against the cool glass of the window.

"The last time you ran away I had animal control insert a tiny GPS tracking devise into your neck while you were unconscious," explained Dr. Whitmore.

"So it wasn't Mr. Doodles?" said Ortega.

"Who is Mr. Doodles?" asked Dr. Whitmore in a bewildered voice.

"No one," mumbled Ortega, giving his teddy a ferocious squeeze.

"I thought the GPS tracking device would prevent you from ever being able to escape undetected," continued Dr. Whitmore, "but unfortunately we were unable to pick up a signal until just half an hour ago."

"I was hiding in the basement," said Ortega, wiping his runny nose on the window.

"I see," replied Dr. Whitmore, who hadn't noticed him do it. "Anyway, I don't think I have to tell you how upset I am by the behavior of you and your friends, Ortega, or that the consequences will be severe, but I must say that this demonstration of your resourcefulness has had an extremely positive effect not only on your long-term prospects but on the prospects of Project Ortega as well."

"I thought Project Ortega was over," sighed Ortega.

Dr. Whitmore laughed shrilly. "Hardly!" he cried. "The truth is that there were some very important government people at that conference we attended, Ortega. *Very* important government people. They'd come to watch you in action and to explore certain theories they had about the application of the technology I've developed."

"By 'technology,' you mean me," said Ortega.

"Correct," said Dr. Whitmore. "They felt that in certain situations, they could have a use for a trainable, non-human with language abilities, provided it was able to demonstrate an ability to cope with extreme stress."

"By 'it,' you mean me," said Ortega, as they pulled into the back parking lot of the lab.

"Yes," chuckled Dr. Whitmore. Then he grew serious. "Unfortunately, I didn't have the data I needed to demonstrate that you had an ability to cope with stress. The government people were under a tight deadline to make a decision about you one way or another, so I was forced to introduce artificial stress into your environment."

Ortega coughed wetly without bothering to cover his mouth. "What are you saying?" he asked, giving the seat beside him a halfhearted slap.

Dr. Whitmore parked the car, wiped Ortega's spit from the side of his head and shrugged. "Project Ortega was never in danger," he explained. "You were never going to be sold. It was all part of a bigger plan! And I am pleased to report that on the whole, your performance has once again exceeded my wildest expectations."

Ortega stared at Dr. Whitmore's beaming face, unable to believe what he was hearing.

"Did Dr. Susan know about this?" he finally croaked.

"Susan? Oh, my heavens, no," said Dr. Whitmore. "She would have created problems. She is utterly without vision, unable to leave the philosophizing to the philosophers and, worst of all, unable to set her feelings for you aside for the greater good of the project. You see what I mean?" he said, gesturing impatiently toward the lab building. "Here she comes now, demonstrating exactly none of calm, cool impartiality I'd expect from a trained behavioral scientist."

Ortega looked hungrily out the window at Dr. Susan. He had to admit that Dr. Whitmore was right — she didn't look much like a trained behavioral scientist. Charging joyfully toward him with her uncombed hair, her tearstained face and her ugly poncho flapping behind her like a victory flag, she looked like something else altogether.

She looked like someone who loved him — in whose arms he belonged.

"You know what, Dr. Whitmore?" said Ortega. "Suddenly, I don't feel so good."

And with that, he leaned over and — being careful not to hit the plastic sheet — vomited two days' worth of brown sugar and cherry suckers all over the back of Dr. Whitmore's fancy new car. Then he daintily wiped his mouth on the back of the seat in front of him, kicked open the door and was gone.

———

That night was the best night of Ortega's life. After calling Dr. Mike to ask him to make an emergency visit, Dr. Susan helped Ortega into a pair of freshly washed jammies and tucked him into bed without asking him to brush and floss even though his breath smelled like vomit. After that, she refused to leave his side except to run for snacks and to fill Dr. Mike's prescription (antibiotics to treat the infected wound in his shoulder, antibiotics to treat his lung infection and an extra-large banana split with plenty of whipped cream to soothe his jangled spirit).

His room was back to normal — all his toys and books where they belonged (scattered on the floor), all his pictures set neatly on his bedside table.

"Look," smiled Dr. Susan. "I even stuffed the candy wrappers back into the hole in your beanbag chair."

"Neat," sighed Ortega, nestling deeper into his freshly fluffed pillow.

Dr. Susan reached out and smoothed the hair at his temple — something she'd done over and over again since their reunion. He hooted contentedly for a while and was about to ask her for a lullaby when he changed his mind. Opening his eyes, he asked, "Where were you all this time?"

With a tentative smile, she reached over, opened the drawer of his bedside table and pulled out a yellow envelope. Curious, Ortega sat up a little, wincing slightly at the ache in his shoulder.

"I went back to the zoo where you were born and spoke with the zookeeper personally about your interest in learning more about your birth parents. I also got pictures of your mother, father and two younger brothers," she explained, tipping the envelope to reveal a small handful of photographs.

Ortega's mouth dropped open. "I have *brothers*?" he blurted, suddenly not feeling sick at all.

Dr. Susan nodded. "Two full brothers, and at least three half-siblings. Your father has four mates."

Ortega wasn't sure how to react to the news that his father had a *harem*.

Seeing the uncertainty on Ortega's face, Dr. Susan gently explained that it was normal for a male gorilla to have multiple mates. "From an evolutionary standpoint, it makes sense for a strong male to pass his genes on to as many infants as possible, because it will help improve the gene pool and increase the species' chance for long-term survival. The best way for a male gorilla to have lots of children is for him to have lots of mates."

"But don't they ever get jealous of each other?" Ortega couldn't help asking.

"Not in the way you're thinking," said Dr. Susan carefully. "Gorilla families are highly structured. Sometimes a female might try to move up in the pecking order, but this is probably not because she's jealous. More likely, it's because the chances that she and her offspring will thrive and survive improve the closer they are to the dominant silverback. It's ... it's a different world, Ortega. Not better, not worse. Just ... different."

Ortega thought about this for a long moment. Then he held out his hand for the pictures. Wordlessly, Dr. Susan handed them over.

The first picture was of a female gorilla. She was pretty, in a gorilla sort of way, with her soft, bright brown eyes and dainty little ears. Ortega stared at his mother, trying not to notice that she wasn't wearing any clothes, trying to feel something more than a curious sort of detachment. He let his eyes wander over the rest of the picture — the fake boulders nestled amid the lush greenery, the fake waterfall gushing down into the fake stream, the high cement walls and the DON'T FEED THE GORILLAS sign. None of it called to him — none of it. He couldn't imagine living there any more than he could imagine living on the moon. Sighing, he turned over the picture of his mother and scanned the other photographs. The last few showed two young gorillas chasing each other, their mouths stretched wide and their faces wild with excitement. He drank in the sight of his brothers leaping and tumbling together, crashing into things (including their hulking, dour-faced silverback father). With a deep chuckle, he touched the figures in the photos with his thick index finger, and felt his legs more restlessly as though they could carry him into the screeching, frenzied fun in the picture. *This* he could imagine — rolling around, grunting and grappling with young creatures his own size, bashing into things with wild abandon. Never getting scolded for breaking things, never being told to use his words.

"I bet they never have to brush their teeth," he murmured.

"Probably not," agreed Dr. Susan, pushing a lock of frizzy hair out of her face. "There's stuff they don't have to do that you do, Ortega, and stuff that you get to do that they don't."

"Different," he said slowly. "Not better, not worse."

Dr. Susan nodded.

Ortega slipped the pictures back into the envelope, then reached out to give Dr. Susan a tickle under her chin. At that moment, there was a knock at the door, and Glen walked in carrying a coffee and a bag of doughnuts.

"Still trying to butter me up?" asked Ortega, reaching for the bag.

"Always," replied Glen, frowning as Dr. Susan intercepted the bag and whisked it beyond Ortega's reach.

"He's eaten nothing but brown sugar and cherry suckers for two days!" she exclaimed.

"Breakfast of champions," chuckled Glen, holding up his hand so Ortega could give him a high five.

Ortega chuckled, too, and smacked Glen's hand.

"By the way," said Glen. "Loved the clip on Video-Junkie."

"What clip?" asked Dr. Susan.

"Peter used Eugene's cell phone to take a video of me just before the cops showed up at the factory," explained Ortega.

"He shot that video with a cell phone?" said Glen, taking a big slurp of coffee. "I'm impressed."

Ortega nodded. "Peter is really good. He thought that if he could get a shot of me looking sick and hurt, talking about everything I'd gone through, maybe people would feel so sorry for me that the company wouldn't let Dr. Whitmore sell me to some mad scientist whose goal in life is to find out if my body would keep swimming if my head got cut off above the brainstem."

"Ortega! I would *never* let Dr. Whitmore do something like that," spluttered Dr. Susan. "The very idea makes me want to be sick to my stomach!"

"Tell me about it," he said.

───◦◦◦───

The next morning, Ortega awoke to the sound of Dr. Whitmore's office door slamming. Sliding out of bed, he knuckle-walked slowly down the hall. He had just pressed his ear against the door in the hope of hearing something he could later use against Dr. Smarty Pants, when the door flew open and Dr. Whitmore came charging out of the office so fast that he slammed into Ortega and the box of papers and books in his arms went flying.

"Watch it!" complained Ortega.

Instead of reprimanding Ortega for eavesdropping, Dr. Whitmore scrambled around him on his hands and knees, shoving things back in the box, and muttering, "Who are they to judge me ... sitting in their ivory tower ... nothing gets done without sacrifices ... I made a judgment call ... their duty to support me ... no idea the economic benefit this could have ... opportunities like this don't come along every day ..."

Ortega backed away slowly, just in case this new, demented Dr. Whitmore had a concealed weapon. "Everything all right, then?" he asked.

Dr. Whitmore's head snapped up. "They fired me. Fired *me*," he said, his whole face contorted in rage and disbelief. "Said I'd crossed the line doing what I did to you — said I could no longer be trusted! Well, of course I told them that this experiment was never just about you and that they had to look at the bigger picture, but oh, no!" His shaking hands were clenched so tight the knuckles were white. "They put Susan in charge of the lab. Susan!" he cried, giving a bark of laughter. "Not only that, but they've agreed to consider her recommendation that they begin voluntarily giving you some basic rights and freedoms in order to stay one step ahead of any legal challenges that might be instigated by headline-hungry animal lovers — *and* they're going to let her hire that crazy mother of hers as a part-time handler!" Dr. Whitmore shook his head back and forth in much the same frantic fashion that Ortega had the night he'd been told he was going to be sold. Then he staggered to his feet and, looking wildly around the lab, said, "History will judge me kindly, Ortega. I will receive credit for the advances that come as a result of my work. Mark my words — other scientists will undertake other experiments with other primates. Progress will continue. All is not lost."

For a long moment, Ortega just stared at the man who had never shown him the least kindness. Then he yawned and said, "All may not be lost, Dr. Whitmore, but it must be a real kick in the head to find out that this experiment was never just about you, either."

And with that, Ortega turned on one knuckle and wandered off to see what Dr. Susan had laid out for breakfast.

It was two weeks before Dr. Susan would let Ortega go back to school, and then she let him go only because she said he was going to be spoiled beyond redemption if she didn't get him away from Grandma, who'd shown up every day with fresh baking to eat and new movies to watch. It felt strange walking into school again after everything that had happened, but it also felt unaccountably precious. All of it — the spitballs, the schoolwork, the unpleasant discovery that he had four old lunches rotting at the bottom of his locker — all of it was a part of what he had come so close to losing.

"I will never take anything for granted ever again," he announced at lunchtime as he sat in the tree house with Eugene and Janice, waiting for Peter to hurry up with the sandwiches. "Not even when I'm in charge of a dangerous military operation or manning a craft on a mission into deep space."

"They are *not* going to let you do something like that," huffed Janice, who could not believe that someone was actually considering training Ortega to undertake top-secret government projects someday when she was so clearly the better candidate.

"They definitely are," said Ortega, who had absolutely no idea if this was true or not. "Of course, I still haven't completely ruled out becoming a brain surgeon, so those government eggheads are really going to have to butter me up if they want my help saving the world from alien zombies."

Janice rolled her eyes and returned to her book. Eugene started chortling just as Peter scrambled up the ladder shrieking that Derek Blackheart had e-mailed him to say that he'd seen the clip on VideoJunkie and thought Peter had a promising future as a documentary film director. Ortega hooted with delight and crashed about the tree house with such enthusiasm that he toppled Eugene over and nearly knocked out a wall.

"You are, like, the second weirdest friend I've ever had, Ortega," panted Eugene when he finally managed to sit back up.

"Oh, yeah?" said Ortega, still grinning happily at Peter. "Who's the first?"

Putting his finger on his lips, Eugene nudged his head toward Janice.

"I saw that," she said, without looking up from her book.

———

That night, as he lay in his nest behind the beanbag chair, Ortega hugged Mr. Doodles and sleepily wondered what his future would really hold. He was glad to have the pictures of his gorilla family, and he thought he might even want to visit them someday, but he knew in his heart that his future didn't lie in their world. He'd stepped too far into this world of books and beanbag chairs, of clothes and friends and forks and words. Of Dr. Susan, and Grandma, and people who loved him for who he was today, who he'd been yesterday, and who he would be tomorrow. And while it was true that he was a pioneer in a strange and sometimes dangerous land, it was also true that there was really no way to know what the future held for anybody, and so, in that way at least, Ortega was the same as every living creature on the planet.